THE STARLIGHT DEMON

Key to Maps

ASHTEAD

- 01   George's House
- 02   Footbridge over the Rye
- 03   Railway Footbridge
- 04   Ashtead Railway Station
- 05   The Astronomers House
- 06   To Roman Villa (remains)
- 07   The Rec
- 08   Emily's House
- 09   To Park House School

LONG SUTTON

- 10   Aunt Muckle's House
- 11   To Salt Marshes and Sea Defences
- 12   Old Bull Hotel (derelict)
- 13   St Mary's Church
- 14   Home Guard (7c) Auxiliary Unit (boy scouts hut)
- 15   To Gedney Railway Station

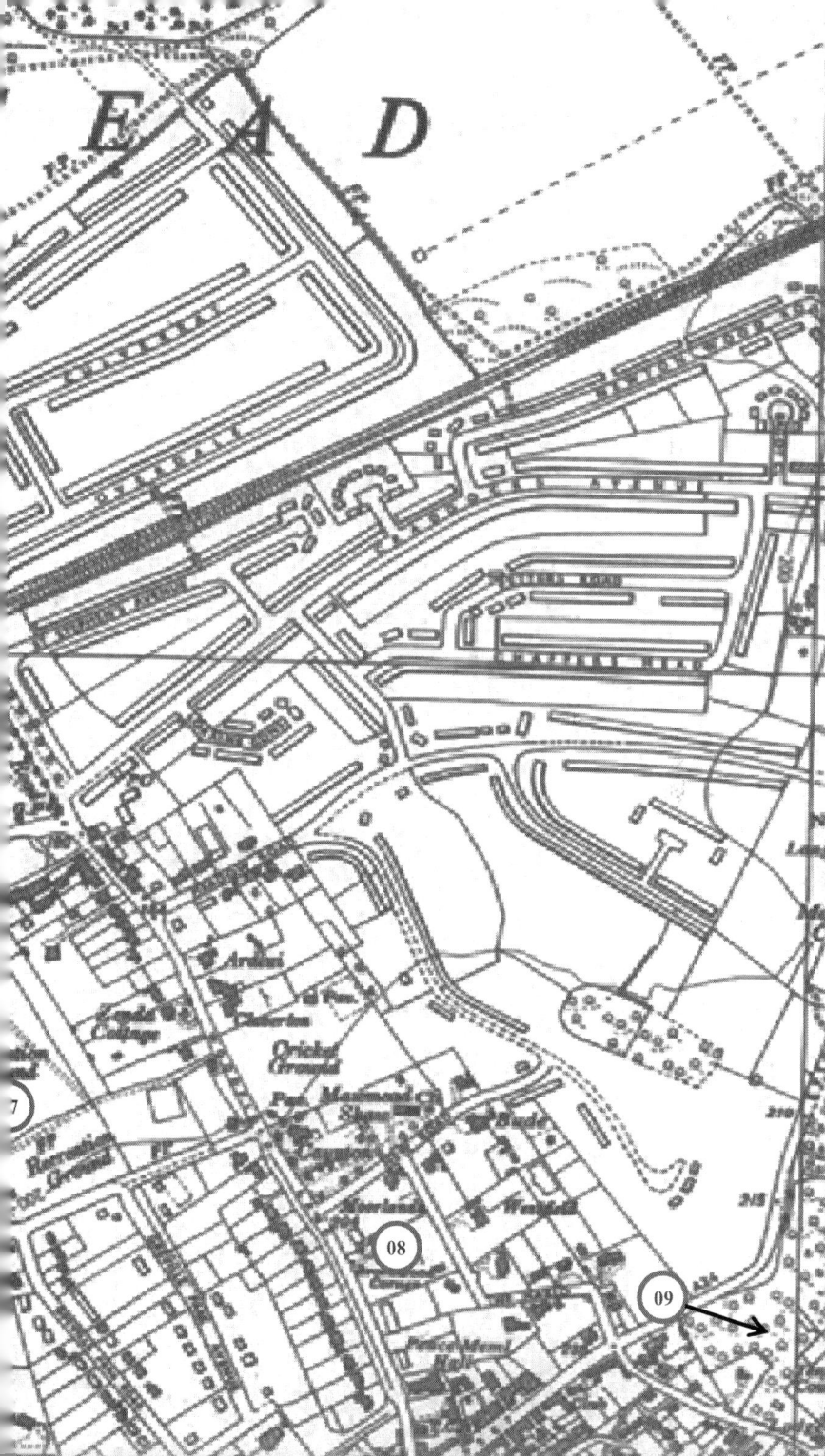

THE STARLIGHT DEMON

AT Richens

First Edition
This paperback edition published November 2021
ISBN: 979 8-6572-5140-1 PB

Copyright © 2020 by AT Richens
This is a work of fiction. All characters appearing in this work are fictitious. Any resemblance to real people, living or dead, is purely coincidental.

Village maps reproduced with the permission of the National Library of Scotland.

All right reserved. No part of this publication may be reproduced, distributed or transmitted in any form or by any means, including photocopying, recording or other electronic methods, without the prior written permission of the publisher, except in the case of brief quotations embodied in critical reviews and certain other noncommercial uses permitted by copyright law.

To my Princess, Sarah-Jane,
a million thank-yous for saying 'yes' to me
on a very cold night in Paris

'grá go deo'

Nothing is real. What we believe to be the truth is simply an opinion in flux, captured within a moment of our thoughts. It is simply an individual's biased perspective of the world; a single point of view.

It changes from person to person.

Chapter I

June 1939

It was a pleasant Saturday morning, even though Mother had not left the house. Regardless, I played in the garden with my father's spring-powered air-rifle. Mother hated the thing. When dad died, it became mine. I had been pushing several twigs into the ground along the fence line for target practice. Advancing enemy soldiers, intent on invasion. I would defend the land. Defend England. Beat back the tyranny. It was my favourite game.

I lay prone upon the lawn, aiming at my foe. Although not a potent rifle, it was accurate nonetheless. I could hit a tin can a hundred yards away, most of the time.

Mother stepped out into the garden. She stood behind me, hanging damp washing onto the line. It stretched across the lawn, from fence post to shed, displaying our intimate apparel for all to see. I held my fire as she pegged out the garments. Mother disapproved of me shooting, especially when she was nearby. I took the opportunity to hold my aim upon the last remaining twig. I knew that it would fall. I knew that as soon as Mother returned to the house, the twig would be hit. I smiled. I could not help myself. A voice in my head sang a tune, over and over. A nursery rhyme. A torment from the playground.

'I know something you don't know. I know something you don't know...'

Mother returned inside, the back door closing. The sound of sliding locks, securing me in the garden. I squeezed the trigger and the twig fell with a plink. The slaughter was complete.

Reloading another pellet, I scanned the garden for my next target. A juvenile blackbird landed on a branch to my right. A male, singing the most beautiful song. The tune carried across the garden, proudly staking its territory to anyone who cared to listen.

I stood. Without thought or care of consequence, I took aim. The foresight sat squarely upon its black chest. I had never killed before. Not yet. I was curious. Curious to experience the excitement of the act. I studied the bird, the delicacy of its feathers.

My mind drifted. Memories of my father. I wondered if he had felt the same apprehensive exhilaration. I imagined him on the battlefield with his rifle. Aiming at the chest of a German. Slowly squeezing the trigger.

The voice of my mother barked loudly from behind. The blackbird took flight.

'George,' she yelled, 'Give me that damn thing now.'

Mother slapped the back of my head.

'Nasty little child,' she said, kicking my tin of pellets across the lawn with great force. They scattered, lost in the grass.

I rubbed the back of my head. Reluctantly, I returned the rifle to the garden shed, propping it against my father's work table. The shed was full of spiders, they hide in every nook. I don't like spiders, but I miss my dad. That's why I still go in there, from time to time.

* * *

Constable Billet knew instinctively that something was wrong. The heavy curtains were drawn tight across the windows, despite the lateness of the afternoon. He stood at the entrance of the short gravel driveway that led to the front door of the little bungalow. Four milk bottles stood neatly to attention beside the doorstep. Mrs Stride only ever had two bottles delivered, more than enough to supply visiting policemen with a steady flow of hot tea. He had certainly never seen so many bottles before. Since her husband passed away, the old lady had become lonely. She looked forward to visits. Sergeant Wells had discouraged such calls. He feared her hospitality was being abused by his officers. Regardless, Constable Billet attended the address twice a week.

The policeman's shoes crunched upon the gravel as he approached. A blue-tit pecked at the foil cap of a milk bottle to reach the cream. It flew away as the constable reached the door. A knock was met with no answer. Lifting the letterbox, he called through.

'Hello, Mrs Stride. Are you in there, Betty?' Again, nothing.

The policeman looked for gaps between the curtains, but there were none. Opening the side gate, he entered the rear garden. The lawn was immaculate, like a lush green rug. Garden furniture rested welcomingly upon the patio, beneath the kitchen window. Peering through the glass, he saw the breakfast table. It was laid with toast and jam and tea. He tapped on the glass with a knuckle.

'Hello Mrs Stride,' he said, 'It's Harry. Constable Billet. Are you in, love?'

Nothing.

He tried the handle on the back door. It pushed open and he stepped inside.

'Mrs Stride,' he called again, 'Just popping in to use your loo. Is the kettle on? Hello.'

The bungalow was silent. He placed the back of his hand against the teacup - stone cold, the toast, untouched. He moved through the bungalow, along the long narrow corridor. Passing the old lady's bedroom, he saw the door, wide open. Her bed was made neatly with tight hospital corners.

The next door led into the bathroom. It was cramped and smelt of lemons and dried lavender. A watercolour painting of a seaside resort hung unevenly beside the toilet cistern. The constable straightened it.

Resting on the toilet seat he noticed a white envelope. It bore the name '*E. Stride*' in bold, clumsy letters. It was unsealed. Protruding, a single black feather. He placed the envelope into the window sill, next to a vanity mirror and a tin of talcum powder. He lifted the toilet seat lid.

'Jesus,' he gasped.

Stumbling backwards, he fell to the ground, banging his left elbow hard against an iron radiator. Placing a hand over his mouth, he got to his feet and peered into the toilet bowl. Half submerged within the crimson water, the battered head of Mrs Stride. It stared up at him with open eyes. Exposed flesh and fat around her neck, jagged and torn. Her mouth, missing her dentures, gaped at him. Her face was dreadful. The look of fear, of pain. Her eyes capturing the final moment of murder. The pungent smell of death coated the back of his throat.

A clattering sound, brief but distinct. It came from elsewhere within the bungalow. Reaching into his pocket, the constable withdrew his truncheon. He wrapped the leather strap tightly around his wrist. Slowly, he stepped out into the hallway.

'Police!' he announced. He cleared the fear from his voice. 'Police – come out now.'

Silence.

The constable edged his way along the hallway in short, tentative shuffles, truncheon resting upon his shoulder. He reached the living room. It was dimly lit. As he flung open the curtains, the afternoon light flooded in. He scanned the room. Nothing untoward. Nothing, save for a small vase lying on its side, atop a nest of tables. The constable lowered his weapon and returned to the kitchen.

A fly landed on the toast. Another flew above the sink. It buzzed against the windowpane.

A clattering sound again, this time much closer. The policeman spun on his heels to face a door. He knew it led to the scullery. Raising his truncheon again, he took hold of the doorknob. Bracing himself, he yanked the door wide open.

He ducked. A yellow bird flew from the room, a budgerigar. It fluttered frantically against the kitchen window behind. A rancid stench forced him to recoil. He peered through the doorway at the carnage that lay before him. The dismembered body of the elderly woman, torn and discarded, as if by some wild animal. He returned the truncheon to his pocket and placed a white handkerchief tightly over his mouth.

The stone-tiled flooring was covered by thick, congealed blood. It had set like dark jelly around the contours of the skirting boards. The carcass and organs of the lady, tossed upon the draining board as superfluous waste. Her intestines dangled over the edge, snaking to the floor whereupon they rested atop a pair of severed legs, cast within the juices of congealed blood.

Beside the torso, protruding from the sink, the lower arm and hand. Constable Billet stared at it. He could not help himself. The fingers, snapped sharply backwards, one digit missing. Defensive wounds. He had seen them before, but only in photographs, never in person. The station kept an album of such things. A macabre catalogue of human depravity.

He felt sick. He had never seen anything like this. Not in fifteen years of service. The wretched smell. It permeated his uniform, his skin, his lungs. He brushed away a fly as it tried to crawl into his nostrils.

The constable withdrew himself into the garden. He took his fill of fresh air, but the stench was overpowering. He vomited onto the pristine lawn. As he wiped his mouth clean with the handkerchief, the yellow bird darted into the open. Free from captivity, it lost itself beyond the rooftops of suburbia.

* * *

I stayed hidden in my bedroom. I did not leave it until the late afternoon, when Mother left the house. As the front door closed behind her, I relaxed. I had not eaten since breakfast so I indulged myself with bread and some of her favourite jam. And then I ventured into the village. I was going nowhere in particular, just anywhere away from the house.

I headed off across the Rec - the Ashtead recreation ground. It lay alongside Barnett Wood Lane, not far from home. It was a reasonable expanse of land. Set aside for football matches, cricket and lawn tennis. A children's play area occupied one corner. It had a wrought iron merry-go-round, a slide, swings and a red rocking horse. The horse was my favourite ride. It was designed to seat five children but it could hold over fifteen, provided they could cling on. Nickolas Hopwood once chipped his front tooth on it. I did not like him much.

On the opposite side of the lane was the start of the Common. It had been protected by ancient laws for centuries. It allowed the residents of Ashtead to graze their livestock and gather firewood. During my entire life, with the brief exception of one small pig, I only ever saw people walking their dogs on the Common. Highly manicured villagers promenading their equally manicured dogs.

A small number of dirt tracks crossed the common, converging at the railway station. To much fanfare, the line had been electrified a few years previously. Although some of the new electric stock passed through on occasions, the majority remained passenger steam trains or diesel freight. Very little was electric. Still, from here, a gentleman could travel north to work in London, a distance of some twenty miles. Or, if he so wished, head south, to Brighton or Littlehampton on the coast. Indeed, from the ports, a short ferry ride could deliver the more adventurous traveller across the Channel and into France – returning him safely home before the day was out! To me, the station was magical. A gateway to the wider world. A world just beyond my reach. The chance to flee, never to return.

Stretched elegantly over the railway lines stood an intricately sculptured Victorian iron bridge. From atop, if timed correctly, I could stand above the tracks, just as the fast train to London hurtles through. It sends dense, choking plumes of steam and soot high into the air. The blast engulfs the bridge and chokes anyone brave enough to remain there. It is exhilarating as the train thundered beneath one's feet. The station porter usually tries to chase me away but he is hopelessly lethargic. He can never catch me.

On this occasion, there were no trains as I crossed the bridge. The Common extended outwards on both sides of the track. This vast, open space was edged by a narrow stream, the Rye. It was passable by a low brick-built footbridge. On the other side, I made my way onwards, aimlessly strolling along a bridleway. Beneath the canopy of the woodlands, I felt free. I enjoy my own company. If I could keep away from others, I would. The bridleway was ideal for this.

I trekked for an hour or so, finally reaching the remains of the old Roman Villa, long forgotten and overgrown. I had been here before, several times, but it was not easy to find. Hardly anybody came here so it was generally undisturbed. The ruins were not much to look at. The outlines of the foundations were still visible, though. Thick tree roots, bracken and ferns pushed up through the stone. Fragments of red brickwork randomly littered the ground – each one carefully handcrafted some two thousand years ago. The villa always had an eerie feel to it. The rustling wind and the crunching of dry wood litter underfoot often set my imagination ablaze.

Living wild within the clearing were giant Roman snails, easily four or five times larger than the native ones. They had been brought to Britain as a delicacy, to be consumed by an invading army. The snails clung to the red brickwork of the villa. The Roman Empire had not yet released its grip upon the nation.

I imagined myself being transported back in time. Back to an ancient epoch of oppression and enslavement. It was easy to do, something about the clearing. I stood for a moment as the remnants of my enemy's last meal slithered beneath the rotting decay of fallen oaks.

I rested beneath a tree; alone with my thoughts. The summer was slowly drawing to an end. Of late, the village had become awash with talk. Another war was coming. I hoped it would. I hoped my school would be closed if hostilities were declared. I would finally be left in peace to read my books.

The snap of a branch. Startled, I froze. At the far side of the villa, a gentleman walked into the clearing. He had not seen me so I remained stationary, partly concealing myself behind a throng of saplings.

The man was dressed in rather drab, dark clothing. A vagrant. I studied him intently. Secretively. From time to time he snacked upon some small morsel, scavenged from the ground. The woods were host to numerous edible berries and nuts if you knew where to look. I have a book on such things. Everything he picked up was examined carefully. Sometimes he used a small handheld ocular. And then he would eat.

As I spied, I noticed the gentleman's left hand. It was missing two fingers and a portion of the palm. A sudden recollection, vivid and fresh. I had seen the man before. I recognised his wound. He had been with my father when dad was still alive. I was much younger at the time, but I still remembered him.

I stared at the man across the clearing. He began to gag. Bent double, he cupped his hands in front of his mouth and retched violently. His back flexed in waves, like a poisoned dog. I shifted my position to get a clearer look. Thick, porridge-like vomit ejected from his mouth. It filled his hands, overflowing. The vagrant remained bent. He sniffed at the mixture before raising his hands to his mouth to devour their contents. He feasted enthusiastically as if he had never eaten before. Slurping. Chewing.

I heaved involuntarily. Reflux filled my mouth. The man spun swiftly on his heels to face my direction. His eyes fixed on mine, through the dense ferns. Methodically, he wiped his chops clean. I froze, too afraid to run. Then, in an instant, the vagrant dropped to the ground. He was gone from sight, hidden within the undergrowth.

I spat, clearing the bitter taste from my mouth. I tried to contain my panting but I could not. The ferns ahead of me began to shake and rustle chaotically. Through them, the outline of the man, charging towards me on all fours like a beast. I saw his eyes - wild and vacant. I braced myself. And then he was upon me, slamming his body into mine, hurling me onto my back. A wave of pain travelled through my spine. He pushed his forearm into my throat, painfully restricting my airway. His damaged hand held tightly over my mouth. I smelt his vomit, his sweat. I kicked out wildly but could not break free of his grip. Removing his arm from my throat, he raised a clenched fist above my head. I flinched and turned my face, awaiting his blow to be struck.

'No,' I pleaded, gulping for air. The pain of burning lungs. I closed my eyes.

A pause. Silence. The blow did not come. I turned to face the man again.

'Please,' I said.

The stranger bent close towards me, his face almost touching mine. The smell of warm sick hung on his breath. Slowly, methodically, he licked my face from chin to eyebrow. I gasped, terrified.

The man withdrew his face. He sniffed the air in sharp sips. And then he smiled.

'You're different,' he said.

I thought of calling out but was too afraid. Afraid of how he would react. I felt myself trembling.

'I know who you are,' the man said, 'You're Engle's boy. You don't belong here.'

He sneered at me, drawing his face close to mine once again. 'The cleaners are coming,' he whispered, 'one by one.'

The foulness of death was cast upon his face. I could see it. A madman. An animal.

'The light in me is old and dark,' he said, 'but yours, Engle, yours is just beginning.' He smiled again, his filthy teeth stained with sputum. 'You should rejoice. While you still can.'

Then, in the most vulgar way, he licked my face again. I wet myself.

The stranger stood up. He towered over me as I lay motionless. Too afraid to flee. Too afraid to call out. I thought he was going to kick out at me, to smash my bones. But he did not. He just turned his back on me and ran. I watched as he fled through the trees. Squawks of startled crows filled the air as he darted through the woodland, zig-zagging sharply about, twisting and ducking through the branches until he was gone from sight.

Slowly, the sound of startled birds receded. I listened to them. Their laughter mocked me. When they became silent, I could only hear the sound of the breeze pushing through the foliage and the thumping of my heart.

I found the courage to stand. I coughed. My throat was painful and hoarse. My trousers were heavy with urine; the darkened material clung to my legs. I thought of heading home but I was too afraid. Afraid my mother would be angry at the state of my clothing.

I stayed in the clearing for a little while. I became curious to examine the area where the man had first stood. Rising to my feet, I brushed the leaf litter and debris from my trousers. I found the patch of ground, splattered with vomit. Thereabouts I saw nothing but discarded fragments of brickwork and roofing slates. Disgusted by the man, I kicked at the ground until my anger began to wane.

Something caught my attention. My eye had been drawn to an object glistening nearby. It lay discarded amongst the leaves, out of place. It was not ancient. Rather, it was a somewhat ornate fountain pen. I picked it up and examined it closely. It had been exquisitely crafted in blue and green enamel with a golden nib hidden beneath a weighty cap. Upon it, emblazoned in bold, almost vulgar gold text, were the letters '*SS.*'

Chapter II

I did not mention the incident to my mother. That night, as I lay in bed, I thought about the stranger. I thought about his injured hand. I had been no more than six years old when I first saw him. My parents and I had been walking in the village. Passed the small row of shops in Lower Ashtead. The gentleman had stepped out into our path having exited Goldings, the grocers. Father recognised him immediately but he did not greet him warmly. The stranger looked frail. Broken. I had seen several men like this. Products of the Great War.

I was shorter then and my face had rested close to the gentleman's waist. As the adults exchanged awkward pleasantries, I studied his hand as it dangled loosely before me. The skin was pink and thin, like dry, brittle, tissue paper. A jagged, triangular portion of his palm, missing. It extenuated the length of his remaining fingers, the tips of each ending in a stumpy callus. Only the thumb retained its nail. It was crusty and twisted, like some ancient seashell or cloven hoof. On seeing my curiosity, the stranger hesitated briefly. He apologised to my father before concealing his wounds discreetly behind his back.

In a low voice, the stranger spoke.

'What was it like, after the gas?' he asked, 'Did it take long? And what about the nightmares, do they still visit you?'

Father never spoke of the war. Not to us. Not to anyone. We knew little of his conduct, save he had been sent to the front as a young man in 1914. He returned the following year, broken and without vigour. Nothing was said. That is why I recalled the stranger so clearly. This was to be the only time my father spoke of the war.

The stranger had a foreign accent. Slight, but noticeable. I could not place it with any certainty, I knew so little of the world beyond the village.

Mother had tensed up at the boldness of the man's questioning. No one asked of such things. It was an unspoken agreement, adhered to across the nation by civilised convention.

Father let go of Mother's hand as if not to taint her by his recollections. In a slow, deliberate tone, he spoke, like a well-rehearsed script. Prepared in his mind a million times over. I listened as he spoke of his wounding.

'Ghastly stuff you know,' he said, 'I thought nothing of it at first. Just a brown mist. Rather innocuous really. It was a beautiful day. No shelling or gunfire or any of those dreadful sounds. It was so peaceful. It really was a beautiful morning. And then it drifted in. Engulfing us. Covering us in the filth and muck of war. One has so very little time to react, you understand. I didn't know what to do. So, I laid my rifle down and knelt on the grass. And then I prayed.'

I reached out to hold my father's hand, but he would not take it.

'The smell is very distinctive, you know. Like damp hay. Not at all unpleasant. And the effects are very mild, at first.'

Mother looked pale, uneasy. But Father continued, nonetheless.

'It washed over us all. Like a shroud to cover the dead. The chemicals are slow to take effect. It burned our eyes and our lungs. It flung us to the ground like poisoned rats. But it never took me. I hoped that it would. I prayed for it. But I had no soul to gather. Not anymore. I was already dead, deep inside. You understand.'

The stranger smiled. But it had been a mournful kind of smile, the kind only seen at funerals. And then the stranger looked at me.

'He's a big lad now, your son,' he had said, ruffled my hair with his good hand.

Father became enraged. He shoved the man away from me, causing him to stagger backwards.

'Don't ever fucking touch my son again!' Father barked.

Mother anxiously looked around at passers-by, giving a forced smile to whoever looked our way. She began to shuffle me along the pavement, away from the wounded man. An awkward pause, then we parted. I never saw him again. Not until the clearing.

* * *

A few days had passed since my encounter with the stranger in the woods. I was in the garden, lying with my back to the lawn, looking up into the evening sky. The long summer days meant it did not get fully dark until almost ten o'clock. I was not allowed to stay up late so there was little chance of seeing the heavens.

I began to think of school. I loathed the end of the summer holiday and my return to Park House. It was a private school for boys, set within extensive grounds and woodlands. Mother taught there. I like the look of the building and I like its library, but that is all. I have attended there since I was four but I do not have any friends there. I have a reputation for being different. I hate sports but I excel in physics and mathematics. If it were not for the library and my science lessons, I would never survive the drudgery of the place.

I do not understand why, but people with an interest in science are viewed somewhat as a peculiarity. Someone to be ridiculed and mocked. I do not think it is limited to Park House. I fear it is commonplace across England. I can offer no rational explanation. All I know is that it has led to my persecution both inside and outside of school. Morning assemblies are particularly loathsome. To be bullied amongst the entire school is something of a familiar routine. Whoever sits behind me, cross-legged upon the floor seems almost duty-bound to torment me. I do my best to tolerate them, to blank them from my mind. It is usually nothing more than a few prods and pokes to my back. I can cope with that. But some boys are more spiteful. They pull my hair or jab me in the bottom with pins. I never turn to face them though, that would solve nothing. They bully me to get a reaction. I can deny them the satisfaction. Besides, school rules state students must sit quietly and face the front at all times. Without rules and order, there is anarchy. So, I sit quietly and face the front at all times.

Once, last spring, in assembly, someone burnt my ankle with a magnifying glass. I did not move then either, despite the pain. I knew the sun would slowly cross the sky, changing its position as the Earth rotated. It would be ten minutes at the very most. Ten minutes before the sunbeam no longer fell on my skin. Six hundred seconds. I counted them in my head. Most people can endure discomfort for six hundred seconds, if they stay focused. I can.

There is a certain amount of flexibility regarding the classes taught at Park House. If a child shows a particular aptitude for a subject, it is possible to devote more time to it, and less on others, within reason. The Headmaster, Major Lucas-Smith, believes some subjects are core to the development of a young gentleman. It is forbidden to neglect the study of these fundamental subjects; English, Mathematics, The Arts, History of the Empire and, most importantly, cricket.

Mathematics has been my salvation. It has enabled me, as far as reasonably practicable, to replace the study of much of the non-scientific drivel. Unfortunately, my aptitude for mathematics could not shield me from such a preposterous sport.

I loathe cricket. Yet despite my level of derision, I am still required to play. To be a team player. To be a good sport. To represent Park House. If I had the remotest regard for the game I would, perhaps, be mortified by my incompetence. My skill in bat is clumsy at best and the subject of much ridicule. Regardless, it has never dampened their relentless efforts to enthuse me. To make me fit in. To conform. To fill the same dreadful mould that has created countless thousands of identical, wretched children. A production line of sheep. Ready for the next generation of slaughter.

By the time I turned eight, the Major conceded a partial defeat. From then, until now, I am required only to remain in the position of deep-field, far away from the action, regardless of who is in bat. My allegiances can swap in a heartbeat, often without even my knowledge.

Fielding in cricket presents the opportunity to let my mind wander. Sometimes I bring a selection of books onto the pitch. Nobody objects. Not anymore. On one occasion I forgot myself entirely and strolled aimlessly away from the grounds altogether. I found myself back inside the library. I was gone for hours. No one noticed.

The worst compulsory subject taught at school is the arts. I hate the arts. I hate the fact it is my own mother who teaches the subject. I get frustrated by the scientific inaccuracies of the old masters. If I get too angry my legs begin to fidget and twitch involuntarily. Still, I remain silent, face the front, speak only when spoken to. Mother is a stern teacher. It pays to adhere to the rules in her class.

The chime of a clock. I heard it from the garden as I lay on my back. My mind snapped into the present. Seven chimes. I rose to my feet and headed indoors.

Mother had already unlocked the back door to let me in. As I stepped inside, she appeared by my side like a wild tempest. Without pause, she struck the back of my head with her open hand. A verbal torrent of indistinguishable yells and shrieks. The strikes to my head continued with increasing magnitude. I cowered and turned my back. It was the wedding ring on her left hand which caused the most pain, hard, cold metal. My mind began to race.

Seizing the opportunity, I dashed across the living room and up the stairs. Mother chased after me as I shielded my bottom with my hands. I reached my bedroom. Mother followed.

I saw my chest of drawers, each one pulled open. Their contents of shirts, trousers and underwear, strewn across the floor. And there, resting in the middle of my bed, was the fountain pen.

'Where did you get this?' Mother yelled, grabbing my arm and twisting my entire body so that my head was bowed low.

'I found it, in the woods,' I replied, surprised at how nervous my voice sounded.

'Liar,' she screamed.

She pushed harder on my shoulder. My legs buckled and I dropped to my knees. Mother changed her grip on me. This time her right hand grasped the back of my neck. I was now at the mercy of her wedding ring. Her nails dug into my skin as she pushed my face onto the bedding.

'Where did you steal this?' she demanded, her voice lowered but more vitriolic.

'The man, in the village,' I said. 'The man with the injured hand, from the war.'

Mother released me. Regardless, I remained motionless, bent over on the bed. I did not wish to provoke her further.

'Him? He's been in no bloody war. Filthy bloody German, that's what he is,' she said, her tone reduced, almost conversational.

'Men are bastards,' she said, 'Always fighting pointless bloody wars whilst we're left at home, trying to make ends meet!' She paused. 'He's Mr Simpkins. I don't want that bloody thing in my house. Take it back to him. Go on, get out of my bloody sight.'

I grabbed the pen and dashed from the room, relieved to be free of the house.

* * *

Constable Billet sat uncomfortably in the C.I.D reporting room at Leatherhead police station. Uniformed officers rarely ventured into the lair of their plain-clothed colleagues. This section of the building was unfamiliar to most of them, including Constable Billet. Sat casually opposite him were two scruffy looking detectives. The younger was Porter, a handsome chap who many considered rather arrogant, despite having served less time in the job than most. The older detective was Mare. Unshaven and overweight, Mare was already nursing a glass of whisky and a cigarette well before lunchtime.

'Look, Billet,' he said, 'I don't want uniform trampling all over the place. It's got nothing to do with you lot. Mrs Stride is our job. I don't want you messing it up.'

Mare kept his eyes firmly on the constable. He liked to intimidate uniformed officers with his gaze, scrutinising their faces for signs of weakness. Constable Billet felt uneasy. He blinked momentarily. The detective grunted triumphantly before taking a swig of whisky.

'I've known her for years,' Billet said, 'Everyone in the street knew her. I could do a door-to-door. Might turn something up.'

'Whoever killed her wasn't some fancy snob from Ashtead,' Mare said, 'They bloody shredded her, sick bugger. Some nutter from the lunatic asylum I reckon. Nothing taken from the house. Hadn't even fiddled with her, not that you'd want to.' He smirked again, 'Norman and I are going to the scene today. Straight after lunch.'

'You might still need some uniform,' Billet said, 'Visible presence. Reassure the public. Keep the local press in order if they decide to run with the story.'

Detective Porter leaned forward in his chair. 'Public don't know yet. Neither do the press. Besides, we've already got a uniform allocated to us. Some spinster sent from HQ. We don't need anymore tripping us up.' Shifting in his chair, he called out into the hallway. 'Oi, Doris, get your arse in here.' He beamed a broad smile to his colleague.

A uniformed woman in her mid-forties appeared at the door holding a notepad and pen.

'My name's not Doris,' she said, 'It's Woman Auxiliary Barlow. What do you want?'

'Cup of tea please, love,' Porter said, giving her a wink. She rolled her eyes and disappeared from view. 'She used to be a copper during the war,' Porter added.

Mare swigged at his whisky. 'What one,' he said, 'Crimean?'

The detectives grinned at one another.

'Mrs Stride's old man used to be a copper,' Constable Billet said, 'Investigated the Ashtead Ripper, back in the day. She told me about it. Pretty gruesome. A bit like this one, really.'

Porter chuckled. 'Hardly think they'd be linked. Before I was even bloody born,' he said. 'If the Ripper's still at large, he must be ninety-odd by now.' Porter looked smug. 'You reckon the old dear was pulled apart by some toothless geriatric from the 1800s? Sort yourself out.'

'No. But it could be a copycat killing though,' Constable Billet said. 'I'd like to get involved, all the same. I knew her. And it's on my beat.'

'Alright,' Mare said, draining his glass, 'Look, she did some house cleaning from time to time. An hour or so once a fortnight. You can have a word with her last client. Get a statement from them. Just don't get in our way, clear?'

Detective Mare rummaged through the items on his desk and opened a small receipt book. He thumbed through the pages. 'Here you go,' he said, 'Looks like she only had one client at the moment. You can pay them a visit. Might be able to say what mental state she was in.' He smiled at Constable Billet dryly. 'You know, so we can rule out suicide.'

The detective slid the receipt book across his desk. 'There you go,' he said, 'some bloke called Simpkins.'

* * *

I wandered around the quiet lanes of Lower Ashtead feeling nauseous at the prospect of seeing the man again. I contemplated discarding the pen in a bin but the thought of Mother finding out discouraged me.

After an hour or so I became tired of walking. I sat down on the kerbside of Barnett Wood Lane, not far from home. The shops along the row had all wound in their awnings and pulled down their blinds for the night. I felt hungry.

I began to think of my mother. When Father died, I became a burden to her. She told me. She always said I was like him. But she said it in a bad way, as if it was wrong to be like him. As far back as I could remember, she spoke ill of him, ridiculing him. Perhaps he *had* been a coward to take his own life. Perhaps he *had* been unfair to leave us. Yet I always remembered him as a caring man. Perhaps I was wrong.

Memories are never real, no matter how vivid. They become twisted and contorted over time. The truth can become a lie and a lie can become the truth. It is whatever best suits your needs at the time. The best version to support your own opinion. Perhaps Mother was right. Perhaps people *are* better off alone. You don't need family or friends. The world was on the brink of war. A war so that one group of people could stick a flag into a patch of land belonging to someone else. It was all pointless. Pointless because, one day, they will all die. They will own nothing, and they will be dust.

I arose from the kerb as a horse-drawn cart approached. It was driven by Mr Johnson. He worked at the bank in Epsom. Ashtead was void of any banking service. So, twice a week, Mr Johnson drove his cart into the village. He often let me ride alongside him. He would take me either into Epsom in the evenings or out into the surrounding villages of Leatherhead or Cobham in the mornings. He was a friendly, smartly dressed gentleman. I liked him. The cart came to a halt. I made a fuss of his horse as it stood obediently in the road.

'Hello George,' he said, 'Off to Epsom lad?'

'No,' I replied, 'My mum wants me out of the house. I'm on an errand.'

'Well, you'll not get anything done sat by the road, will you,' he said, 'She been hitting you again, son?'

I stopped making a fuss of his horse. I did not like our family being judged. 'No,' I replied, 'She just wants me to give something back to Mr Simpkins – the man with the war-wounded hand.'

Mr Johnson sneered at me. 'He's not been in any war son, you can be sure of that! God knows how he injured himself, but it wasn't from fighting. You know he's a German do you?'

I nodded.

'You'll do well to stay away from that man,' he said.

'He lost a pen. Looks expensive. Mum says I'm to give it back to him,' I said.

'Well,' Mr Johnson said, 'He lives down Agates Lane. The bright red house. I suggest you don't hang around there too long, though. Just put it through the letterbox and scarper.'

I nodded. 'I know the one,' I said.

'I thought you would,' he replied.

I thanked Mr Johnson for his time and watched as his horse and cart clip-clopped off along the road towards Epsom.

I knew the house he meant. It looked out of place nestled amongst the mock-Tudor homes scattered amongst the treeline. Many children passed along Agates Lane. It linked the two sweet shops in the village - *Henry's* in Upper Ashtead and *The Wendy House* in Lower Ashtead. We all had stories to tell about the red house. Great yarns of psychotic murder and gruesome tales. Stories of how the house became drenched in the blood of the madman's victim's. Children would knock upon the front door and run away, hopeful for a glimpse of a killer. Yes, I knew the red house along Agates Lane. We all did.

I reached into my trouser pocket and withdrew the fountain pen. I examined it closely. It was expensive. Carefully crafted. Carefully maintained. There were no marks or scratches upon the surface – it was in fine condition. It would not have looked out of place within the British Museum, I imagined. And yet, despite its beauty, I felt unnerved as my fingertips ran over the letters '*SS*' inscribed upon the cap. This strange man was a German. Perhaps, I thought, he was a Nazi sympathiser; a member of the Schutzstaffel. An S.S. soldier. Maybe he was hoping to return to the Fatherland if war was declared. Perhaps he was a spy, sent here by Hitler himself no less, to disrupt our defences. If war came, I wondered what he would do. Where would his loyalties lie?

I placed the pen into my pocket. I would post it through his letterbox. And then I would run.

It was a short walk to Agates Lane, a narrow route that offered no footpath for pedestrians. It was a pleasant, almost picturesque part of the village, sheltered under a dense canopy of birch and sycamore. The lane was barely wider than a motor car. Most children were discouraged from taking this particular route, despite its abundance of conkers during the autumn.

I walked along the lane, beside the wooden fences and brick walls that marked the boundaries of each grand property. Eventually, they gave way to a field on the right. I paused to pamper a familiar horse that came to greet me. I like horses. This one was called Star. Chestnut in colour with a large white flash upon his forehead. He was owned by a gentleman from the livery stable. In the Great War, both man and horse had taken part in the last ever cavalry charge before such actions became mechanised. Redundant. I did not know the gentleman's name. But his scarlet face was unmistakable. A web of broken capillaries stretched across his cheeks and nose. They looked like a street map of London. He had an emotionally vacant glass eye in his right socket. People in the village say he lost it in the war. But he did not. I asked him about it once, when I was collecting conkers. He had fought from 1914 right through to armistice with barely a scratch. On his first day home, he got drunk on cider and inadvertently blinded himself on the prongs of a pitchfork.

Quite unexpectedly, my right ear was struck by a hard chunk of dry mud. The side of my head began to throb. My ear was burning hot. I scanned my surroundings. A group of older boys stood some distance away. I recognised two of them. Charles Fenton and his friend, Martin. They had probably followed me. I didn't like either of them. Together, they could be particularly nasty. They were scouring the ground for more missiles to throw so I did not hang around. Despite the painful throbbing in my ear, I did not react. You should never react. The horse was twitchy though. She turned and cantered off across the field, leaving me alone. I continued onwards at a brisk pace along the lane. Fenton and the other boys did not follow, they were too intent on searching for stones.

The lane began to narrow as I approached the red house. The front of the building was set at ninety degrees and commanded a dominant position.

On the opposite side of the lane was a black Labrador dog. He rested patiently beside a brick wall. This was Toby, a friendly animal well known and loved by the children. He was somewhat overweight and tended to move slowly and lethargically. His tail always wagged at any approaching children. Always hopeful they may share a treat from the sweetshop.

Toby slowly rose on all fours and padded towards me. His tail wagged, inducing a slow wriggle that travelled the full length of his spine. Only his head remained still, transfixed to my pocketed hand. I made a good fuss of him but once satisfied I had no sweets, he returned to his old blanket beside his water bowl.

I pushed open the small wooden gate of the red house and passed through. Crossing the lawn, I reached the front porchway. The house was in darkness, except for the soft orange glow of a hallway lamp illuminated through a side window. Even in the poor light, the paint looked like blood. I removed the pen from my pocket and lifted the letterbox flap. In an instant, the door swung inwards with great vigour. I gasped. Standing before me was the stranger, Mr Simpkins. Dark shadows cast across his face through the dimness of the evening. His eyes sparkled, wide and wild. His terribly wounded hand dangling loosely by his side. I turned to run but the man reached out for me, gripping my shoulder tightly with his good hand. He pulled me sharply into the house and closed the door.

Chapter III

Held in a tight headlock, I struggled. Unable to pull free, to call out, to breathe. The man dragged me through the house, along a narrow hallway. To my left, a staircase snaked upwards into the darkness. Each step, stacked chaotically with piles of books. At the end of the hallway, a flickering shaft of orange light. It shone through a gap in a doorway. I tried frantically to loosen the grip around my neck so as to breathe, but I was too weak.

A door pushed open and I was pulled through. I found myself in the lounge. The man released his hold on me, shoving me in the direction of an armchair. I wheezed painfully, instinctively clutching at my throat.

The room was cluttered with strange instruments. More books – periodicals and scientific papers. They lay upon every surface. Heavy, dark curtains, drawn for the evening. A smouldering log fire the only illumination.

'Sit down boy!' the man demanded.

He stood between me and the hallway, blocking my exit. Too afraid to make a dash, I stood motionless beside the armchair. It too was laden with books and manuals.

The man lent over the fireplace and stoked the flames with an iron bar. The fire sprung to life, releasing a thousand tiny shards of light. As the flame grew, it cast long flickering shadows across the room.

I began to remove a large book from the armchair.

'Not there,' the man snapped, 'The stool, boy.'

Beside the armchair, pushed into the corner, a metal stool. I removed a heavy steel ball-bearing from its seat and placed it on the floor. I sat, using my foot to prevent the bearing from rolling away. It would make a good weapon should the need arise.

The man turned to face me. He held the poker like a sabre. The red glow, pointing towards my face. I tried to calm myself. Mr Simpkins stared at me as the fire crackled and spat behind him. I remained motionless, silent. Then he turned his back on me, plunging the poker into a bucket of ash beside the hearth. I took this opportunity to roll the metal bearing out of sight with my foot.

'I wondered how long it would be before you came here. You're Alfred Engel's boy, aren't you? George, isn't it?' he asked.

I nodded.

'Well then,' he said, 'this calls for a celebration don't you think?'

The man briskly departed the room, leaving me with nothing but the sound of the crackling logs. I bent down and picked up the bearing. I hid it under my thigh.

As the flames intensified, the room grew brighter. Curtains, old and dust-laden. Peeling paper clung to the walls like the decaying shroud of an Egyptian mummy. A burgundy rug by the hearth was scorched and threadbare. To the right of the fireplace, a pile of cut logs. A brass scuttle held a few chunks of dirty black coal. Beside it, the fire poker handle protruding from a metal bucket, filled beyond the brim with grey ash.

Mr Simpkins returned with two drinks glasses. He thrust one containing milk into my hand. 'To Alfred Engel!' he toasted. He downed his glass, a clear liquid of some apparent potency.

I sipped at my drink. My stomach immediately heaved. At first I thought it was poison. I sniffed the glass. The milk was sour and lumpy. The palms of my hands became clammy at the smell.

'Can't you handle your drink?' he said.

I lent down and placed the glass on the floor, keen not to expose the bearing under my leg. 'I'd like to go home now, please,' I said.

The man smiled. It had the outward appearance of being warm and friendly, but I knew it was not.

'I knew your father,' he said. 'Alfred and I go back a long way.' He smiled again before correcting himself. '*Did* go back.' He threw a log onto the fire and lent against the mantle.

As the firelight grew, I saw the man more clearly. He no longer looked dirty and wild. No longer the disgusting vagrant from the woodland. He looked respectable, like a teacher. An educated man perhaps, in his early thirties. Yet to have been in the Great War he should be closer to his fifties.

I sat and glared at him. His face was thin and gaunt with tired-looking eyes. Distant and melancholy. His suit was smart but somewhat dated and fraying at the cuffs. The jacket and white shirt hung loose as if he had lost several stone in weight. I made a concerted effort not to look at his hands but I did, nonetheless. Both were concealed by thick black woollen gloves. I went to the pictures once, in Epsom. I saw a film about a murderer. He wore gloves too, for concealing his fingerprints.

Mr Simpkins stirred himself. He pushed a stack of books from an armchair in one swipe. They tumbled to the floor in a heap. He sat, illuminated by the burning fire, and relaxed.

'Well then,' he said, 'I don't care much for visitors. So, what brings you into my house, uninvited?'

I withdrew the fountain pen from my pocket and offered it to him. Mr Simpkins said nothing. He gestured for me to place it down, to which I obliged.

'I found it,' I said.

'Rubbish!' he replied, 'You were spying on me, in the woods – don't deny it, boy!'

'No,' I said, 'I was resting, by the trees. Then you came. I wasn't spying.'

Mr Simpkins looked unconvinced. 'At least your mother gave you a hiding,' he said, gesturing vaguely towards my neck. 'She's still got a temper on her, I see.'

I rubbed the back of my neck, dislodging a crusty scab. The tip of my finger dabbed in a spot of wet blood. I wiped it across the leg of the stool - a clue to aid the police, should they need to find me.

'The letters SS,' he said, 'Do you know what they stand for?' He paused. 'Well?'

A burst of anger welled up inside. It caught me by complete surprise. I could not help myself. I jumped to my feet. With no regard, I found myself yelling.

'It means you're a filthy bloody German!' I shrieked, reaching for the steel bearing. I held it above my head, ready to hurl.

In an instant, the man leapt to his feet. He towered above me. I was taken aback by his speed. His good hand gripped my wrist and twisted it painfully, forcing the bearing to fall. His face crimson, he kicked the steel across the room, beyond my reach.

'A filthy German?' he yelled, 'What, like your father? Sit down, boy!'

Unarmed, I stood my ground.

Mr Simpkins shoved me in the centre of my chest. I stumbled back onto the stool. I sat in silence, shocked by the strength of the man.

Mr Simpkins returned to the armchair and sat.

'Stanley Seabrook - S.S. He was a friend of mine. And a good friend of your fathers too,' he said.

I rubbed my wrist to recover the circulation.

'Stanley was a keen motorbike rider,' he said, 'All the girls thought he was rather dashing, of sorts. At least that's what I've been told. No doubt there's some truth in it. He was keen on your aunt. Nice enough chap but a damn menace on that blasted machine of his.' Mr Simpkins stared down at his two gloved hands. 'The local police, including your father, tried to calm him down. Stop him being so reckless. He liked the thrill of the speed, you see. That's how they met, your father and Stanley.' Mr Simpkins shuffled himself in the armchair. 'I knew your father beforehand. Before the war.'

The man turned his face away, staring into the dancing flames within the fireplace. 'They both volunteered for the Ashtead pals brigade, you know. Went to the front almost immediately. Except for me of course. Not permitted to fight. Not trusted. German parents you see. Your father was alright though. Grandparents don't count, apparently.'

Mr Simpkins struck the arm of his chair firmly with his fist. A plume of dust became airborne, suspended within the flickering firelight. For the briefest of moments, I caught sight of his wrist as it protruded from the top of his left glove. The skin looked blackened and rotten. I had seen flesh like that before, visiting the convalescence home with Mother. I had seen men with such terrible trench-foot. Black, dead flesh that clung to the raw wounds of the living.

'When Stanley was on leave,' he said, 'he'd drag his blasted motorcycle into the house. Into this very room, just to tinker with it.' He rubbed at his gloved hands as if he were stroking a pet.

'So no, I never went to war,' he said. 'Stanley left me that pen as a keepsake. Until he returned. Except he never came back, of course. It's quite expensive, I believe,' he said, 'but I doubt it's worth a chaps life.'

The light from the fireplace danced across the face of Mr Simpkins. Regardless of the multitudes of angles at which it fell, he would always look tired. Tired and sad. But this sadness was not transient. I had seen this kind of sorrow before, in my father's eyes.

'We are so much alike, George,' he said, 'You must know you're different, from the rest.'

I said nothing.

'Do you feel it? Coursing through your veins. Burning you. I can help you, George. I can set you free.'

My leg began to twitch.

Mr Simpkins smiled again. 'Yes,' he said, 'you've felt it. Your anger. Your strength. Don't be afraid of it. Use it. I can help you. I can make you magnificent.'

I was confused. I knew I was different from the others, from everyone. From everything. I cannot explain it. I do not like to dwell on such things.

'Well,' Mr Simpkins said, 'We can discuss this further when you're ready,' he said. 'Now then, before the war, I developed a fondness for dabbling in electricity. Electrical pulses and radio waves, to be precise. Nothing too complex you understand. But it certainly got me noticed by the army. It was your father's idea. He suggested it to them. After he joined the Intelligence Corps, he made the proposal. Consolation for my inability to fight. So, I became involved in a secret project. To encrypt the telephone lines.'

'Encrypt?' I asked, not knowing the word.

Mr Simpkins continued. 'So,' he said, ignoring my question, 'I spent the war years working in this very room. Far from the bullets and the mud. But I did my bit. Of course, no one knew. You see, the telephone lines along the Front were easy to eavesdrop into. The Germans did it all the time. Learning our plans of attack. So, I designed an electronic device to detect any meddling.'

The man threw a lump of coal onto the fire. 'I worked on another project too – encryption. That is,' he said, 'the application of a mathematical function. It enables a verbal message to be transmitted in code, meaningless to everyone. Except for the intended recipient of course. Someone in possession of the cypher key.'

A hint of a smile appeared on the man's face. 'I hear you're something of a mathematician yourself.'

'Yes,' I said, 'calculus.'

Mr Simpkins stared at me. Scrutinising me. I felt as though the slightest involuntary twitch or blink would somehow betray me, revealing my urge to flee the house. But I was intrigued. I knew I was different. but I did not know why. Perhaps he did.

'Of course, a fundamental understanding of mathematics is merely a tool to define the physical world. Don't you agree?' he asked.

I did not reply.

'Mathematics is nothing but a means to an end,' he said. 'It is the language of science. You see, one needs a rudimentary grasp of English in order to read the works of Shakespeare. But to fully understand Shakespeare, to truly love his work, one must possess a deep and thorough understanding of the complexities of language. So too is it with mathematics.'

Mr Simpkins stroked his gloved hands once more. 'Something wicked this way comes,' he said theatrically. 'Likewise,' he said, 'only a profound understanding of mathematics can reveal the true mysteries of the universe.'

I was cautious of the man, yet I felt myself warming to him. Captivated by his scientific standing. I knew that I should flee but something in my heart stirred me, enticing me to stay.

'Encryption and the war effort were of vague interest to me,' he said, 'The real science, the science encapsulating all others, is astronomy.' His face became alive. He ceased caressing his gloved hands. 'The one truly fundamental science. It defines everything. From the very large to the very small. What greater science can look out into the vast, endless universe of stars and, with that knowledge, reveal the workings of every cell within our bodies. And then, go beyond that scale, to the atomic level?'

'I like astronomy,' I said, 'but it's not taught in school. I'm reading a book at the moment though. It's about Charles Messier.'

'Well,' Mr Simpkins said, 'anyone can read catalogue numbers. Books and journals are fine for basic principles,' he said, tapping a gloved finger upon a nearby pile of literature, 'but to understand astronomy, to feel astronomy, you need to see it with your own eyes. To open your mind to the universe. That's what your father did. You should follow in his steps. The things I could show you! Come now, outside.'

Mr Simpkins stood. He gestured for me to rise and follow him. As I did so, he leant over and seized the glass of milk by my feet. In a single gulp, he enthusiastically drank the lumpy contents.

'Marvellously good for you, milk, you know,' he said, placing the empty glass on a pile of books. He wiped his mouth clean with the back of his hand.

Mr Simpkins escorted me along the hallway and out the front door. I was relieved to be free of the house and surprised by the coldness of the evening air. The temperature had fallen noticeably since my arrival. We stood together in the centre of his front lawn, looking up into the night.

There was no moon in the sky, only drifting layers of low-level clouds. I watched as Mr Simpkins scanned the heavens, peering through occasional gaps.

'There. Up there. Do you see it?' he asked with a sudden burst of excitement.

At first, I saw nothing. Then, for a moment, a bright star sparkled through the clouds.

'That's Deneb,' he announced, 'part of the constellation of Cygnus, the swan. Now, that particular star has a diameter two hundred times greater than the sun. Imagine that. Yet it's so far away we see it only as a pinpoint of light - a single photon transmitted mainly in the blue part of the electromagnetic spectrum. That photon, George, has travelled across our tiny section of the galaxy for two and a half thousand years. Moving at the speed of light, for all that time. And now, it reaches our eyes at this very instant.' He smiled again. 'Our retinas have evolved in such a manner as to be sensitive to this particular wavelength. It sends an electrical signal along the optic nerve, directly into our brains. What information may be concealed within those photons, I wonder!'

I watched as the rolling clouds concealed the star. My intestines began to rumble. I had not eaten for some time and I wanted to get back home.

'Are you interested in astronomy, at an academic level?' Mr Simpkins asked, his tone suggesting my reply was of great importance.

'Yes,' I said, 'I've got a pair of binoculars, my father's. I've seen the Orion nebula through them. They show it quite well.'

'I'm not surprised by that,' Mr Simpkins said, 'I expect your father was keen to point it out.' He looked away from the gathering clouds. 'I prefer,' he said, 'to observe through a rather splendid twenty-four inch reflecting telescope in my observatory. It's in the rear garden.' He smiled again. 'Perhaps you'd care to take a look through it one evening when the skies are clear?'

I do not know why, but I nodded. A sense of excitement leached into my heart. Compared to binoculars, the views through such a large telescope would be spectacular. I smiled. I could not help myself.

Mr Simpkins pulled a scrap of paper from his pocket and wrote his telephone number onto it. He handed it to me with a sense of ceremony.

'Call me, when the sky is clear,' he said, 'and I'll show you something that will astound you. But you must telephone first. Never come here uninvited. Not ever. Do you understand?'

Mr Simpkins patted the side of my arm with his good hand. 'You're a bright boy, George,' he said, 'You should rejoice and revel in the wisdom to come.'

I thought for a moment and felt emboldened to ask the man a question. That had been playing on my mind.

'In the woods,' I said, 'you spoke of something. The cleaners. What did you mean?'

Mr Simpkins stood closer to me. He spoke in whispers. 'You don't need to know about the cleaners. Not yet,' he said, 'but they're coming. They're coming, for you.'

My mouth dried. 'I'm sorry, but I don't know any cleaners. Why would they be looking for me?' I asked.

The astronomer smiled again. 'You'll find out soon enough, when they find you! Good night George.'

The man turned his back and retreated into the red house. I stood alone, listening as half a dozen locks and bolts slid across to secure the house for the night. I stood alone, gathering my thoughts, and then headed home.

Agates Lane was in darkness save a few widely dispersed lampposts. All was silent except for my footsteps upon the roadway. I paused, taking the opportunity to listen to the sounds of the night. I heard nothing. Yet, for a fleeting moment, I sensed I was being watched. It was a strange feeling, based upon no discernible facts. But I felt decidedly ill at ease nonetheless.

I did not wish to meet Fenton and his gang at this late hour so I increased my pace. The sound of my wide strides and rustling clothing reassured me somehow. I was about halfway down the lane when I heard a distinctly crisp sound, like footsteps on dry leaves. I paused again. Listened through the shadows. It was unmistakable this time. The sound of rustling leaves a short distance behind me. I began to run but after only a few paces I drew myself to a halt. This time the noise was ahead of me.

'Piss off, Fenton,' I called out, 'I'll tell your mum. Go on, clear off.'

Silence. And then another sound, closer. I turned and headed back towards the red house. I could make my way to Upper Ashtead and find a longer route home. To Hell with Fenton!

No more than fifty yards and I froze mid-stride. Ahead of me, standing in the centre of the lane, was a dark figure, some ten feet to my front. From the darkness stepped a creature. It growled as it approached. Some kind of dog, as black as the night with white snarling teeth and bubbling white froth about its mouth. Its brown eyes glinted, transfixed onto my own. With hackles raised, it lunged at me. Having no time to shield myself, I closed my eyes tight. My outstretched arm, offered up in the hope it would latch onto a less sensitive part of my body. The dog obliged. It sank its teeth deep into my forearm. It clung on tightly, shaking my arm like a rag. I did not feel the pain at first, only the clamping pressure of its jaw. Globs of drool flicked in every direction as the beast shook at my arm.

I was scared. Scared that I may be pulled to the ground. I had to break free. Raising my captured arm, I lifted the thing onto its hind legs. The smell of its warm breath upon my face, its frenzied eyes distorted by rage. It was the devil's dog. And then I saw it. The leather collar around its neck. This frenzied dog, this animal violently shaking at my arm, was Toby. His eyes glazed in raw anger. This gentle, lethargic pet, transformed into a wild, vicious creature. I kicked it as hard as I could in its genitals, momentarily lifting both hind legs off the ground. The dog yelped and let go of my arm. I turned my back on Toby and walked away as quickly as I could. I did not wish to run, for fear of encouraging it to give chase. It did not follow. The dog wished only to tend to its injury. It sat in the lane, licking itself.

I arrived at the junction with Barnett Wood Lane. A street light allowed me to examine my arm. The sleeve of my jacket was torn and missing a button from its cuff. My arm revealed two deep puncture wounds, each filled with dark congealed blood. The area around the bite was grazed, the skin already starting to form a purple bruise. It was very painful.

Toby was such a friendly, welcoming animal. I had shared my sweets with him. Yet he had stalked me in the darkness. He had hunted me, waiting for the ideal opportunity to attack.

I thought about my torn jacket. Mother would be furious.

Chapter IV

As Constable Billet passed along the corridor of the station, he caught eye of detectives Mare and Porter. They were sitting alone in the small canteen, waiting for the service hatch to open. The policeman drew a chair to the table and joined the two detectives.

'About the Stride investigation,' he said, 'I spoke to her last customer. Chap called Damien Simpkins. Seemed decent enough.'

Porter thumped on the table. 'Shop!' he called out, ignoring the constable.

The service hatch screen rattled upwards. It revealed an elderly man dressed in white.

'Three bacon rolls, grandad,' Porter called out, 'Stick it on the slate will you, cheers mate.'

Constable Billet continued, despite their obvious lack of interest. 'She only cleaned there once a fortnight or so. Wasn't due back 'til Thursday morning. He didn't notice anything unusual about her mood. Didn't know she was dead.'

The detectives remained disinterested.

'I tell you what was funny though,' the constable said, 'That bright red house down Agates Lane. I've been checking through the old records. Turns out it was owned by a bloke called Tony Ambrose, years ago.'

Mare became agitated. 'And who the bloody hell is Ambrose?'

'He was the main suspect,' Billet said, 'In the Ashtead Ripper killings. Disappeared in 1880. Never seen again. Four random murders, all in Ashtead. Each of the victims torn apart. No one was ever charged. Not in sixty years.'

'Is Simpkins, a relative of his then?' Mare asked.

'No,' Constable Billet replied, 'As far as I can tell they've nothing in common. Apart from living in the same house. Records show Simpkins purchased the property in 1910. Before that, it was derelict for years. The council wanted to pull it down.'

The elderly man through the hatchway began humming a tune to himself as he fried rashers of bacon. Carol Barlow entered the canteen. She was struggling to carry three cups of tea whilst gripping a large brown envelope under her arm. She deposited the tea onto the table as she seated herself.

'There's no bloody spoons anywhere,' she said, 'You'll have to stir it with a fork. Here, you've got some internal mail. There you go.'

The woman placed the envelope next to Detective Mare's hand. He pushed it aside and reached for his cup of tea.

'So,' Mare said, facing Detective Porter, 'what can you tell me?'

'Epsom lunatic asylum is probably a dead-end,' the detective said. 'None of their residents are missing. But, they do let 'em out every now and then. Some were out, around the time the woman was murdered. Not many though. No one of real interest, except for one. A nutter in his fifties. Bloke called David Rollingson. Once tried to smash his girlfriend's skull with a claw hammer. Staff said he's been in a funny mood for the last week or so. They're keeping an eye on him.'

Mare stirred his tea with the fork. 'Did you get his fingerprints?'

Porter stood up to collect the bacon rolls from the hatchway. 'No I bloody didn't - you should see the size of the bugger. I'm going back later though, after he's had his sedatives.'

'Right then,' Mare said, with a mouth full of food, 'Your man Rollingson, do you reckon he's capable of ripping someone's head off?'

Carol Barlow shifted uncomfortably in her seat. 'Oi,' she said, 'not when I'm eating.'

Mare continued. 'We need to check on all the local slaughterhouses. See if they employ any funny characters. Someone used to working up to their elbows in blood and guts. And I want to know how much the old woman's house is worth - who gets the inheritance.' He opened the brown envelope, spreading several photographs of the Stride murder scene across the table. Graphic images of the mutilated body of the old woman. Some showed her autopsy, words carved into her blackening skin.

Barlow rolled her eyes. 'For fuck's sake,' she said, pushing her half-eaten roll aside.

Mare gave the photos a cursory glance.

'Looks like he's got a bit of a foul mouth on him. Likes his obscenities. Reckon your man could do something like that?'

Porter glanced tentatively at the photographs before nodding.

Detective Mare finished his bacon roll. 'Good. Check that he can read and write. Get him to jot down a few of these swear words for comparison. I don't care what they are. There's quite a list.' He pushed a photograph across the table towards Detective Porter.

'Jesus Christ,' Porter said.

* * *

I had successfully concealed the torn sleeve from my mother. The bite mark on my arm had formed two dark scabs, each a quarter of an inch or so in diameter. They were very itchy. I tried not to draw attention to them.

Over the following days, I began to think about my father. If he had still been here he would have flashed me a smile, beyond the vision of my mother. He would have repaired the jacket for me. He would have kept it a secret; tell me everything would be alright. I liked my father. He had been a kind man and I had looked up to him. Not because of his conduct during the war, but because, despite his pain and his nightmares, he found time to care for me. He nurtured my fascination in the sciences not by forcing his ideas upon me, but by combining our interests. Of course, Mother had no such interests. I remember one evening, dad and I were rinsing muddy stones in the kitchen sink. Mother was furious, but regardless of her anger, the vitriol, Father winked at me. It was almost imperceptible, but it was there, and I felt safe again. To be loved by a parent is a wonderful thing. When dad died I had nothing. My entire heart ripped from my body. I would give anything to have him back. Still, Mother looked after me now. She kept me warm and dry and fed. What else did I need?

Dad taught me how to handle a knife when I was five. He was keen that I knew how to defend myself. Once, a few years ago, I had been playing out in the garden with an old steak knife. I had been throwing it into a chunk of wood. I remember I had missed the log completely and the knife became embedded in the ground nearby. I ran over to retrieve it. As I pulled it from the soil, I grabbed the serrated blade by mistake. As I slid my hand upwards along the teeth, they cut deeply into my four fingers. The tendons on my index finger were exposed and my hand began to drip red. I tried to look at the wound but it was difficult to open out my hand. As the pain intensified, I ran indoors. I ran to my mother, crying hysterically. She was furious.

I still have scars across my fingers. They are hardly noticeable now but they hurt if I grip a pencil too tightly when I'm sharpening it at school. Some scars can be better hidden than others. That was the first time I considered running away from home. But no matter where I hid, I would still be alone. I would still be unloved. And so that day ended and the next began. Each merging into one another, forming the boundaries of my life.

On the first Saturday morning after the dog bite, mother woke early. She suggested I should leave the house; play with children my own age. I had noticed of late, she was paying more attention to her appearance. Her hair had been done and she started to apply make-up and perfume every day. A mask to hide behind.

After breakfast, Mother stated I need not return until late. I was to let myself in. I concluded she had taken it upon herself to entertain a gentleman friend. She did this from time to time, since my father's death. I felt he was being betrayed. I felt that I, by remaining mute to the entire charade, had become complicit in the act.

I made myself a packed lunch of jam sandwiches and two red apples. Mother stood in the hallway, by the front door. She was clutching my jacket but had not seen the torn sleeve. And then she kissed me on my forehead. I wiped it off.

'Now, off you go dear,' she said, handing me the jacket, 'I'll be in bed when you get back, so don't make a sound. And don't forget to lock up. I'll put the key under the stone.'

I had the presence of mind to smile back at her. She opened the front door for me but I dashed into the kitchen. Here, on the Welsh dresser, Mother kept her knitting and sewing equipment in a small wicker basket. I stole a sewing needle and a length of black cotton and wrapped them in a scrap of paper I found in my pocket. I then left out the back door before the theft had been detected. I unlatched the side gate and headed out into the street.

I walked away from the house as briskly as I could, eager to repair the jacket and get on with the rest of my day. I knew of several public benches around the village but I could not risk being seen by any of my mother's friends. The gossiping old hags would report back in a heartbeat. So, I decided to go to the common.

The warm morning light was pleasant. On the common, I saw a gentleman trying to place a lead around the neck of his German Shepard. The dog was sniffing at the rear quarters of an elegant looking whippet. The lady with the whippet was trying to wave the other dog away.

I crossed over the railway bridge. The platform below was busy. A strange mix of young families, suited office clerks and a few soldiers. I had not seen soldiers at the station before. I stopped at the summit of the bridge and peered over the railings at them. Ten or so troops. They were waiting for their train to arrive. I was disappointed not to see any rifles. Instead, they carried kit bags and sandwiches from the station tea shop.

I crossed over the railway line and headed towards the little footbridge over the Rye. It marked the start of Ashtead Woods.

The Rye is little more than a narrow, slow-flowing stream. But I was bored. I imagined it as a fast-flowing, crocodile-infested Amazonian adventure, majestically carving its way through the jungle. Provided there had been no heavy rainfall, it was possible to clear the stream in a single bound but I did not wish to risk getting wet.

The bridge, only twenty feet or so in length, was paved with loose gravel and bore no handrails or edging. I often felt uneasy crossing it. Once I had seen a dog lose its footing and tumble in. It had let out the most ghastly yelp.

As I sat upon the crest of the bridge, dangling my legs over the side, I listened to the babbling water. I allowed the morning to unfold. With the jacket tied around my waist, I examined the torn sleeve. Retrieving the needle and thread, a light gust caught the paper that concealed them. It blew down onto the water's surface below. I watched as it sailed down the stream like a toy battleship. I pretended to be a naval Sealord in charge of the big guns. I threw numerous stones, one at a time, at the fleeing enemy ship. Each stone sploshed tantalisingly close to the paper vessel. They sent ripples across the Rye with a plop. The ship bobbed chaotically, but it managed to slip out of range without a single hit. I watched as it escaped downstream.

After the excitement of the sea battle, I returned to the task at hand. Apart from the missing button, I managed to repair the garment reasonably well. I relaxed and began to enjoy the rest of the day.

From time to time I spied small gatherings of stickleback fish. They congregated within the calmer edges of the bank, so I decided to do some fishing. I fashioned a rod from the remaining length of cotton and a suitable branch taken from a birch tree. I bent my mother's needle inside a crack in the brickwork of the bridge. This made an excellent fishing hook. A small twig tied to the line acted as a float. This worked surprisingly well. A search of the embankment unearthed a thick worm as bait. I even found a discarded milk bottle, filled with mud and the pelt of a dead mouse. I rinsed the bottle in the stream and filled it with clean water.

After an hour or so, I was rewarded with my first tiny catch. I placed it inside the milk bottle. I watched as the little fish darted about inside, examining its new prison. This kept me amused whilst I continued to fish. After a while, the worm looked less animated. It wriggled and contorted slowly under the water. Numerous small fish swam near the morsel but none fell for my trap.

A girl yelled out. She was calling my name from a distance, from way over by the railway line. I turned to look. As I did, someone grabbed my hair. They pulled me backwards onto the bridge, painfully twisting and yanking. Instinctively, I held their hand firmly to my scalp. I wriggled frantically on my back, the sunshine dazzling my eyes. Beyond the glare, I saw my attacker. Charles Fenton. His shirt was untucked, scruffy. His rolled-up sleeves displayed crusty scabs on his elbows. Parts of the scabs had flaked away revealing bright pink blotches of new skin beneath.

'Freak!' he cursed, making a fist, pulled back ready to punch my face.

I seized the opportunity to grab his little finger as it clawed at my head. I bent it backwards at an unnatural angle. Fenton let go. He stepped back, examining his hand. I rose to a sitting position but before I could climb to my feet, the boy kicked me in the middle of my back. I was sent flailing into the stream, landing face down. The water stung my eyes. The shock of the cold stream took my breath away.

Fenton laughed boisterously.

Gasping, I got to my feet, ankle-deep in water.

The girl ran to Fenton's side. It was his younger sister, Emily. She had a boyfriend, James. He was in the year above me at school.

Emily was breathing heavily, having run across the common. She rested an arm on Fenton's shoulder to steady herself.

'Leave him alone Charlie,' she yelled, 'He's half your size, don't be such a ruddy bully!'

'Been fishing have we?' Fenton said to me, picking up the fishing rod from the bridge and snapping it in two.

I took a step toward him in anger. Realising my face was now aligned with his shoe, I stepped back again. Fenton picked up the milk bottle and shook it vigorously, taunting the little fish. Then, slowly, he poured the contents, out onto the dusty bridge. He flung the empty bottle at me. I deflected it painfully with my elbow.

I saw the fish, helplessly gasping on the gravel. Fenton smirked. Slowly, deliberately, he crushed it under his foot. Emily struck him in the arm. She turned and left, heading back across the common.

Fenton scooped up the moist remnants of the dying fish and flung them into my face.

'I'm telling mum!' the girl called out, some way off.

'Wait up, Emily!' Fenton yelled, 'Don't tell.' He ran off to catch up with his sister.

I wiped the fish entrails from the side of my nose. The tiny creature's innards continued to wriggle and convulse in the palm of my hand. Tiny intestines twisting and contorting. I watched as they finally gave up on life.

By the time I washed my hands and face in the stream, Fenton and his sister were specks in the distance. Insignificant. I headed off into the woods, hoping the trees would swallow me from sight and sound of the entire world.

I followed the bridleway which wound ever deeper into the woodland. Despite the temperature of the day I wore my jacket, hoping my body heat would dry it. My clothes were still damp when I reached the Roman Villa. The clearing was empty.

Feeling hungry, I removed the soggy sandwiches and apples from my pocket and laid the jacket on a sunlit branch. Water dripped from the cuffs. The apples tasted delicious but the jam sandwiches were damp and gritty.

I sat by the base of an old oak. Growing nearby was a clump of lords-and-ladies. I know their Latin name. It is *Arum maculate*. It was decorated with shiny plump green berries. During the latter parts of the year, the berries change from green to orange and then a vibrant red. It has a rather unusual appearance and I knew it was poisonous. Simply touching the plant could result in a rash. If one were to rub one's eyes afterwards, it could, I have been told, cause blindness. I remember Father telling me. Anyone foolish enough to eat the berries would suffer a slow and agonising death. I untucked my shirt and used the material to pluck some of the fruit. I placed them in my pocket.

After a while, I picked up a stick and brandished it wildly like a sword. I spied a dense patch of stinging nettles almost as tall as me. I imagined I was a soldier. Heroically felling Germans with each swipe. I hacked at my foe, cutting them down into a blanket of green. I advanced, crushing them underfoot.

Within the centre of the nettles, I saw a rock. It was about the size of a footrest. I chose this to be my military objective for the morning. Several blisters were already forming on the palm of my hand but I fought my way forward regardless. Father would have been proud.

As I reached the rock, I stopped, forced to cover my mouth and nose. The most disgusting smell. My sword fell to the ground. Laid atop the rock were hundreds of dead snails. Their shells smashed to reveal wads of gooey mollusc flesh and shell splinters. It was all bound together in revolting globs. Flies fed upon the carnage. No thrush or similar bird I knew would have done this. Nor a fox. I retreated from the stench. Four or five pounds of rotting snail flesh deposited on a rock. I had never seen anything like it before.

By the afternoon my clothing had dried so I headed back into the village. I made my way to the *Wendy House* and purchased a quarter of jelly babies. I ate them as I made my way through the village into Upper Ashtead. A match was underway at the cricket grounds. The scoreboard announced that Ashtead was playing Epsom. Who was in the winning position I neither knew nor cared. The sound of a ball being struck firmly by the bat, followed by a soft ripple of applause.

By the time I reached Upper Ashtead, all my jelly babies had gone. It was only three o'clock and I did not wish to return home until well after dark. I made my way to the paper shop and purchased a copy of the Hotspur comic. I sat down on a bench and read it. It was not very funny.

I began to feel bored so purchased an open bag of chips for my supper. I ate them as I strolled along the shopfront, peering into any window which took my fancy. The sky above was clear and blue. An ideal night to observe through the astronomers' telescope I thought.

I placed my empty chip bag into a bin, beside a payphone box outside the shops. I checked my money. I had enough to telephone Mr Simpkins. I picked up the receiver and rummaged through my pockets for his number. However, I discovered the scrap of paper that held it, was the very same piece that escaped my naval battle along the River Rye. I called the operator for help. The lady could not place the call. Mr Simpkins was not on the directory.

I made my way over to the red house. The closer I got, the more apprehensive I felt. But the sky above looked so clear. Perfect, beautiful. My fear of calling unannounced was swept away by the excitement of the stars.

I stood outside of the gentleman's front door. No signs of light from within. Perhaps he was not in, or he was sleeping, I thought. Perhaps he was already working inside the great observatory, preparing the equipment for the night ahead. To observe the heavens through such a glorious telescope; I could not wait any longer. I knocked on the door.

Inside, a hallway lamp became illuminated. It shone through the narrow glass panes of the door. The sound of a multitude of locks and bolts sliding free. And then the door swung open. Mr Simpkins stood before me. His face looked stern. His eyes were somehow vacant as if staring into the distance. I felt uneasy. I should not have knocked. I should never have returned. I had been unbelievably stupid. I considered turning on the spot, fleeing. Yet somehow I was captivated by the strangeness of the man's eyes. A smile erupted across his face.

'My dear fellow,' he said, enthusiastically shaking my hand, 'Marvellous to see you. Absolutely marvellous. So glad you came. Splendid conditions tonight, you know. Come on, in you come.'

I followed the man inside. He paused in the hallway with his back to me.

'You know, George,' he said, 'you really should have called ahead first. You'll have to wait here a moment. I need to tidy up.'

Mr Simpkins left me in the hallway as he entered the kitchen. He closed the door firmly behind him. I stood politely, listening to the hidden sounds. A window, or something similar, was being opened. A few seconds later it was closed again. Then Mr Simpkins returned.

'Well then young man,' he said, 'I expect you'll be wanting to see the observatory!' He leaned in closer. 'Come on then, it's a marvellous thing.' He beckoned me to follow him.

The kitchen was disgusting. Dirty plates, some coated in dried food residue, lay haphazardly about. Filthy clutter. One cupboard, above a countertop, was missing its door. It held a ramshackle stack of crockery.

To the right of the back door was a Butler sink. As I followed Mr Simpkins out into the garden, I glanced into it. It was filled with the foulest smelling brown, greasy water. Protruding from the surface of the murky liquid were yet more grimy plates and utensils. I wondered how any human could live in such a state of affairs.

A plump, white maggot wriggled aimlessly across the draining board. The most obnoxious stench, my throat tightened.

'My cleaner would only do the hallway,' he said, 'Refused to do anywhere else. She's gone now. Still, not to worry, I'll hire another one soon enough.'

Then, picking up the maggot with his gloved hands, he slowly crushed it between his thumb and index finger. 'There,' he said, 'that's better.' He began to examine the residue. Then, he wiped the gummy mess, in its entirety, into the top pocket of his suit. I did not see this to be the actions of a sane gentleman. Yet I had seen my father conducting himself in a similar manner from time to time. No doubt a consequence of his experience in the war. It often bred antisocial behaviours and peculiarities in men.

Outside, the fresh air was welcoming. The garden and lawn were immaculate, bound within a brick wall. Rose bushes and apple trees lined either side, alternating along their length. An ornate armillary mounted upon a marble plinth marked the centre of the lawn. Beyond, towards the rear of the garden, stood a most impressive observatory dome. Perhaps one of the finest in England. The walls of the structure were red brick but embedded with bold chunks of black flint for decoration. The base was hexagonal, perhaps twelve feet or so in width. Resting atop the structure was the grand dome. It was constructed from sheets of curved copper, tarnished green with time.

Sunset was still a few hours away. The air was crisp - excellent viewing conditions. I could not conceal my excitement of such a prospect, and nor would I have wished to do so. I smiled broadly.

Mr Simpkins unlocked the metal door. Unlike smaller, privately owned observatories I had seen in books, we didn't need to stoop low to gain entry underneath the rotating dome, such was its scale.

Inside was illuminated with soft light from several electric bulbs. A curved desk swept elegantly around the circumference of the structure. Everything appeared impeccably clean, neat and in its proper place. Three study chairs were tucked neatly beneath the desk. Overhead, the great observatory dome stood like a cathedral to the pursuit of scientific knowledge.

Rising from the very centre of the floor was an iron pier. It was some twelve inches in diameter and about three feet in height. Upon this, sat the bulky iron mechanics of the telescope mount. I had seen mounts before, but never one so substantial. This particular device looked to be powered by a hefty clockwork mechanism. Several counterbalances, each no doubt weighing several pounds, were attached to the end of an iron bar. It was exquisite engineering, designed to smoothly synchronise the movement of the telescope with the rotation of the heavens above. And there, bolted securely onto the mount was the telescope. It was a magnificent thing. My delight was immeasurable.

The observatory door clanked shut.

Chapter V

The telescope, which rested horizontally from the mechanical mount, extended across much of the observatory. It was simple in design yet substantial in its construction. Consisting primarily of a large steel tube some ten feet or so in length and over two feet in diameter; open at one end. Starlight entered through the aperture and fell upon the large primary mirror at the rear of the instrument. The glass had been ground and highly polished to form a curved, parabolic surface. It directed the gathered starlight back towards the very centre of the open end. Here, the light struck a much smaller secondary mirror, suspended across the opening by means of four thin metal struts; spider veins. This mirror was cut into an ellipse and angled to direct the light into a focusing device at the side. By placing any one of several removable eyepiece lenses into the focuser, one could vary the scale of magnification. A fine-tuning knob brought the image into focus. It was a truly wonderful construction, based upon the designs of Sir Isaac Newton over 270 years ago.

'It's beautiful,' I said, 'I didn't know there's anything like this in Ashtead. Is it old?'

Mr Simpkins nodded. 'It's old – eighty or ninety years, give or take. There used to be a substantial refractor telescope here but it was too damaged to be of further use. Even the mount was in a pretty poor state when I purchased the house. Your father helped restore it, you know.' Mr Simpkins ran his fingertip along the contours of the mount. 'Hand-built,' he said, 'by a very skilled engineer. Unfortunately, he's long gone. He used to live here, in the red house. Worked tirelessly within these very walls. The things he saw through this telescope!' Mr Simpkins paused for the briefest of moments. He let out an almost inaudible sigh. 'He was fascinated by the Orion nebula, you know,' he continued, 'I still have some of his original observational notes. Very fascinating. Certainly gave me a head start in my research. Unfortunately, the old man had gone. No one knows where or why. He just disappeared one day. Everything fell into ruin after that. The house included. That's how I could purchase the place so cheaply. The restoration became a passion of mine. And your father's too. We all had our part to play.'

I looked around, imagining my father tinkering with the mechanics of the hefty mechanisms. He would have been happy here, I knew it. Enjoying every aspect. And yet Father had never mentioned the observatory to me. He knew I would have been enthralled by it all. Yet, he had said nothing.

In my earlier years, before his death, Father would hand me his binoculars in the darkness of our garden. He would point out the locations of the planets; Mars, Jupiter and Saturn. Even with such simple binoculars, it had been possible to see the Galilean moons of Jupiter. On countless clear nights, I watched their celestial dance around their parent body. Tiny dots of light. They jostled for position around the formidable gas giant. The thought of observing such splendours through a wondrous telescope made my heart race.

'It won't be dark for a couple of hours,' Mr Simpkins said, 'Happy to show you the basics. You can be my honorary assistant for the night, if you'd like.'

The gentleman handed me a blank notebook. He instructed me to record, in considerable detail, the operational procedures of the equipment as he explained them to me. He drew my attention to the location of a large wall clock mounted close to the observatory door. This clock, he stated, was to be accurately maintained at all times; kept in exact keeping with Greenwich Mean Time. He explained the workings of the mount, with its cogs, worm gears and counterweights, all crucial in maintaining the tracking accuracy of the telescope. This was the workhorse of the entire observatory. I was enthralled. Learning the skills of a professional astronomer. Mr Simpkins was obviously a skilled mechanical engineer and possessed a great command of mathematics, far beyond my comprehension. I was his eager apprentice. Absorbing the knowledge and practical skills required to gently slew tons of delicate scientific equipment towards any astronomical body in the night sky. The universe, in all its grandeur, stood before us.

I listened intently as Mr Simpkins explained to me the astronomical coordinate system. Right Ascension and Declination; the method by which any object within the night sky can be readily located. It is similar to that of longitude and latitude applied to any traditional map of the world. He explained the workings of a secondary clockwork mechanism that also rotated the aperture of the observatory dome, keeping it, and the telescope, in perfect synchronisation.

To observe, it was necessary to perch upon a rather uncomfortable seat atop a wooden platform. The seat was accessible via a narrow ladder. Periodically the entire platform was moved manually to keep pace with the slow movement of the telescope as it tracked the heavens. It was built upon heavy, lockable, caster wheels for this very purpose. It was the duty of the astronomer's assistant to nudge the platform whenever needed.

As dusk fell, Mr Simpkins extinguished the white lighting and replaced it with a soft red glow from additional electrical lamps upon the walls. To observe the faintest of objects, an observer's sight must not be compromised by unwanted pollution. Red light causes the least disruption to one's dark-adapted vision.

I watched the astronomer as he turned a cranking handle positioned close to the tracking mechanism. The dome's two vertical shutters slowly slid apart to reveal a thousand stars sparkling from horizon to zenith. The telescope had been perfectly balanced upon the mount. Its entire bulk could be manoeuvred into any position with a gentle push of a single finger.

When employed in observation, a clutch contrivance was engaged in the plane of Right Ascension. This process locked the telescope onto its current coordinate and engaged the clockwork mechanism. This ensured the entire instrument would automatically guide in near-perfect harmony with the rotation of the Earth. Thus, any object placed within the view of the eyepiece would remain fixed and visible for the duration. I could not have been more excited. I found my eyes dancing around the observatory, absorbing all its wonders.

As the air temperature began to fall, Mr Simpkins sat me down beside the desk. He spoke to me as an equal – a fellow scientist. A scientist about to embark on a voyage of discovery. He explained to me the importance of recording observations within my notebook. Briefly leaving the desk, he cranked the entire dome towards the southern sky. He then drew my attention to a set of dials attached to the telescope mount. They displayed the current astronomical coordinates at which the telescope pointed. Numerous catalogues on the desk listed the positions of tens of thousands of stars, nebulae and galaxies within the universe. One needed only to release the clutches on the mount and push the telescope by hand until the required coordinates were displayed upon the dials.

The astronomer studied the telescopic view through a much smaller finder telescope attached firmly to the side of the main instrument. I watched as he made minor alterations to the positioning with the aid of two hand-adjustment knobs. When he was satisfied, he engaged both the clutches.

'I have a gift for you, George,' he said, 'I doubt your father would have wanted me to keep it.'

The astronomer extended his arm and handed me a pen. It was Seabrook's fountain pen. I stared at the initials on the cap.

'Thank you,' I said.

I felt hesitant as I took it. It was bound to infuriate my mother.

Mr Simpkins gestured for me to look through the eyepiece. Despite being positioned almost horizontally, it was still too high for me to view from the ground. The observation platform was pushed forwards and its height adjusted accordingly. I climbed up onto the viewing seat, five feet or so above the floor. Now, *I* was the astronomer. Mr Simpkins was my assistant, gently pushing the ladder and platform into position. I felt ecstatic.

Closing one eye, I peered into the small eyepiece in the focuser. I felt disappointed, nothing but a fuzzy orange blob. A blurry anomaly. As I turned the focusing dial inwards, the orange blob melted into crystal clear grandeur. The broadest of smiles crept across my face. Enthralled by the anticipation of the night ahead, I recorded the very first entry into my notebook:

'Saturday 23rd August 1939. 9.40 pm. Observations of Mars'.

As the night proceeded, Mr Simpkins showed me how to slew the great instrument around to the next target of the evening, the planet Jupiter. Despite the gibbous moon in the southwest, its glare did not obscure the gas giant. The view was spectacular. The planet appeared much larger than Mars, I could even see several bands running horizontally across its disc. By three o'clock, the famous Great Red Spot began to rotate into view. A violent stormcloud some twenty-five thousand miles across, wider than the Earth itself. Within my notebook, I sketched the positions of four of Jupiter's moons. Callisto and Ganymede to the left and Io and Europa to the right. The swirling mechanics of the Solar System were laid bare before my eyes. I was a god, watching over my vast empire. Of all the billions of inhabitants on Earth, I was, perhaps, one of only a tiny handful looking upon the moons of Jupiter at that moment. It was a humbling experience.

'Time for a cup of tea, I think!' the astronomer announced as he assisted me down from the ladder.

I sat by the desk.

'You've worked well tonight, George,' Mr Simpkins said, 'Wait here, lad.'

The astronomer departed into the darkness of the garden, leaving me alone. I took the opportunity to peruse the sheets of notepaper on the desk. Complex mathematical calculations, excitedly scrawled in pencil.

Stacked neatly upon the desk, snug against the brick walls, was a substantial collection of black notebooks. They were stored chronologically, based upon the season and year. The periods were indicated along their spine. They ran from the winter of 1910 right up to the present. Out of curiosity, I examined one of them, opening it at a random page. On the left-hand leaf, the most exquisite colour sketch of the great Orion nebula. Vast pink, purple and green clouds of gas, illuminated at their heart by the birth of newly igniting stars. And yet it was the drawing to the right of this which caught my attention. It was rendered in such a strange style. Dark pencil marks scratched across the page in sweeping arcs and jagged angles. The page was creased and worn as if produced in a great hurry. Yet within the shadows of this sketch, strange figures could be seen to lurk. I did not notice them at first. A single pair of eyes peering back at me. I had never been moved by artwork before, but this sketching was different. I felt uneasy. I do not know why, but I could not look away from this ghastly scene. Something about those strange, demonic eyes. They were staring at me. Familiar, as if from a distant nightmare. A dream I did not wish to recall.

The observatory door opened and the astronomer entered, carrying two cups of tea. I began to return the book to its rightful place.

'Stop,' Mr Simpkins yelled. 'Don't you ever touch my notes without permission, you filthy bloody rat!' His German accent evident in his tone. He hurried across to where I sat, placing the cups hastily onto the desk beside me. His eyes scanned along the collection of books.

Seeing spilt tea, I pushed aside the sheets of mathematical calculations to ensure they were not soiled. I mopped up the tea with my sleeve. It was then I noticed the gentleman's hands. They were un-gloved. The fingers of his wounded hand were blackened and shrivelled. Blotchy. A mat of scabs coated his wrist and what was left of his palm. It looked to be decaying, spreading along his arm like the roots of a tree. But it was the sight of his right hand which shocked me most. Here, the skin had been roughly peeled back from the flesh. The muscles and tendons were exposed and enflamed. I could see they were weeping and the taste of decay clung to my mouth.

The astronomer hastily turned his back. When he faced me again, he had donned his gloves.

'Well then, young man,' he said, 'I think it's time you learned a lesson or two. About the cosmos!'

The astronomer made himself comfortable in the chair beside me. He smiled as if nothing had happened. A veneer of normality. I found this more unsettling than the sight and smell of his decaying hands.

I sipped at the hot tea. It tasted particular. Very sweet, but with a rather bitter aftertaste. I did not want to anger him, so, I drank it and did not make a fuss.

'A gentleman's notes, on scientific research,' he began, 'are a private and personal affair. One must endeavour to protect such things, you understand.'

I nodded slowly, hoping that it would appease him.

'So,' he said, rather abruptly, 'what can you tell me about the equation E equals m c squared?'

The question caught me somewhat off guard. 'It's Einstein's equation,' I said, 'E represents energy and m is mass and c is the speed of light.'

The astronomer rolled his eyes. 'C represents the cosmological constant,' he corrected, 'the speed of light in a vacuum – something which never alters, regardless of where you happen to observe it within the universe. Obviously, that's what the equation represents, but what does it actually *mean*?'

I paused, trying to understand his question. I could tell my hesitance irritated him. He was fidgeting in his seat.

'Let me put it another way,' he said, 'The equation five times two equals ten. What does that tell us?'

Mr Simpkins looked at me coldly. I felt confused.

'It means,' he said, 'that everything in the equation is balanced. Interchangeable. It means that not only does ten equal five times two, but that five is equal to ten divided by two, and that,' he continued, 'two is equal to ten divided by five.'

The astronomer slumped back into his chair. 'So then,' he continued, 'what can you tell me about Einstein's equation now?'

'Er, well,' I began, 'it means the mass of an object is also equal to its energy divided by the speed of light, squared.'

The astronomer smiled.

'Good,' he said 'and likewise the speed of light, squared, is equal to the energy divided by the mass. Now then,' he continued, 'the speed of light is naturally a very large number. If you multiply it by itself, you arrive at an even larger number. Since energy is equal to this large number, multiplied by mass, that tells us that energy is the largest variable in the equation. Even greater than the speed of light, squared!'

Mr Simpkins reached across to the desk and took his cup of tea.

'You see, George, what this equation *means* is that if you take something small, which has mass, say, a metal coin, it could be converted from matter into pure light and energy.' In an almost hushed voice, he added 'vast, vast amounts of light and energy. Energy such as heat. A fireball in fact. Greater than you could ever imagine.'

The astronomer fell silent in his thoughts. I did not wish to distract him.

'A war is coming, George,' he said. 'One side will win and one side will lose. I suspect it may be a very fine line between the possible outcomes.'

The astronomer finished his tea. 'The powers that be,' he said, 'believe that certain efforts should be made. Efforts to pull matter apart. To release the heat and light upon our enemies. A new era of weaponry. The next generation of carnage. They aren't content with the mechanised slaughter of men. They want to expand their skills of destruction with the application of physics.'

Mr Simpkins paused again. 'I propose a rather different approach,' he said. 'Rather than disrupt matter to create energy and light, we should combine light and energy, to form new matter. New mass. We should be the masters of creation, not destruction. Your father agreed with me. That's why he assisted me for so long. If it hadn't been for the Great War, perhaps, well, who knows!'

I glanced at the long row of notebooks. 'Did my father write any of these?' I asked.

The astronomer nodded, 'Yes, your father made notes for me. From the beginning. He was an excellent student. You would do well to follow in his footsteps.'

I have often thought about this moment. The astronomer, the man who would one day become so intrinsically entwined in my life. If I could go back, if I could re-live those hours. I could change the course of events. I would gladly sell my soul to the devil himself for such an opportunity. I could have simply walked out of the observatory and never returned. I could have set about the man, clawing out his heart with my bare hands. Or I could have ripped my own eyes from their sockets, blinding myself so that I may never gaze upon the stars again. I could have burnt the place to the ground, the entire village even. Such actions would have been just. But I had not yet realised my fate. Not yet. Instead, I remained. An assistant to an astronomer. An accomplice to an unnatural, wretched and unearthly deed.

Chapter VI

By the time I returned to the eyepiece, Saturn had risen. It was high above the horizon towards the south, ideally situated. To view the planet's magnificent ring system through such a splendid telescope filled me with excitement. I had seen them before, through my father's binoculars, but they had been barely visible. But it became apparent Mr Simpkins was not willing to indulge in any such folly. He had other plans. He glanced over his shoulder, remaining vigilant of the hour. It was now one minute past four. In little over an hour, the first light of dawn would bring an end to the proceedings.

'My interest,' he said, 'lies in the constellation of Orion.' He paused and smiled dryly as if he had inadvertently divulged more than he intended. 'You see, George,' he continued, 'your father, together with Stanley Seabrook and myself, had studied this particular region of the sky for some time. Since 1910, in fact. The very year I acquired this house, this observatory. I expect,' he said, 'it was your father who encouraged your study in such things.'

I nodded.

'My university education,' he said, 'is in mathematics and physics. But I hold a particular fondness for the science of astronomy and the electromagnetic spectrum. That is to say,' he explained, 'the wavelengths of electromagnetic radiation of visible and invisible light, and their associated energies, of course.'

The astronomer looked towards the stars. They sparkled brightly through the open aperture of the observatory dome.

'Out of little more than curiosity,' he said, 'I examined the research notes written by the previous owner of the house. With these notes, I made the most astounding discovery. I can scarcely believe it myself. You see, George, I discovered something. Something wonderful.'

Mr Simpkins did not offer further details. Although curious, I did not wish to push him on the matter. Regardless, the thought that my father had been involved in a significant scientific discovery, was exciting. Strange therefore that he had never alluded to such things.

'Sometimes George, when I study the stars, I forget to acknowledge their beauty,' the astronomer said. 'Science, you see is about understanding. Humanity is about looking. About feeling. About thinking. It's so very easy to forget how to be human, don't you find?' He looked directly into my eyes. 'Don't ever let science hinder your humanity.'

'There are trillions of stars in the universe,' he said, 'I wonder how many hold host to planets. How many of those planets are conducive to harbouring life.' He paused. 'Perhaps, life not unlike our own. Take the Orion Nebula, for example. It's a fascinating object to study you know,' he continued, 'It's called M42 in the Messier catalogue. A rather cold name for something so delicately beautiful, don't you think? The birthplace of new stars.' He smiled again. 'Your father and Stanley were fascinated by the Orion Nebula. They made some wonderfully detailed sketches. Gas clouds stretching out for light-years, illuminated by burning stars.'

The astronomer began caressing his gloved hands again.

'Located above the nebula,' he continued, 'is a line of three bright stars. The belt of Orion. From that belt, hangs the sword of Orion, M42.'

Ever since I was a very young boy, I had known of these three stars. They are a prominent feature in the winter sky. Even the great gas nebula is visible to the naked eye. A glowing smudge, almost the same apparent size as a full moon. Yet most people never even notice it though. People do not bother to look up at the sky, not properly.

'Those three stars,' the astronomer said, 'are named Alnitak, Alnilam and Mintaka. But it is the middle star, Alnilam, which proved so remarkable.'

The astronomer was animated as he spoke.

'Your father and Stanley lacked my interest in Alnilam,' he said. 'In fact, Seabrook would have no part in it. He only wanted to observe the aesthetically pleasing objects. He was naïve.' The astronomer smirked. 'But at least your father offered some tangible assistance.'

Mr Simpkins continued to caress his gloves.

'I've told you of my fascination with light and energy,' he said, 'Alnilam has both, in great abundance. It's a pulsing star, you see. For almost thirty years I've studied it. The wavelengths of light emitted at each peak. I've found it possible to split its spectrum of colours. A unique fingerprint of light. It reveals the very structure of the star. From this spectrum, we can infer so much knowledge. Temperature, distance, mass. Even the composition of the atoms within its core. It is all revealed to us in the starlight.' The astronomer smiled. 'And this particular spectrum of Alnilam,' he said, 'has revealed something wonderful. You see, your father and I observed a phenomenon. Something rather strange.'

I was intrigued but felt great unease as I sat underneath the metal dome, listening in awe of the man.

'We noticed,' he said, 'over a period of only a few seconds, a sudden increase in the star's brightness - its magnitude. I couldn't explain it at first. A transient event. But I was, nonetheless, able to image it. I took several photographs in fact. A record of the star's spectrum. I have them here, look.'

Pulling open a drawer, the astronomer removed a single glass photographic plate. It had been secured within a small storage rack within the drawer. The image, monochrome and slightly faded towards the edges of the glass, consisted of a set of long bands of varying shaded densities. Scattered amongst these bands were several lines. They were thin and irregularly spaced. Most were faint but some were very dark and prominent. They had been annotated. I saw the labels Hα, Hβ, OIII and SII written above. One particular cluster had been circled in pen. Above it, the words '*transient anomaly - equipment leaching?*'

'You don't understand do you boy; it's fundamental physics,' the astronomer said. 'You see, those strong emission lines simply shouldn't be there. No atoms absorb or emit wavelengths in those combinations. And the energy! The energy in the emission lines, phenomenal. I couldn't explain them. Not at first. When we took a second image, they were gone. Only the familiar markers of the lighter elements remained. An unknown transient event.'

The astronomer looked at me and smiled. 'Of course, we assumed it was due to a piece of faulty equipment. The camera or stray light, trapped within the imaging train. But a week later, the anomaly returned. Only for a few minutes, seconds even. We practically rebuilt the entire imaging path within the telescope, looking for the cause of the error.'

Replacing the glass plate into the drawer, the astronomer looked at the wall clock. 'But you see George, there was no error. It was your father who made the connection between the emission lines in the spectrum and the pulsing of the star.'

'My father?' I said, 'He never mentioned it.'

Rising from his chair, the astronomer began to pace, constantly rubbing his hands. 'I would be surprised if he did,' he said. 'You see, Alnilam pulses every six and two-thirds of a day. We call this '*one period of pulsation*'. It was your father who noticed the pattern. The correlation between the transient anomaly and the period of pulsation. You see, the anomaly didn't occur at every peak. That was the curious thing. Only on the second, third, fifth, seventh, eleventh, thirteenth and seventeenth pulse. And then the sequence repeats. Every 110 days.'

The astronomer grasped the rear of my chair, 'Primary numbers,' he said excitedly, 'They're all primary numbers. In fact, there are seven of them. That is, in itself, a primary number. It's inconceivable that such an anomaly could occur naturally.'

The astronomer's eyes seemed to sparkle as he looked at me in delight. 'A signal. A message even. Deliberately transmitted towards us,' he said, 'And the energy within the broadcast, it's phenomenal. A message from the stars. A gift.'

It was the dream of every schoolboy. To hear tales of aliens, space adventures and the like. Yet, as I listened to the astronomer, I felt no such excitement. I felt uneasy. I felt uneasy with the universe and of my place within it. My mind raced. Intelligent life from a distant star, transmitting a signal towards the Earth? It would be a fantastic achievement. A feat surely indicative of a phenomenally advanced society. And then, of course, there is the issue of distance. The great void across space in which the signal must pass. The light reaching Earth would have travelled for almost two thousand years. Could it *really* be a signal reaching out to us, across both space and time?

'Alnilam is such a young star,' the astronomer said, 'Far too young for any life to evolve there I suspect. I believe the sender was not native to such a place. That suggests a nomadic civilisation. Travellers through our grand galaxy.'

It was such a fantastic notion.

'Seabrook would have none of it,' the astronomer said, 'But your father continued to assist me nonetheless. Until the Great War of course. That rather put a halt to things. Stanley became obstructive. He disapproved of our research, you see. In fact, he even tried to sabotage it.'

'If you've been studying this for thirty years,' I said, 'you must have discovered more about its origin, what it means!'

The astronomer motioned for me to stand.

'Indeed I have,' he said.

I followed Mr Simpkins over to the telescope. I watched as he disengaged the Right Ascension and Declination clutches and pushed the great instrument towards a low region of the southwestern sky. The observatory dome rotated in unison until I could see the recognisable pattern of the Orion constellation. After locking the clutches, the telescope began to track.

'It is, perhaps, no coincidence that you chose to visit my observatory on the very occasion of the first cycle of the transmission cycle!'

I watched as the astronomer peered through the small guiding telescope, directing the main instrument onto the central star within the belt of Orion. To Alnilam. The light of dawn would soon be breaking. It would mark the end of the observing session. And yet I sensed great urgency in the man's actions. He looked anxious in his hasty undertakings. As if a great deal depended on it.

When the telescope had been aligned, the astronomer ordered me to climb the ladder onto the observation platform. He continued to monitor the passing of each second, watching the hand silently sweep across the clock face. I felt uncomfortable at the sudden change of his demeanour. He had become consumed, as if the rest of the world had been blocked from his mind.

I settled myself into the observing seat. Under his instruction, I replaced the eyepiece for one with greater magnification. As I brought Alnilam into focus, the clockwork mechanism of the mount kept the blue-white star stationary within my central field of view.

'What do you want me to record?' I asked.

'I don't require you to record anything, George,' he replied, 'I merely require you to observe.' The astronomer spoke clearly and distinctly, like a teacher. 'When I say so, I want you to fix your gaze on the star. When I tell you to look, you shall look. I don't wish you to speak. You must only I do as I say. Do not take your eye away from the star, not for a split second. In fact, I don't even wish you to blink. Not once! Do you understand?'

I sat obediently beside the telescope. Below me, the astronomer, staring intently at the wall clock. He began to pace again, at the foot of the platform.

The wall clock showed three minutes before the hour of four a.m.

'Now!' the astronomer barked. 'You are to observe now. And don't dare look away. Or Blink. Or talk!'

In my foolish youth, I fulfilled his request.

Holding my left eye to the eyepiece, I watched the shimmering image of the distant star. The instability of the atmospheric disturbance made it sparkle beautifully. It shone in brilliant white and blue. But I also saw brief flashes of reds and greens. After a minute or so, I began to grow bored. The star looked identical to any one of the tens of thousands of other stars. I shifted myself to a more comfortable position within the seat.

'Concentrate!' the astronomer yelled, banging his fist on the side of the platform, 'keep your eye fixed, damn it, boy!'

I continued to look at the single point of light. I saw nothing but the mundane. But then, as the minutes passed, the star began to increase in brightness. It was very slight but it was noticeable. I had not been certain of the change at first, but by comparing its relative magnitude against other fainter stars in the field of view, I could tell it had brightened. I smiled. My first observation of a variable star. They are common throughout the night sky but I had never seen one before. I felt an exhilarating rush of adrenalin.

As I continued to stare, I become aware of a subtle, rhythmic pulsing within the light. It was a strange effect. Almost hypnotic. It lasted only a few seconds. A brief pause, and it would repeat. But each time, it grew in intensity, ever brighter. It was obvious now, it shone like a torch, making it difficult to see any other stars. Soon, the light was so bright, it became painful. I had never seen anything like it before. Like staring into the sun!

I tried to look away but I could not. Compelled to peer relentlessly into the eyepiece of the telescope. I blinked involuntarily. To my surprise, I found I still saw the pulsing light as if it were etched onto my brain. I listened to the astronomer. He was yelling at me. Yelling vile obscenities. Ordering me not to look away from the telescope. I felt nauseous. I closed my eyes tight, but still, I saw the shining starlight of Alnilam.

The astronomer's rantings became an incomprehensible burst of thunder in my skull. I opened my eyes again. I could not help myself. The star shone much bluer now. I could no longer look away. The beam flickered so rapidly. I felt a pain in my head. It grew in intensity, deep behind my left eye. It was like a magnifying glass burning at my skin.

As the dancing light continued, I felt myself staring into the very core of the star, as if I were somehow being pulled into its raging heart. The pain behind my retina was unbearable. It spread through my brain like wildfire. Unsteady, I grasped firmly onto the seat rest. The fire within my head grew to a white-hot inferno. Yet I felt compelled to maintain my gaze upon the light, like a moth attracted to a candle.

A sense of weightlessness washed over me. I saw only the light. Even the mad rantings of the astronomer were lost to me in the hypnotic glare. The telescope no longer existed. I was oblivious to it all. The observatory, the house, the village. Everything ceased to exist. I saw nothing within the entire universe save for the dazzling light from the burning heart of Alnilam. The inferno raged through my body.

I do not know how long I had been at the eyepiece. Perhaps no more than a minute. Fear and anxiety washed over the back of my head. It doused my body. It covered my face in a shroud of darkness. I had never felt so afraid, so alone. Unable to break free from this pulsating force.

I vomited violently onto my lap. But the light continued to burn. The pain was unbearable; as if my organs were to explode from my chest. I began to panic. With all my strength, I pulled my face from the eyepiece. I felt a sudden icy coldness, and then I passed out.

Chapter VII

Constable Billet had been on duty since eight o'clock that evening. On parade, Sergeant Wells instructed him to give the landlord and patrons of the Woodcutter public house some words of advice. Of late, their revelling's at closing time had drawn several complaints from local residents. He was also to conduct a welfare check on Constable Turner. Turner was a keen nineteen-year-old and, as the newest recruit to the station, had been allocated the more mundane duties. Tonight, Turner was to spend his entire shift on cordon duty, guarding outside the late Mrs Stride's bungalow.

Despite the pleasant weather, Constable Billet only saw a few members of the public as he set off from the police station. It was almost ten o'clock when he reached Lower Ashtead. The onset of darkness had cleared the streets of pedestrians. Outside the row of shops along Barnett Wood Lane, he shone his torch through the windows. Golding's, the grocers, was securely locked up for the night. A hand-written notice had been fastened to the entrance. It read:

'*Sorry, no flour until next week*'.

The village hall was nestled in the middle of the shops. The policeman rattled the doors to satisfy himself all was in order. Then he checked the chemist's and the newsagent's stores at the far end of the row. All was quiet.

A clunking sound nearby. The policeman stopped and listened. He heard it again. It came from the narrow path running along the side of the shop. The sound was followed by rummaging. The torchlight drifted towards the sound.

'Police,' he said, 'Who's there?'

Silence.

Constable Billet pulled the chin strap down from his helmet rim and secured it. 'Come on, don't mess about now,' he said, slowly making his way along the pathway.

Movement.

'Alright,' he said, 'out you come sunshine.'

A figure in the shadows bolted towards a wooden fence at the far end of the path and began to scramble over. The constable dashed forward. He took hold of their wrist with one hand and pushed it into the small of their back.

'Stop,' he barked, 'Stand still.'

The torchlight illuminated the silhouette. It was a thin, middle-aged man. He wore a long dark coat and a flat cap. The man tried to wriggle free.

'Stop resisting,' the policeman yelled, tightening his grip on the thin man's wrist.

The thin man continued to struggle.

With the torch raised above his head, the constable brought it firmly down upon the man's arm. The man yelped as he was pulled sharply to the ground.

'Alright mate,' the thin man said, 'take it easy.' He sat himself up in the middle of the driveway, nursing his shoulder.

Constable Billet shone the torchlight into the man's face. He was unshaven with wild hair that cast bedraggled shadows across the sidewall of the newsagents. The man squinted, shielding his eyes from the glare.

'So then,' the policeman said, 'what are you up to, Robert?'

The man shrugged. 'I ain't up to nothing,' he said, 'I'm just having a look in the bins, that's all. It's just rubbish. I ain't doing no harm.'

'But it's not your rubbish to take now, is it!' the constable said, helping the man to his feet. 'Come on, turn your pockets out.'

The man mumbled his objections. Nonetheless, he pulled his coat pockets inside out. They were empty. His trouser pockets revealed nothing more than a box of safety matches and several cigarette butts. Some were flat and twisted. Others held red lipstick marks from their previous owner.

'Are you wanted for anything at the moment?' the constable asked.

The man shook his head. 'I don't think so.'

'You can put your stubs away now,' he said. 'Right then, stand up against the wall. Keep your hands out so I can see them, alright?'

The man placed the cigarette butts back into his pocket.

Constable Billet withdrew his pocketbook. 'Why aren't you out on the common, getting drunk with your mates? Fallen out with them again, have you?'

The man shuffled his feet in the gravel. 'We don't go there anymore. Not at night,' he said. 'None of us do. There's some right strange things going on in the woods these days. Particularly at night. You should look into it, Harry. Not keep harassing me all the bloody time. Victimisation that is, mate.'

'What kind of strange things?' the policeman asked, writing into his pocketbook, the torch held awkwardly underneath his arm.

'Just sounds,' the thin man said, 'But godawful ones at that, mind. Enough to give ya the willies. I ain't never heard sounds like them before.'

'Didn't know you're afraid of the dark, Bob,' the policeman said. 'I'm not putting that in my report. Go on, bugger off home. If she'll still let you back in the house at this hour.'

The thin man said nothing. He straightened out his coat and turned to depart. Constable Billet reached out and took the man's arm again.

'Hold on a minute,' he said, reaching into his tunic, 'you can have one of mine.' The constable handed him a cigarette from his own packet.

'Cheers mate,' the thin man said, tapping the brim of his cap in acknowledgement. He placed the cigarette behind his ear and scurried off into the darkness of the village.

Outside the Woodcutter pub, the familiar faces were already leaving the establishment. The church clock had only just chimed eleven. It was unusual to see the patrons so punctual.

Once the pub had emptied, Constable Billet went inside. The landlord and his wife greeted him with a cup of tea. It was already waiting for him. He sat down and rested his feet as the landlord counted his takings for the day. The policeman relaxed, keen to keep his tunic sleeves clear of the puddles of sticky, stale beer covering the table.

Half an hour later, he resumed his patrol. It took another half hour to reach Mrs Stride's bungalow, over by the village pond. Constable Turner was standing at the front gate. He smiled as Billet approached.

'Thank god you're here,' Turner said, 'I'm bored out of my head. Hardly seen a soul. Just a couple of nosey old dears wanting to know what I'm doing here. I've eaten all my scoff. Dying for a pee though.'

'Off you go then,' Constable Billet said, 'Stretch your legs for a bit. But I want you back here by two, clear?' He stood himself to attention, besides the gate. He had not attended the address since discovering the body.

Turner marched himself off into the darkness.

Constable Billet stood silent and still. He enjoyed point duty, it allowed him to clear his mind. He listened to the silence of the village.

It was almost two o'clock when Constable Turner returned to the bungalow.

'Cheers, mate,' he said, 'I owe you one!'

A shriek.

'Bloody foxes,' Turner said, 'They've been at it all night, Randy buggers.'

'Didn't sound like foxes,' Billet replied. He looked out, across the common, towards the railway station. A light flickered from a distant window, near the ticket booth entrance. 'Better pay 'em a quick visit,' he said, 'See who's about.'

Leaving Turner alone, the constable made his way across the common. Reaching the perimeter of the station, he squeezed himself through a gap in the fencing and made his way onto the southbound platform. It was in darkness, save for the single illuminated window. An adjacent door bore the words *Staff Only*.

'Put the kettle on,' Constable Billet called out as he rattled the door open and stepped into the ticket office. It was warm and inviting.

'Shan't be a tick mate,' an unseen voice replied.

The policeman sat himself down in a comfortable armchair beside a small occasional table. Removing his helmet, he stretched out his legs.

The stationmaster appeared from an adjoining doorway. He carried two cups of tea. 'There you go mate,' he said, 'white and two.'

The stationmaster was an older gentleman. He sat opposite the constable and removed his cap, revealing a bald head. He was a weathered man in his mid-sixties, grubby from the grime of the station. He puffed enthusiastically on a tobacco pipe as he produced a pack of playing cards from his top pocket.

'What's it to be then, Harry,' he said, 'gin-rummy alright?'

The two men began to play. They chatted idly about the gossip of the village. The stationmaster did not ask about the murder of Mrs Stride.

'I raise you,' he said, sliding a dry biscuit across the table to join the pile.

The men studied their cards.

A shriek, like the one before. This time it sounded closer. It jolted the constable, forcing him to sit smartly upright. The stationmaster ignored the sound, barely looking up from his cards.

Constable Billet rose and stepped out onto the platform. The old man muttered under his breath and followed.

'That's not foxes, is it,' the constable said. 'What on earth is it?'

'It's nothing Harry,' the stationmaster said, 'Often hear strange things out in the woods. You know, at night. Puts the right wind up you sometimes. Expect it's badgers or something, I reckon.'

The two men stood on the edge of the platform and listened.

Another shriek, this time more distant. It sounded pitiful, like an animal in pain.

'Sounds more like a dog or something,' the constable said.

They stared out into the darkness, listening.

Then, on the opposite side of the tracks, movement. The unkempt undergrowth beyond the iron fencing began to rustle and sway. The constable withdrew his torch. He shone it out across the tracks.

'Out you come, then,' he called out, 'Come on, show yourself.'

Slowly the undergrowth parted. A pair of unblinking eyes reflected in the light. Green and wide. They advanced no further.

'Look,' the constable said, 'I'm not telling you again. This is Southern Rail property.'

The torchlight remained fixed on the reflective eyes.

Then, in a single bound, a creature broke clear. It leapt over the fence onto the opposite platform. It was joined by another, and then another. Wild deer from the woodlands. A herd of twenty or so adults and fawns. They frantically made their way down onto the tracks, kicking and bucking at invisible predators. Their eyes bulged with fear, venting water vapour from their heated lungs. Skittish and wild, they ran chaotically along the track until they were lost in the darkness.

Another distant shriek. Then silence once more.

'Guess something spooked them,' the old man said, before returning to the card game.

* * *

In my stupor, the darkness which fell upon me was the blackest of any dream. Depraved thoughts and visions bled into my soul. They charred a crust around my heart. Never had I seen such horrors. A landscape of death and torture. Of fear and pain. The vividness was repugnant. A vision, for something that can have no words. Wretched thoughts and emotions leached into my mind, rotting away the innocence of my youth. No person should endure such raw torment as I did that night. But I knew this nightmare was not of my making. My mind was torn and raped by the most wicked and vile of demons. My brain burned. Filled far beyond its natural capacity. Violated by sordid evil. The blood flowing through my body, tainted by bitter hatred. I could never be clean again. Nor could I ever forgive the instigator of this unearthly crime.

A nightmare unfolded before me. Visions appeared as strange amalgamations of hell and reality. So tightly bound, I was unable to unravel their disorder.

My soul was embraced by death. A hopeless void. A nothingness, for all eternity. Pain and fear erupted from every cell in my body, tearing me apart. It belched from my mouth. It seeped through my skin until I was nothing. Nothing but the memories of my tears.

My understanding of the universe was lost. Everything had changed at a fundamental level. There is no right or wrong. No good or evil. No science or belief. There is only blackness. Before this day, I did not believe in God or angels or elves or fairies. And yet, in that observatory, in the darkly hours, as I lay motionless beside the telescope, I believed in the Devil. I had looked into the mind of a demon. This hellish beast taunted me with his power. I was afraid as I bore witness to his dark magic. I will never be loved. I will die alone. And I am nothing.

I became immersed in a wave of fear. It soaked my body like a tidal wave. I shivered uncontrollably. Clammy hands covered my face to hide me from my shame. But my shame was my own. I could not hide from it. I was trapped within the darkness of my mind.

My heart pounded. Veins bulged within my wrists as thick lumps of congealing, rotten blood surged through my body. I was disgusted, claustrophobic. Confined within a body which was not my own, a wretched veneer of flesh. Repulsed by my physical form, I wanted nothing more than to tear at my skin. To free myself. I dug and clawed at my wrists. I sank my nails; pulling away elasticated strips of flesh. Despite the pain, I persevered, determined to rid myself of this repulsion. I lashed out at myself in a frenzy. Probing the wound, I located a thick blue vein. The flesh was warm and slippery with blood. Ashamed, I forced my index finger deep beneath the rubbery vein and hooked it. When at last I could command a firm purchase upon the tendril, I gripped it within my clenched fist. A pulsation of blood surged through my body. I was repulsed, not by the wound, but by the hideous grotesqueness of my mechanics.

Fear boiled over into anger. Anger at the abhorrent creature I had become. Rejoicing in my freedom from my form, I laughed as I pulled sharply upwards. The vein stripped from my body like a fishing line zig-zagging through the water. It pulled free from my arm, my neck, before finally snagging behind my ear on some such obstruction of my anatomy. I tried to tug further upon the cord, but I could not free it. With each pull, my left eyeball spasmed and convulsed. I let go my grip. The vein dangled loosely, still attached to my neck and wrist.

I knew I shall never be free. I smelt the iron within my blood as it trickled from my arm. My clothes were wet. I felt nauseous, not from the pain of injury but from my senses. Overwhelmed by colour and sound. I wanted the sensations to end. I closed my eyes and pleaded for death to take me. But no god heeded my call. No god saved me. I heard only the voice of the demon. His foul stench. He was everything. He was the universe, the light and the dark, the heat and the cold. And I was nothing. Less than a mote of dust suspended in an infinite universe.

I opened my eyes. I found myself standing within the depths of a dense and green forest. It was night. I could see the stars all about. But they were not in the heavens above. Instead, they drifted slowly through the air before me. No more than single points of light. Green, blue, red, white. They flocked together. Some in spiralling arms, others in fuzzy clumps. And in the vast space between the light, was the blackest of blacks. And this is where I stood. In the coldest, darkest place.

Dizzy by the intoxication of the tainted air, I become unsteady on my own clumsy feet. I tumbled to my knees, onto the dry, dead foliage of a woodland floor. At first, I did not recognise my surroundings. It was Ashtead woods, the clearing by the old Roman villa. The exposed vein dangled from my neck, soiled by dirt. It hung from my body, trailing upon the ground. My left arm no longer in pain. I trembled. Not from cold but from fear. In my heart, I knew what was to come. I wasn't brave. I wanted the comfort and mercy of death to offer me escape. But still, I burnt cold in this inferno.

I began to gag. The smell of decay. The smell of the woodland. I sensed the presence of scuttling bugs beneath me. Of the microbes, deep within the filthy soil. Even the breeze which blew across my face carried a vile and unfamiliar scent. The revulsion. Not just of my surroundings but of my form. The detestable smell and texture of my own body. The stench of stale blood, damp clothing and skin bombarded me.

I found myself fighting the urge to breathe. To keep the rancid, poisonous air from filling my lungs. And yet my own body betrayed me, forcing the action regardless. The foul-tasting air sucked deep into my chest. It left a bitter aftertaste that stung my throat. With each vile breath, yet more blood pumped painfully through my veins to nourish this sickening vessel of man. I was disgusted and ashamed.

I do not know how much time had passed. A second, or an hour, or a lifetime. But the realisation of my circumstances became clear. Anger and rage welled within me. Strange memories entered my mind. Uninvited memories. Yet these vivid recollections were not mine. A great punishment had been bestowed upon me. Draconian and unjust. Strange, ungodly creatures entered my mind. A violent struggle. A brutal murder, administered by my own hands. The murder of not one, but of many. An entire culture. An entire race. The silencing of a hundred billion lives.

The darkness continued. I felt overwhelmed. The feeling of great loss, as if everyone I ever knew had been lost within an ancient past. They were nothing but dry dust, hidden from me across the void. Yet here, somehow, within the lair of my exile, amongst the ruins of an ancient building, I felt at ease. This was the one place in which I held the slightest of links to my true belonging. The crumbling brickwork strewn upon the ground was not of my world. But it was, I felt, of my time.

Abstract flashes of strange and distant memories. I saw rivers of pale orange. Viscous matter, flowing through a landscape of yellow rock and dust. Scattered alongside a valley were complex structures rising upwards from the land, reaching high into a green, shadowy sky. I saw twisted, darkly shapes festooned with a thousand lights shining brightly from within each structure. I could judge neither their size nor distance having seen no familiar features within the landscape in which to define their scale. At first, I thought these strange protrusions to be rocky outcrops upon an alien landscape.

But a strange feeling of intimacy fell upon me. I was calmed by their presence. These structures, I am convinced, were dwellings within a kingdom of unearthly origin. My home. Confused by my familiarity with this sulphurous vision, it melted into obscurity.

My mind became clear, as if witnessing a mirage fade into reality. Now I saw Emily. She was with her boyfriend, James. They stood boldly before me. But somehow they were different. Their clothing was strange in design and their faces derided me with ugly, uncaring eyes. Unkempt billowing hair drifted unnaturally around them. They towered above me. Like an immovable tower. I could not comprehend their strange sounds but I knew they jeered me. Mocked me.

James pointed in my direction. His sneer turned into a cackle. His face began to melt away. It formed a painful, disfigured mixture of both his face and mine. An amalgamation of our flesh. Likewise, I felt my head melt and contort. Distressed, I held my hands tightly to my face but I could not hinder my deformities. My fingers fumbled across my features, feeling for something familiar. I felt nothing but an open, weeping wound as if my face had been torn from my skull, exposing my eye sockets and nasal cavity to the poisoned air.

James and Emily continued to grow in stature. They stood before me as ghostly apparitions. I was dwarfed and intimidated by their bulk. James's face continued to morph into the most hideous of forms. Too afraid to feel my disfigurements, I uncovered my face. I held my wounded arm close to my body, cradling the injury like a sickly child. I caressed the back of my hand to console myself but to no avail. Such pain and heat. My face contorted in unison with James's. I was truly, truly broken.

The apparition of Emily began to speak in slurs. Unlike her boyfriend, she spoke English but with the strangest of accents. She smiled at me with deeply loving eyes. I found myself transfixed by her beauty. I could not tear my eyes away from her. In an instant, I knew that I loved her. But it was more than love. It was lust. In all its vile, debasing forms. I would have her. And then I would mutilate her. I could not explain this violent urge. I knew I should feel shame, but I had none. Then I felt my stature increase in size. I grew, empowered. As I became physically equal to her, she placed her hand softly upon my own. It was the most gentle of touches and I felt at peace.

'My dear George,' she said, 'I have travelled so very, very far.'

James began to speak, clearly this time too. 'To your paradise,' he said with a mocking smile.

The apparition of Emily giggled.

'Yes, to your beautiful little paradise,' she said.

Her gentle hold upon my hand became a painful, spiteful, grip. She crushed and twisted my fist into a sharp knot of pain.

'To your stupid, decaying, filthy fucking paradise,' she bellowed.

I tried to pull free but found I could not. Looking down, I saw her arm. It was fusing into mine. Binding us together by our own flesh. I could no longer see where my body ended and hers began. I felt her cold, thickly blood coursing from her body into mine. Forcing me to take this deathly transfusion. The sensation was abhorrent. Trapped within the space that lies between life and damnation. The excruciating torment of pain. I wished only for death to tear me away from her brutality. I whimpered and cried.

James laughed hysterically. A madman. I closed my eyes tightly but I still saw him. His laughter grew louder and more crazed. I felt an equal rage and repulsion grow proportionally to his madness. I watched his face. His ever-changing features. They melted into some wild unearthly creature. I was transfixed by the spectacle. His form began to melt like stalactites of wax, dripping from the altar. This thing of Hell. It took on a spider-like form. Strange appendages, vile and jagged, buckled and contorted in rhythmic, hydraulic motions. The head of the creature, this ungodly, satanic beast, resembled a wild dog. A vicious, rabid dog. Drool dangled from its chops. Its vacant eyes, wild with war. James's mocking laughter, now a snarl.

I wanted nothing more than to flee from this abomination. Not to preserve my life; I knew I could not be saved. I wanted to goad them. To enrage them so that they would end my suffering. I thrashed and pulled violently at my merged arm. It tore away from the vile entwined limb of Emily. A sickening crack of splintering bone within our wrists. I pulled free from her. The bond was broken and I saw the creatures for what they were. Evil, savage, filth. They had entered my mind like a disease. Poisoning me. A germ that needed to be destroyed. A rage welled from deep within me. The intensity. A primal force of which I had no control. I held in my heart such hatred and anger towards these beasts. I was unstoppable. Despite my wounded arms, I attacked this strange creature which James had now become. I kicked and punched and tore. The more the creature yelped in pain, the more alive I felt. Invigorated by my newfound empowerment. I gouged out its eyes. I tore its cheeks from its face. I revelled in the smashing of its bones. The sound of a splitting skull, like a coconut, cracked upon a pavement. I found myself laughing. Rejoicing as this vile beast pitifully begged for mercy. Yet my assault continued. Darkly powers coursed through my soul. Surrounded by death, and with the voice of Emily cajoling me. I had never felt so free. So alive. I indulged myself. I become drenched in the warm blood and entrails of my victim. My thirst for violence and revenge was my salvation.

I awoke from my nightmare to the bright light of morning. Lying naked upon the floor, I found myself tightly wedged beneath my bed within my father's house. I felt sick. Slowly, I extracted myself from underneath the bed. My forehead felt itchy as if stung by nettles. I rubbed at the skin above my left eye. It was sensitive to the touch so I desisted. Crawling upon the floor was uncomfortable. My limbs and neck were stiff. As I rose, I examined my arms and legs for injury. I saw none. My skin looked radiant. Blemish-free, like a newborn baby.

The deep bite marks, inflicted on me by the dog, were gone. Not the slightest trace remained. The wound had not healed, it had vanished in its entirety. I did not believe it at first. In my drowsy state, I checked both arms. There was nothing. It was a miracle. The bite had been deep and painful with ugly scabs. Yet even the bruising had gone, leaving only healthy skin that radiated with vibrancy. Yet they had been present only hours before. I felt uneasy. It made no sense. I began to doubt my recollections of the past few days. But I knew I had not dreamt about the dog bite. It was not a figment of the imagination. It was a fact. Something extraordinary had happened to me. I could not explain it and I was scared.

My clothing from the night before lay strewn across the floor. They were damp and splattered in mud. I hid them under my bed. My jacket was missing. I had no recollection of where it may be. Nor could I recall my journey home from the astronomer's house. Yet the ghastly dream remained fresh and vivid in my mind.

I located clean clothing from the chest of drawers. I found that touching the metal knobs produced the strangest of sensations, as if my fingertips could feel every single atom within their surface. My mouth filled with a metallic, tingling taste so powerful that I chose to open the drawers using a cotton handkerchief.

Getting myself dressed took over fifteen minutes. My entire body was tender to the point of discomfort. I took short breaks from the task. My hands and feet were particularly sensitive. Walking was almost unbearable. I placed two pairs of socks on each foot to alleviate the discomfort a little.

When dressed, I stood motionless in my bedroom, fearful I would irritate my skin on the roughness of my clothing. A sound. Deep and slow, like puffing bellows. I looked but saw nothing. Still, it continued as if only inches away. The sound of air being sucked into the expanding lungs of an unseen creature. I could discern every single molecule of air as it dissolved into the moist, watery membrane of the lungs. I sensed oxygen being plucked free by pulsing blood, circulating through an unseen body.

I stepped out of my room, onto the landing. The sound intensified. And then I knew. It was the sound of my sleeping mother. The sound of her slumber behind closed doors. The clarity of each inhalation repulsed me. I could not bear to stay in the house a moment longer.

I stood upon the pavement outside. The sunlight burnt my skin. My eyes watered excessively at the brightness of the day. A single tear trickled down my cheek. The droplet veered left and right as it traversed the intricate undulations of each single-celled pore of my face. With each blink, my eyelids scraped across the surface of my cornea. They dragged shards of dust and pollen across the moist surface of my eyeballs. I could feel every atom in contact with my flesh. I walked slowly from my father's house. My clothes rubbed painfully across my joints with each step.

As I reached the shops in Lower Ashtead, I saw a few people in the vicinity. I did not wish to mingle with any of them, so stayed on the opposite side of the road. But even from this distance, I was irritated by the sound of their movements. Their wretched breathing and clatter. As I shuffled myself along the footpath I caught sight of their inquisitive glances. They judged me, resenting my existence. One woman, pushing a newborn baby in a pram, smiled at me from across the street. I had the urge to smash her skull wide open. I could not help myself. I wanted to stamp my boots upon the contents of her skull. To squish her brain into the treads. To leave her rotten carcass abandoned by the roadside in the company of her crying orphan whelp. But then, my thoughts shocked me. I felt disgusted. Ashamed. Breaking eye contact, I walked on by.

I retreated into Ashtead woods. Somehow the old Roman Villa was calling me. Enticing me nearer. I had no choice but to fulfil the desire but my pace was slow and cumbersome. When I finally reached the clearing, the sky was blue and the sunlight cast intricate patterns of dappled light upon the ground. The world around me remained unchanged in every detail. Yet I saw the universe through different eyes. Ungodly eyes. Every atom of the universe could now be seen for what it was. A clumping of fundamental particles, binding together the cosmological scab of existence.

Within the clearing, I detected the most delightful of scents; like a subtle mixture of baking bread and sweet, warm honey. My stomach rumbled. I sniffed the air to seek out its origin. It led me to a patch of stinging nettles. A narrow pathway had already been cleared through them. The pathway led to a rock, coated in crushed and rotting snail flesh. The fragrance was intoxicating. I plunged my hand deep into the sticky mess. Lifting a handful of the sweet-smelling meat, I inhaled deeply. It was delightful. I salivated. I could not help myself. I placed a slither into my mouth. It was exquisite. Without pause, I forced a fist of the meat into my mouth. I couldn't control myself. The urge to devour. The more I swallowed, the more I craved. I dropped to my knees and pushed my face deep into the slop. I gorged myself. I ate like an animal, only pulling my face free so as to breathe.

Something caught my attention, from the corner of my eye. A few feet to my left, amongst the flattened nettles, lay my jacket. Dreadful memories returned to my mind, filling me with loathing. I looked at the contents of my hand. They dripped in foul-smelling repugnant decay. I flicked the rotting snails from my hand and wiped the mess onto my trousers. Removing their smears from my face, I began to wretch.

The jacket lay rolled up and discarded. A dark recollection. So abhorrent was this memory, I sought to examine the jacket to dispel the notion. I knelt beside the garment and studied it closely. It was heavily stained in wet mud. I trembled at the thought of what I would discover. Slowly I unwrapped the jacket. Within it, the remains of a mutilated dog. Torn to such an extent it was nothing more than slop. The liver and intestines lay glistening in the light, surrounded by protruding strips of fur, a paw and a section of the animal's head. A single eye peered out at me from amongst the offal. Like the eye in the astronomer's sketchings. No matter how I scrutinised it, no matter how I looked, I could see only fear and pain.

In heartbroken remorse, I dug a shallow grave with my own bare hands. In the silent isolation of the woodland, to the sound of laughing crows, I buried the jacket and its contents into the earth.

I returned to the rock. To the pile of rotting snails. I kicked them in anger, scattering the morsels into the undergrowth. I wanted to be free of the clearing. Never to return. I wanted to be free of the nightmare that filled my brain. I wanted to go home.

I found a flat stone which lay nearby. Using the sharp edge of another, I carefully scratched the name *'Toby'* onto its surface. I placed it upon the shallow grave and began to cry.

Chapter VIII

I could not eat. I detested the foulness of such things. Periodically, I forced myself to sip at rancid tasting water from the glass beside my bed. I stayed in my room, shielding myself from Mother, from the world. Not afraid of what she may say, but of what I may do. I avoided sleep as best I could, too frightened to let the visions return. But even my waking hours were filled with darkness. Depraved thoughts of the vilest atrocities. Yet they enlivened me. Empowering me, despite my sense of utter shame. And then I would think of Emily. The more I thought of her, the less my mind contorted. Her pretty smile. Her blue summer dress. The loving care she held for her family. My thoughts of her calmed me. They reminded me who I *really* was.

A week passed since my vision of the demon and a deep lethargy took hold. When I could no longer fight the urge to sleep, I was taunted by thoughts of ridicule and derision. I felt the entire world conspiring against me. I was an unnatural abomination, a caged animal. Something to be observed through iron bars. To be poked and prodded. To be scrutinized, dissected. They saw me not as a child but as a parasite. A crawling beast upon on its belly. Something to be crushed from existence. Something to be destroyed before it spread disease upon the land. They were right to fear me.

At night, I dreamt of creatures. The strangest I had ever seen. Slug-like things. They were not wild animals like cattle or dogs or birds. They were intelligent, like us. Beyond us. They lived in a world of their making. Each, an individual in their own right. And the things in their world were so very different from ours. I felt uneasy by the knowledge of their existence. I had no understanding of their culture or advancement. But I knew they were something to be feared. It was a natural instinct of repulsion.

I dreamt of a strange land. A society unchanged for aeons. No want. No need. No fear. No crime. And then it came. Like a tempest, to destroy them. This creature, unlike any seen before. It tore at them. A cyst, feeding on their decadence. Violent, torturous. It had no other intent than to spread its hatred and destruction. In my nightmares, the blood flowed so freely. It flowed without end. An unimaginable scale of death. It was relentless. Unstoppable.

I saw their world through the eyes of a killer. I had been held down by force, strapped within a cylindrical tube, barely able to move. Beyond the tube, I heard laughter. I was frightful of it. It mocked me. And then the pain began. The tube contracted tightly around my body, griping me tightly like a second skin. Forcing the air from me. The material of the tube became thin and translucent. Through it, I could see them in their hoards. Pointing and cajoling. A vast crowd of onlookers. Rejoicing in my capture. My binding contracted to such an extent, I was fearful my body would rupture. Unable to breathe. Unable to move. I could do nothing but await my fate.

Through the skin of my tomb, a light began to grow. It intensified, burning my eyes and passing through me. Through every atom in my body. It imaged me. It captured my essence in every detail. Not just my physical form, but the very contents of my mind. My memories. My plans and schemes. My anger. A mathematical construction of my entire being. A recording to be kept. Data to describe every aspect, in the finest detail, to be stored within a vast electronic machine of metal and meat. And then, the end. A blast of heat burned into me. It scorched me from existence. Save for my electronic facsimile, I was gone.

From time to time I dreamt of Emily. I tried to clear her from my mind. I knew that my affections for her would place her in danger.

She was my voice of reason. Reminding me of my true self. Without her, my rage would run free.

Awake, I felt so very angry. Angry with the world and all its abhorrent content, as if everyone was in contempt of me. Despising me for what I was. And so I turned my back on them. I denounced all that had once been familiar.

Days and nights merged into one. My sleeping hours were filled with violence and depravity. Awake, I felt alone and frightened.

I forced myself from my room. Mother watched me from the corner of her eye. She did not speak. I listened to the rhythmic sound of a clinking spoon as she stirred her tea. A slow, rhythmic, predictable motion, like the limits of her intellect. I found the slightest things would enrage me. I dug my fingernails deep into my forearm, hoping the pain would quench my urge to smash her to a pulp. I smiled and offered her a biscuit.

I began to accept these dark thoughts. My new normality. Repetitive, constant nightmares. But despite their horror, in time they became familiar. Less impactive. I had hardened to their brutality. Conditioned. I began to accept them for what they were.

On some nights, if I could not face the torment of sleep, I sat motionless on my bed. I would listen to the sounds of the universe, expanding, cooling. Slowly heading towards its inevitable demise. I no longer belonged to this place. I needed to break from the house, the village, the world. From the confines of my skull.

On the tenth day after the visit to the observatory, my left arm became painful. It happened, quite unexpectedly, at mealtime. I excused myself from the table. Mother was keen to see me leave so I retreated to my bedroom. I pushed my chest of drawers across, blocking the door. I felt vulnerable. I needed to hide. The discomfort in my arm became unbearable. My cheeks felt hot. Droplets of cool sweat began to drip from my forehead as I shook.

Dizzy, I lay on the bed. My arm burned, as if on fire. As the pain intensified. I began to twist and contort. Sweat and silent tears dampened my pillow. I bit hard onto clenched fists, stifling my yells of pain. I was weak, exposed. I panicked. I panicked at the thought of Mother attacking me as I lay vulnerable. To rip me limb from limb. To rejoice in my death. I remained silent in my pain. I would overcome my suffering. My distress would pass, and I would grow. All humans are born out of great pain. So too would be my rebirth.

The illness of my body ceased abruptly. Only the raging fire within my arm remained. And then I saw them. The lesions. They pushed up through the skin of my arm and popped, squirting globules of foul-smelling blood over my face and bedding. My arm throbbed. Captivated by the macabre display, I studied it. I watched, mesmerised. Within seconds, the dog bite and surrounding bruising returned as if freshly cast. My arm was sore and tender. The deep marks bled freely. I applied pressure to allow the flow to congeal. The bloodied ooze squelched between my fingers. Before my eyes, the dreadful marks returned in full, like stigmata. I found myself giggling. Unable to stop. My laughter confused and scared me. I sat up on the edge of my bed and sobbed.

Over the following days, I became more withdrawn. I wished neither to see nor be seen. I stayed in my room as much as possible. From time to time, Mother carried meals to my door. She would not come in. She placed the plate outside, on the landing. She would knock once, then leave hurriedly. She was fearful of me, I could tell. Why, I neither knew nor cared.

There was a knock on my door. A different kind of knock. A gentle kind of knock. I knew it was not my mother. The door pushed open, and I saw Emily. It was the first time I had seen her in weeks. She looked beautiful. Her hair was tied neatly back and she wore a crisp, clean dress that smelt of nothing but skin and soap. She smiled at me but her expression quickly faded.

'You're mum let me in,' she said.

No one ever visited me at home. I felt awkward, exposed.

'What are you doing here,' I asked.

'Checking you're alright,' she replied, 'Not seen you for yonks. I was worried.'

Emily sat down on the bed beside me and looked around my room.

'What's that smell?' she asked.

I had not noticed the smell before. I sniffed at the air but detected nothing. Perhaps it was my clothes I thought. I had not changed them for days. I could not remember the last time I had brushed my teeth. I knew my hair was greasy and tangled.

Emily sniffed the air near me. 'Bloody hell George,' she said, 'Your mum can't keep you like this, the council will put you in care!'

She looked over at the pile of dirty clothing in the corner of the room. Placed there to conceal my excrement. When the flies became too problematic, I would hurl the mess out the window. Mother would gather them all up from the garden. The flies were beginning to become a problem again.

I shook my head. 'She's afraid of me,' I said. 'Stays away most of the time. She's been acting odd for weeks. Why are you here?'

Emily stood up and began to search through my clothes drawers.

'Come on,' she said, 'get yourself washed. I'll pick some nice clothes for you. Well, move it, then!'

I did not stir. I didn't feel like getting washed.

'Move,' she said again, as if I were a disobedient dog. 'You can't stay in this smelly room. God knows what diseases you'll get! I want you to play with me. Outside, in the sunshine. But not dressed like that. Or smelling like that either. You're a mess.'

Reluctantly I got to my feet. The bite on my arm was itchy. I rubbed at it.

'Bloody hell, George,' Emily said, 'How did you get that?'

'It's nothing. A dog bite. That's all.'

Emily took hold of my wrist. 'A dog bite? You haven't got a dog. Here, let me take a look.'

'It was Toby,' I said, 'Down Agates Lane.'

Emily let go of me and I placed my hand slowly by my side. She looked at me for a moment. She knew, I could tell she did. She knew what I had done to the dog. She turned her back on me and began to pull some clothing from the drawers. I felt my fist clenching but I fought the urge to hit her.

'This will look nice on you,' she said, holding a grey flannel shirt up to me.

I took it from her. 'I won't be long,' I said, heading to the bathroom across the landing.

'You'll need these too, silly,' she said, throwing me a pair of clean trousers and pants.

After I had washed and changed, we left the house. We walked side by side through Lower Ashtead towards the common. I felt better in myself for leaving the house and for being in Emily's company. The air wasn't stale outside and it was nice to speak to someone again. We ambled about with no real direction. Eventually, we found ourselves near the railway station.

'Come on, I dare you,' Emily said, catching me off guard, 'Dare you to walk along the top truss of the bridge.'

'I don't like heights,' I said.

'Neither do I,' she replied, 'We can do it together.'

Reluctantly I followed her across the common towards the bridge. Apart from a dog walker in the far distance, we saw not a single soul. We stood at the base of the bridge and looked up. I never realised how tall it was; straddling across the tracks. Emily took hold of my hand and led me up the steps. The sidewalls were made of a thick lattice mesh about five feet high. It was capped with an iron girder which ran horizontally along the full length of the apex. It was dimpled chaotically with rivet heads. I looked down at the platform. It was empty.

'I'll go first,' she said, 'Help me up.'

Emily pushed her fingers through the mesh and tried to climb up. I watched as her shoes slid up and down against the metal. I bent down and took hold of her ankle. I gripped her so tightly I thought I would hurt her. She scrambled over the mesh and heaved herself onto the girder. Kneeling above me, she clung to the cold iron. Her bare knees, coated in dark smudges of grease and dirt.

'Come on,' she said, leaning over to grab hold of me, 'It's great up here.'

My legs felt weak and unresponsive.

'Quick,' she said, 'before we get caught.'

I raised my hands to meet hers as she pulled me up. Elated, I knelt by her side. I examined my hands. They smelt of diesel. Slowly Emily stood upright, her arms outstretched for balance. She began to shuffle her feet along the truss of the bridge.

'Don't be stupid,' I said.

She ignored me.

Not wanting to leave her, I got to my feet. By my right was the deck of the bridge. To my left, a drop of some twenty feet. I peered over the edge onto the coarse gravel of the trackway below. The fall would likely kill a child. I felt unsteady, faint from vertigo. Regardless, I edged my way towards Emily.

When she reached the middle of the bridge, Emily sat down, dangling her legs freely above the tracks. She looked out into the distance. The breeze blew at her hair. She looked so pretty. I made my way to her and sat beside her like a loyal puppy. After wiping the muck from my hands as best I could, I reached out and held her hand.

'I knew you were brave,' she said.

'I don't like heights,' I replied.

She smiled at me. 'I didn't mean the bridge,' she said, looking down at our hands.

Emily's smile made me less anxious. I wanted to smile back at her, but no emotion came. I could not remember how to smile anymore. Not since the nightmares.

'What about James,' I asked, 'He'll beat me up if he finds out!'

Emily grinned. 'Well, I won't tell him, if you don't,' she said.

I felt queasy looking down at the gravel so I settled my eyes onto the horizon. The railway lines cut the landscape in two. To the left, rows of houses. Read Road amongst them. But I could not see my house and I did not care to look for it. To the right, the common. Beyond that, the great expanse of Ashtead woods.

Together we listened to the sound of bird calls. I looked at Emily's face. I studied every strand of hair as it blew. Every cell within every freckle. But when I looked away, I could not remember the colour of her eyes.

Towards the woods, crows, jackdaws and wood pigeons took flight across the grassland. It was so peaceful. We were weightless atop the bridge as if we were flying with the birds. For a moment I wondered if it were possible to leap into the nothingness. To drift safely down, defying the pull of gravity. I could feel it. Pulling me towards the Earth's core. Deep into its centre. Distorting space and time. Crushing me.

'I'm scared he'll not come back,' Emily said, breaking the silence.

'Louis?' I asked.

She nodded.

Her oldest brother was in the army. He had been a few years ahead of me in school.

'I don't know what I'd do if there's a war; if he gets hurt,' she said.

I let go of her, placing my hand on the small of her back, stroking her with my thumb.

'Don't ever join up, George,' she said, 'Never go and fight. Stay here in the village, forever. I don't want anything to change. Not here.'

'If there is a war, I'm sure it won't last,' I said, 'Ashtead will always be Ashtead.'

In the distance ahead I heard the clanking of a steam train. It grew louder, nearer.

'Another few years and you'll be old enough to fight,' she said, wiping at the dirt on her knees.

The steam train turned a corner, into view.

'I'll poke your eyes out,' she said, 'or snip your fingers off with scissors. Anything to stop them from taking you. I don't care about King and country. I just want my brother back.'

My heart was cold. As if it were dead inside. Nothing but blackness. I pushed my hand more firmly against the middle of her back. My heart did not beat. It lay motionless in my chest like a tumour. I felt excited at the prospect of hurling the girl to her death. The thought drifted into my mind with such ease. Perhaps, it had always been there. The urge. The desire. The lust to kill.

The approaching train belched plumes of smoke and soot skyward. Overwhelmed by its mass and speed and noise, my muscles tensed. I heard a voice screaming in my skull.

'Do it,' it said. 'Push her. Kill her. Watch her body tear apart. Let the train disrupt her. Scatter her entrails along the tracks. She's a traitor. Do it. Do it.'

The train thundered beneath our feet, engulfed us in dense fumes. The carriages below, a blur. I gripped the edge of the truss with one hand and began to apply increasing pressure onto Emily's back with the other. The choking smoke stung my eyes. Barely able to keep them open. A high pitched shriek. The train cleared the bridge.

Tentatively, I looked to my right. I had no idea if she would still be there; if she was alive. Slowly the steam dissipated and I saw her. She smiled at me, her eyes alight with the joy of life. I looked down at my left hand. Bleeding fingernails still gripping metal. I leant across and hugged her. I knew then. I knew that she could save me.

I found myself imprisoned inside my bedroom, crippled with anxiety. Like every day before. Sunlight forced its way into the room. I stirred a little but fell back to sleep. I dreamt of rot and decay. Of death and destruction. Of hatred and torture. There was no life or love or happiness in my dream, only suffering and despair. I felt my consciousness drift away until, at last, I was able to look down upon my own body. It was dead and decomposing. Tossed upon scorched earth like discarded rags. The mouth of my corpse was gaping wide. I stared back into hollow eyes. Like tunnels leading back into my mind. A soul at peace.

I awoke, reflecting upon my dream. Somehow it had reassured me. Comforted me. I had seen a path to freedom. I knew the beast that lived within my head could be silenced. I felt in control, no longer fearful. Freedom. Freedom from my self-inflicted incarceration. The dark thoughts remained but I had seen a glint of light.

I had the desire to breathe fresh air once more and so I left the house, without a single thought. I decided to spend the morning exploring the nearby village of Oxshott, some four miles away. I wanted to find a small pond there. I once read in the Leatherhead Gazette that it may have been formed by a meteorite several hundred years ago. I had never seen it and my newfound boldness provided the opportunity. Nonetheless, I was not ready to face the Villa. Instead, I took the longer route to Oxshott, following an unfamiliar bridle path that skirted the woods.

When I finally broke free of the treeline, onto a quiet country lane, I found that I was lost. Regardless, I continued westward, through the warm sunshine. I saw a solitary old lady tending to roses in her front garden. She looked up at me and I felt obliged to acknowledge her. I headed over to her garden fence.

'Excuse me,' I said, 'Is this Oxshott?'

The lady placed her secateurs onto the lawn and made her way towards me. She looked amenable enough. Her skin was pale and deeply wrinkled but she had the bluest eyes I had ever seen. She dragged a wayward strand of grey hair behind her ear and smiled at me.

'Oh, no dear,' she said. 'This is Stoke d'Abernon. Oxshott's over there, somewhere,' she said, vaguely gesturing towards the northeast. 'It's a few miles at least. Are you local?'

'Ashtead,' I replied, 'But I've never been here before.'

'It's only little,' she said, 'but it's in the Doomsday book. You know, 1066 and all that.'

The old lady shuffled closer to me. 'It's an old Saxon word you know,' she said, 'Stoke. It means a holy place.' She raised an eyebrow but I did not respond.

'When the Normans invaded,' she said, 'they obviously liked it here too, they just took it from us. Handed it over to some French family called the d'Aberon's. Cheeky sods,' the old lady tutted. 'Can't even remember what the place was called before that. Expect the Romans gave it another name when they came over too. And the Vikings, probably, if they ever came this way, that is. It'll be the bloody Germans next, given half a chance.'

I watched as she returned to her gardening. Crushing greenfly from her cherished blooms. Her wrinkled, bony fingers slid slowly around each jagged thorn upon the stem, eradicating the infestation. Squashing entire generations of aphids with each ambivalent caress. I could not help but watch as she cleansed the blight. She began to hum a tune to herself. The beauty of the purge. The systematic process of elimination.

History is governed by war. It is the lifecycle of mankind. Perpetual violence interlaced with a few thin strands of peace - short, insignificant, periods wedged between an infinite expanse of war. A time to lick your wounds. To gather your strength. To rebuild your armies. That is the cycle. Life and death and fire. They are all the same. For the rose to bloom, the weak, parasitic greenfly must be crushed.

Life can only be defined at the point of death. Only by dying can a person be said to have lived. But the value of our life, the measurement of the person we are, is found in the words that form in our brain. Perhaps we have no control over such things. Perhaps they simply drift into our minds, like dreams. The good and the bad. The saint and the sinner. Perhaps it is nothing more than chance.

I continued onward, lost in my thoughts. For the briefest of moments, I felt disoriented. It was the strangest sensation, but one experienced before. I had been with my father when it happened last. We had boarded a train at Ashtead, heading into Guildford to see the Christmas lights. I had sat by the window, looking out at an adjacent train. I watched the passengers busily finding their seats and stowing bags. Through the window, I saw a woman in an electric-blue coat. She looked happy and content as she settled herself. Our eyes met and she smiled at me through the glass. There was a clank and our train began to pull away. The blue-coated lady drifted slowly away from view, replaced by a group of smart businessmen. Then they too were gone. Another snapshot of life. And then another. As our train picked up speed, the passengers became a blur - indistinguishable streaks of colour. Meaningless. Faster and faster. Exhilarated, I glanced at my dad and smiled. And then the train was gone. Silence. Beyond the window was Ashtead station. We hadn't moved an inch. An illusion of motion. It had been the other train that had departed, not ours. This is how I felt, as if every experience was an illusion.

I came upon a rather grand, high walled construction. It was adorned with well-manicured creeping ivy that grew both vertically and horizontally along its surface. The wall supported an extensive red-tiled roof that ran along its full length. A few glass windows, protected by iron bars, protruded from the wall. They were placed at regular intervals.

Towards the older sections of the wall, the little windows were replaced by arrow slits for the defence of the property. At the furthest end, a substantial gothic archway marked the entrance. The port was guarded by two heavy slatted wooden gates, each fifteen feet in height. It reminded me of the Hollywood film *King Kong*. I wondered what kind of beast the gates were built to deter. Above the archway sat a brick military-style tower. It was crowned with a wooden spire.

Through the slatted gateway, a gravel driveway led away from the lane and curved tightly, following the contours of yet more buildings. I rattled the gates and found that one was unsecure. Being of slight build, I squeezed through.

I found myself within the grounds of a Victorian farmyard. Several tree-lined fields – some holding cattle and one with grazing horses. The horses became inquisitive at first, even whinnying to me. But they soon lost interest and returned to their grass.

An extensive open-sided hay barn stood to my front, dominating much of the northern skyline. I walked past it, following the curving driveway. It led to a pleasant courtyard with numerous stables and outbuildings. Beyond, I spied a grand farmhouse overlooking the entire estate. Fearful I may be observed, I retraced my steps.

The hay barn stood like a cathedral. To the left, underneath its corrugated iron roof, a small store of loose hay. The floor too was littered with a carpet of hay and crisp straw. It crunched underfoot as I played. I had great pleasure kicking the strands high above my head, darting about playfully to avoid the falling debris. At the opposite end, bales of bound straw were stacked high, almost reaching the roof. I managed to re-stack a sufficient number to enable myself to climb upwards to the very summit. Atop, I felt intimidated by the height and instability of my footing.

I peered through gaps within the rafters, spying upon the farmland below. To the west, near the bend in the driveway, a small row of brick pigsties. Despite the oblique angle, I peered into a small section of their concrete yard. A large sow lay heavy on her side. Pale pink in colour with a head almost as broad as her chunky torso. Nestled around were her piglets, eager to feed on her and to play. One stood out from the rest. A distinctive black mark on its ear, unlike any of the others. From time to time I could hear the grunting from their mother as she called to them. That was their existence. The piglets suckled and played. The sow, I suspected, ate the food lavished upon her. They all gorged themselves, growing fatter by the day. Oblivious to their fate.

A shabby looking wooden trailer stood nearby. It had a drop-down ramp and was attached to a blue tractor, not much bigger than a car. I could just about read the registration number. The same digits were written onto the trailer in chalk. A hand-written registration number is not legal. My father had told me that. This amused me somewhat so I chose to commit the digits to memory.

I remained atop the straw stack for an hour or so, gradually becoming more confident in my footing. I fashion myself a straw table and a golden throne and footrest for my comfort. Relaxing with a strand of straw in my mouth, I was the king of all I surveyed. The air was filled with the sound of cooing woodpigeons and the smell of fresh straw. I closed my eyes and allowed my mind to empty, listening to the soft, constant chattering of nature.

I began to think about my dad. The scars on his body, particularly his legs, caused him great pain and discomfort. As I grew, his suffering did not diminish and his depression waxed and waned unpredictably. I knew the burning wounds of phosgene ran far deeper than scar tissue. He was a broken man. When he passed away, I was eight. A few years later, when I was playing in our little front garden, I overheard a conversation. Two women, standing by our gate. They stared at me as they gossiped. And that is how I found out. How I learnt my father had taken his own life. A leap from the summit of Box Hill. His final view was of the lush green valley below. But I knew his mind was still filled with the mud and pain of Ypres.

Clanking metal. I awoke, startled. Crawling from my straw throne and lying flat on my belly, I peered through the rusty roof. Two farmhands were briskly transporting a wheelbarrow load of horse manure from a stable block. They piled the contents upon a heap against an outbuilding. They were in their early twenties but looked shabby and weathered. They would not see kindly to my trespassing. I knew once the stables were cleared, they were likely to return to the barn for fresh straw. My makeshift staircase of bales would surely betray my location. My heart throbbed painfully. Fearful, I lay silent. When both men disappeared from view, I began my escape.

As I crawled towards the edge of the stack, the entire front section gave way. Unable to prevent myself from falling, I leapt as far from the cascading bales as possible, landing hard on my side. I yelped in pain, covering my head as bales tumbled all around me. They bounced and rolled across the barn floor but none made contact. I arose from the disorder, coughing from the cloud of dust which swirled high into the air. It irritated my eyes and coated my clothes.

Footsteps, running along the gravel driveway. In a panic, I fled the barn and headed out towards the horse field. My left knee was painful and the discomfort impeded my progress. I glanced over my shoulder. The two farmhands were now standing amongst a chaotic pile of strewn bales. They looked out towards me.

'Oi!' one of them yelled, 'Come back here, you little shit.'

I continued on as fast as I could, reaching the gate to the horse field. Propped against a thorny hedgerow was an old rusting bicycle. I picked it up and hurled it over the gate. Then I too followed, landing in thick, oozing mud that swallowed my shoes up to my ankles. Picking up the bicycle, I carried it onto firmer ground, almost losing my footing in the dreadful gloop. The farmhands reached the gate, red-faced and breathless.

'Get back here ya bugger!' the shorter of the two men yelled.

'Stand still!' the other ordered.

I ignored them as best I could. Mounting the bicycle, I pedalled furiously across the field. The land was pitted with deep hoof marks which, away from the site of a leaking water trough, had become baked hard by the sun.

The ride was slow and painful. The saddle had rotted away into a mass of rusting springs and tufts of horsehair. I pedalled faster, sending horses galloping in all directions. The men did not follow.

Once across the field, I climbed over a barbed-wire fence onto virgin pasture. Here, the grass was too thick for me to cycle so I dismounted and continued on foot. When I reached the outskirts of Ashtead Woods, I concealed the bicycle underneath a layer of thick ferns and bracken before finally reaching home by early evening.

Mother acted differently around me. If I entered a room, she would leave. At first I thought she was angry with me but she was not. She was nervous. Frightened, even. We did not converse in any meaningful way. I thought she would be better now that I had started defecating in the toilet again, not in my room.

In the morning, I rose early. The start of September marked the last weekend before my return to Park House School. I did not feel like returning but I looked forward to being free from the house.

Mother was still sleeping as I headed into the village. I busied myself, peering into shop windows in upper Ashtead. I tried to distract myself from the thoughts in my mind but I could not rid them. I looked at my reflection in the hardware store window. I tried to smile but it looked forced and unnatural. I could not see any happiness in my eyes. Perhaps it had never been there, I could not remember.

I saw a note attached upon the glass:

Missing from Agates Lane: Toby the Retriever, very friendly and much-loved family pet. Wearing a red collar and name tag. If seen please call Ashtead 314. Small reward offered.

My face reddened with guilt. I felt like a criminal on the run.

A hand rested upon my shoulder. Startled, I turned around. It was Emily Fenton. She giggled.

'Blimey George, you look guilty as sin,' she said, 'What you up to? Going to pinch something?'

I shook my head. My mind fumbled to concoct an appropriate response.

'I don't want any trouble from James,' I said. 'If he sees me talking to you, he'll bloody kill me.'

'Don't worry,' Emily replied, 'I haven't seen him for days. He's run away from home again. Doesn't get on with his dad. He'll not be back for a few weeks now, I expect. The council will bring him back though. They always do.' She forced a smile. 'Rotten news about Toby,' she said, looking at the notice. 'I reckon we could find him though, what do you think? You may even have been the last person to see him. You know, when he bit you. It's really strange, I've never known him to bite anyone. He must have been ill or something. You know, in pain.' She grabbed my arm in excitement. 'I wonder what the reward is? We could split it!'

I did not want to look for the dog. I knew it was dead. I knew it lay rotting in the woods with its innards torn out. I did not want to return to the clearing. Not to that place. Not ever.

I contemplated telling Emily about my nightmares, even about the dog. About everything. But I did not. I felt ashamed. I did not want her to know how frightened I was. She would never understand. How could she? I liked her, I didn't want her to laugh at me. And so, I played along with the charade. I would help Emily look for the missing dog. A wild goose chase around the village.

'We can look along Agates Lane if you like,' Emily said, 'If that's where you saw him last!'

'I don't think we'll find him,' I said, 'Can't we do something else instead? How about the Rec?'

Emily screwed up her bottom lip. 'Oh come on,' she said, 'It'll be fun.'

I knew I would feel uneasy, seeing the red house again - knowing the astronomer was close by. But despite this, I headed off with her. Not because I wanted to go. Not because there was any chance of finding the animal. I went because she had asked me to go. I liked her. I liked her smile. And I felt so very lonely.

We stopped along Agates Lane and made a fuss of the horses. Star was there, with his distinctive white flash upon his forehead. So too were a few other horses but I did not know them by name. Emily foraged for some treats to give them and found a few windfall apples nearby. They were not too bruised or rotten so she shared them with me.

'Is your arm any better?' she asked, 'Can I look?'

Emily reached across to take hold of my sleeve. I jerked it back firmly.

'It's fine, honest,' I said.

When the horses had their fill of apples, we headed towards Toby's house.

Blackbirds sang from the nearby branches and fencing. The narrow lane looked empty without Toby. A water bowl marked the spot where he once rested. A neglected, metallic headstone. I looked at the thread-bare rug nearby. Every day, without exception, his body had lain there for as long as I could recall. Emily knelt beside the bowl and removed fallen leaves from the water. A *missing* poster was attached to a nearby telegraph pole. I was a villain. A villain returning to the scene of the crime. But it was worse than that. Dirtier than that. I was a monster.

'He had a collar,' Emily said, reading the poster, 'A red one. Maybe he's got caught on some brambles or something. He could be nearby.'

I found myself staring at the red house. 'He knew my dad,' I said, 'Mr Simpkins. He's an astronomer. There's a telescope inside that big dome. My dad used it.'

Emily stood close behind me. We looked at the roof of the observatory, visible above the apple trees.

'He keeps dad's notebooks in there,' I said, 'But he won't let me see them.'

Emily placed her hand on my shoulder.

'Well then,' she said, 'I think you should get them back one day, don't you?'

We searched the immediate area for the dog, in the bushes and along the sides of houses. Emily called out his name, but he didn't come.

Eventually, we gave up and left the lane. By afternoon we had wandered through much of the village. We chatted about this and that but generally nothing of great importance.

'I have to get home before dark,' Emily said. 'Dad'll kill me if I'm late. He's worried. You know, about that madman on the loose.'

'Madman?' I said, 'what do you mean?'

'Everyone's talking about it in the village,' she said, 'Police aren't saying anything, but Dad reckons someone's been murdered. You know, all cut up. That's what the woman at number six told him anyway.'

I escorted Emily to her home. She did not live far from the cricket grounds. We parted company outside her front gate. I listened enviously to the sounds of family life. They were friendly, welcoming and happy. Even Fenton, who gave me a cold glance through the living room window, had rushed to the front door to greet his sister. But when the door closed, I was alone. I turned my back on all of them and headed home.

The next day, being Sunday, saw my mother heading off to church. I told her I felt unwell and it was agreed I should rest at home. She knew I was lying.

I spent much of the morning ensuring my school uniform and books were ready for the next day. I hated moving up a class. It took me most of the year to warm to each new teacher. By the time I became accustomed to their idiosyncrasies, it was time to move on again. My new form teacher this year was to be Mrs Carpenter. She was a sour old hag. A witch of a woman. A whole year spent in her ghastly company lay ahead.

It was late morning when Mother returned from church. As she pushed the front door open, I could tell she was anxious. I followed her around the house like an unwelcome shadow. She did not say anything. She just made herself a cup of tea. I watched as she sat in the living room, fidgeting with the cuff of her blouse. I stood adjacent to an empty armchair, once occupied by my father.

'Sit down,' she said. It was the kind of tone that warranted me to act. 'People are talking in the village. You know, Mrs Hegarty and her lot,' she said. Reaching across to the side table, she turned on the wireless set. It began to play some light music.

I wondered what things were being said of me. What vile tales were being spread. I wondered how much was true. The music stopped, interrupted by the voice of a gentleman. His words filled the room.

This morning, the British Ambassador in Berlin handed the German Government a final note stating that, unless we heard from them by eleven o'clock, that they were prepared, at once, to withdraw their troops from Poland, a state of war would exist between us'.

Mother moved a hand up to her mouth. The crackling sound of the announcement continued.

I have to tell you now that no such undertaking has been received and that, consequently, this country is at war with Germany'.

Mother began to sob. I watched the rising steam from her tea. It dissipated into the air in the most delightful twists and turns. I felt uncomfortable with her so upset. I did not know what to say to her, so I wandered outside into the garden.

The morning was particularly pleasant and not the kind of day on which one would expect to begin a war. The sky was clear and blue. A few thin wisps of cloud hung high above. Standing in the middle of the lawn, near my father's shed, I listened to the sounds of the village. Birdsongs. Nothing else. It was as if the entire nation held its breath. I imagined them, huddled around their wireless sets, in their millions. The world was changing. I was changing.

A rumbling sound. Distant at first. Sirens. They grew louder, rippling across the country, ever closer. I could not detect their direction at first. And then I realised, they were all around.

'Get in here now!' Mother yelled from the back door, 'It's an air raid!'

I did not panic. It was such a lovely morning. Regardless, Mother ushered me indoors and into the darkness of the cupboard under the stairs. We sat together on the cramped floor. Hiding in the dark. It felt a rather cowardly thing to do.

An hour passed and my legs ached. We heard nothing outside. No aircraft. No flak. No bombs. Even the sirens were silent. Eventually, Mother muttered something under her breath and crawled out into the living room, closing the cupboard door behind her. I was alone, listening as best I could to the sounds of the outside world.

I heard the front door open as Mother called out to a neighbour. Muffled voices. Eventually, after a minute or two, the front door closed and the cupboard door flung open, dazzling me in brightness.

'Get out,' Mother said, 'and put the kettle on. It was just a test. Didn't you hear the all-clear?'

As the weeks passed, very little of the war was evident. Nothing changed. Life in Ashtead continued as normal. At school, Mrs Carpenter truly was a witch. I did not warm to her in the slightest.

We had been issued with gas masks, even babies had them. And horses too. Mother sounded funny when she tried hers on. Mine smelt of rubber. It was a requirement to keep them at hand, day and night. At school, we conducted regular gas drills. These replaced some lessons – including sports. The drills irritated Mrs Carpenter no end. The council had constructed a shelter under the playground and the entire school would retreat into the cramped confines. The masks muffled our voices and, due to a valve system, produced a rather rude sound when we breathed. This sent the entire school into fits of laughter. The greater the teacher's anger, the more unruly we became.

The Headmaster screeched at the top of his lungs, 'Boys,' he bellowed through wheezy muffles and grunts, 'These are serious drills. Hitler will send no warning!'

Regardless, the laughter continued. Mrs Carpenter frantically scuttled between this child and that. Torn between instilling discipline and tending to the younger boys who were unable to stomach the smell of rubber and disinfectant without vomiting into their masks.

By the end of November, the war was rather dull and distant. It had all just been talk. When an Anderson shelter was delivered to our house, it finally felt like something exciting might happen. Three men who lived a few doors down helped assemble it near Fathers shed. I helped too. It was rather intriguing. It had arrived in kit-form. Curved corrugated metal sheets. I watched the men dig a small trench in the lawn. They reached the water table almost immediately. When bolted together, the spoil was shovelled on top. It was wet and claggy with thick lumps of clay. Mother planted a crop of spring cabbages into the gloop. Food and camouflage.

As the days grew shorter, the temperature began to fall. On the weekends I was tasked with gathering kindling and logs from the woodland. They took several months to dry before they could be burned. Still, Mother often flung them onto the living room fireplace before they had seasoned. They would spit and ooze hot, sticky sap that bubbled out of their ends. Sometimes I would watch insects crawl out from the bark. The heat would force them to curl up in agony as the flames reduced them to cinder.

One morning, when I was off to collect wood, I arrived on the common to discover a commotion. Two men had erected an iron pen. A small gathering of onlookers had assembled to observe the spectacle. The men unloaded a young pig from the back of a trailer. They carried it, squealing and kicking, into the enclosure. I looked at the registration number written in chalk. It was the very same trailer from the farmyard. The same farmhands who chased me from their land. I kept a low profile and mingled amongst the crowd, my head bowed low.

The cooperative pig. It looked rather small and weedy standing in its new home. It had been paid for by contributions made by several

Ashtead residents. The animal would be cared for and fed on scraps of food wastage until the time was right. When the animal had grown to a sufficient size it would be slaughtered and its meat distributed evenly amongst the members of the cooperative. My mother was a member. I was to take our food scraps to the pig once or twice a week. It would appear that I was to be complicit in the death of yet another animal within the village.

The farmhands drove away. The giant wheels of their little blue tractor flicked sods of mud skyward. I made my way to the front of the gathering to get a closer look at the pig. It was very distinctive with its one black ear. I had seen it before, as a piglet. All the children were eager to pet him and make a fuss. As I waited patiently in line for my turn, I became aware of Emily standing behind me.

'I think it's ghastly, what they're going to do to him,' she said.

I turned to face her. She was wearing her light blue dress again and had her hair tied back to reveal more of her face. She was a pretty girl but I think she had sad eyes.

'Come on,' she said, 'Have you seen the railway station?'

She held my hand, pulling me away from the bars of the enclosure. She ran ahead of me, towards the old iron footbridge which straddled the railway line. We squeezed through the narrow turnstile which led onto the bridge. A throng of adults and children crowded along the top. We pushed our way through until we were able to locate a suitable vantage point in which to look down onto the platform.

The station was chaotic. Several hundred soldiers crammed together. They stood on the southbound platform. None were heading north. I never saw so many men. Each carried a large green kit bag, a rifle and a tin hat. Orders were being yelled. From the bridge, mothers, wives and girlfriends called out the names of loved ones. They craned their necks for a glimpse, pushing and shoving each other. Trying to get one final glance.

'I bet they're going to France,' Emily said over the bustle of the crowd. 'Strengthen up the B.E.F.'

I nodded. The British Expeditionary Force was in France and Belgium, halting the German advance. No one was really fighting though. It all felt rather boring and fake. Emily looked happy though.

'Dad says they're sending a million soldiers over there,' she said.

'I can't imagine what a million looks like,' I said, 'It's a meaningless number. Like nought, or infinity.'

It looked like the war was finally going to do something exciting at last.

Emily tugged at my sleeve. 'Look,' she said enthusiastically, 'over there!' She pointed towards a solitary figure. A man, dashing across the common, towards the woods. I could tell it was Mr Simpkins by the way he carried himself.

'That's the astronomer,' I said, 'going to the ruins.'

'So, no one's home then,' Emily said. She leant close to me and whispered into my ear. 'Fancy getting your dads books back?' She paused, 'Unless you're a coward.'

'I'm not a bloody coward,' I said, 'And neither was my dad. I'm not scared of Simpkins!'

Emily held my hand, pulling me back through the crowded footbridge.

'You're no coward George,' she said, 'Come on, it'll be fun.'

I was keen to reach the red house as quickly as possible. I ran most of the way, but it was difficult to keep up with Emily. She looked unimpressed as I coughed and wheezed some twenty yards behind.

As the red house came into view, my heart flooded with the memories of that terrible night. It was an unnatural place. Toby's water bowl had gone. Even the poster on the telegraph pole was now little more than a shred of torn, illegible paper. It was as if the dog had never existed.

Further along the lane, towards the rear garden of the red house, we found a narrow gap forged between the hedgerow and the garden wall. We pushed through, scanning the area for prying eyes. All was clear. We climbed over the wall, into the astronomers' lair.

'It's alright,' Emily whispered, 'keep calm, we've got plenty of time.'

As soon as my eyes fell upon the observatory, a rage filled my body. The anger took me by surprise. My hatred for the astronomer consumed me. How dare he deny me of my father's notebooks. I felt dizzy, as if a red veil had been pulled over my head, covering my eyes. I struggled to breathe.

Emily tried to calm me down but her efforts angered me further. I barged past her to seize a hefty stone from a garden rockery display. I made my way over to the observatory door.

'What are you doing George?' she said, rubbing my back with the palm of her hand. 'You need to calm down.'

I held the stone aloft and brought it down firmly upon the door handle. Again and again, I pounded. I struck the handle so hard, my hands began to bleed.

'Jesus,' Emily said, pulling at my arm, 'that's criminal damage. Stop it. Please, stop.'

My rage was complete. I shoved her away, as hard as I could. She fell awkwardly to the ground. I stopped to face her. My bleeding hand gripped the stone tightly. She looked scared. Weak. I could have smashed her skull open. Killed her where she lay.

I turned my back on her and continued to strike the handle. Finally, it sheared off and fell to the ground. I turned to face Emily. I saw fear in her eyes. I dropped the blood-stained stone onto the lawn.

Chapter IX

The report-writing room was empty when Constable Billet entered. He sat beside a long desk and began to flick through his pocket notebook. A cup of tea rested beside him. He examined the bank of trays, stacked three high. Each one housed a specific document. A multitude of witness-statement forms, lost property records, case summary sheets, road traffic accident reports and countless others. He removed one. It was labelled '*INT-13 Local Intelligence*'. Referring to his notes, he completed three such forms. He finished his tea and examined his work. Individually, they amounted to little more than gossip. But seen in the wider context, they painted the bigger picture of the criminal fraternity. A known petty criminal seen in the company of another known villain. A drunk, seen rummaging through the bins behind the newsagents. A possible stray dog living wild in Ashtead woods, harassing the deer.

The constable placed the forms into the C.I.D in-tray just as Detective Porter poked his head around the corner.

'Not more shit, Billet,' he said, looking at the pile of overflowing forms in his tray, 'Get yourself down to the palace. The old man wants you.'

Porter often called the dingy C.I.D office '*the palace*'. No one else did, not even Mare. The constable followed the detective down the corridor. He found Mare, sat by his desk, sucking on the final strands of a cigarette. The room was hazy with smoke and the constable's eyes began to blink. Regardless, Mare lit another.

'Sit down Billet,' Mare said, 'I might have a job for you.'

The constable sat awkwardly on a wooden stool. It was usually reserved for photographing prisoners and had been bolted to the floor to hinder non-cooperatives. Porter sat in a comfortable chair beside his colleague.

'We've had a few developments on the Betty Stride murder,' Mare said. 'Not much, but it's a start.' He drew deeply on his cigarette. A shard of grey ash materialised at its tip. 'That feather you found in the envelope, I sent it off to the Natural History Museum. Apparently, it comes from a common blackbird. Said it was plucked out this year, they reckon. As far as we know it's not symbolic of anything in particular. No political affiliations or religious groups or nothing.'

'It was left for us,' Constable Billet said.

'We think it's a calling card,' Mare said, 'To let us know who done her in. But, that gives us a problem, you see. We only have the one body.' He dragged deeply on the cigarette again. 'A calling card is only any good if there's more than one murder. So that means we've either not found it or,' he paused, 'so far, they ain't been done-in yet.'

Porter crunched on a dry biscuit. He wiped the crumbs off this lap, onto the floor. 'We've notified H.Q,' he said, 'They've given us you and Doris to play with. But they want to pass the investigation over to Sergeant Wells in a few days.' He rolled his eyes disdainfully, 'He's ex-C.I.D. More experience than us they reckon. So, we want to get this all wrapped up quickly. Before he takes over.'

Detective Mare shuffled in his chair. 'It's public knowledge now that the old woman was bumped off. I've got Doris working on a press release. If we don't tell the media something soon, the buggers will only make it up,' he said. The detective stubbed out his cigarette into a glass ashtray. He organised a small selection of documents strewn across his desk. 'I want people to be alert. Messing up a body like that, well, it's not normal. Bound to make you a bit peculiar. I want the local rags to ask people to keep their eyes peeled. You know, strange behaviour. Changes in personality. That sort of thing.' Mare poured himself a whisky and stashed the bottle in a drawer. 'Give him an update, Norman.'

'Well,' Porter said, 'I checked to see who'd benefit from her death. You know, financially. Her bungalow's worth a fair bit, almost eight hundred quid. No close relatives, as far as I can tell. She's left half her estate to a bloody cat rescue charity. The rest goes to the police Christmas fund. Bit of a result, that.'

'Her old man was a copper. An inspector. Retired twenty-odd years ago,' Constable Billet said, 'And she had a name, you know. She was called Betty.'

'So,' Porter said, 'unless the old woman was done over by a bent copper keen on a Christmas piss-up or some cat lover fallen on hard times, money probably ain't a motive. Nothing was taken from the house. So, that still leaves the nutter from the asylum. He's probably our best bet at the moment. We don't know for sure if he can even read or write though. Attacked his girlfriend in '33, left her for dead. Then he took the same hammer and smashed his own skull in. The girl survived. Emigrated to Canada. But Rollingson got brain damage. Silly bugger.'

'And the hospital lets him out at night?' the constable asked.

'Yeah,' Mare said, 'but under supervision. Now, the thing is, within the timeframe of the murder, his medication was changed. Sounds like it didn't agree with him. When he was out in the village he assaulted his carer. Bit half their ear off in a struggle. He was detained at Epsom district hospital a few hours later. Found wandering through the wards looking for his girlfriend, daft sod. Thinks she's still in there. Said he wanted to apologise to her.'

'Can't we just nick him?' Constable Billet asked.

'There's no point,' Porter said, 'he ain't going nowhere. The hospital's stopped his outdoor access 'til we tell 'em otherwise. That gives us two days to get our evidence together before Sergeant Wells starts pissing us about.'

Detective Mare studied a document on his desk. 'Got a copy of the coroner's final report back this morning,' he said, 'Not a great surprise. She died 'cause her head came off.'

Mare read from the document:

Severe haemorrhaging from the hepatic artery, brachial artery, renal and common liliac artery. Death from either significant blood loss or decapitation, also resulting in the severing of the carotid artery et al. No sign of sharp implements to disrupt the body – most likely to have been administered by bare hands, pre and post-death. Some defensive injuries to both hands – indicating a brief struggle. The victim killed and dismembered in situ. Mutilation in the form of text upon the subject's back, likely to have been administered by a narrow, slightly curved, penetrative implement such as a fingernail or similar. Severed head then drained of blood and deposited in toilet bowl in bathroom. Level of force applied to victim suggests perpetrator is both physically strong and likely to have been under the influence of a delusional, hallucinogenic substance such as cocaine or similar central nervous stimulant.

The detective lit another cigarette and turned to Constable Billet. 'Porter's getting a record of Rollingson's current medication. I want you to visit all the local hospitals. Find out the names of any known habitual drug addicts in the area.'

* * *

I wiped the blood from my hands and surveyed the damaged door. I had not intended to carry out such an act. The anger within had driven me beyond my control. Emily stood beside me, brushing the dirt from her dress.

'Are you alright?' she asked.

'Sorry,' I said, 'He's no right to take dad's things. I got cross, that's all.'

The door was buckled and difficult to open. We both pulled until it eventually broke free. I went inside. Emily followed. I felt for the switch and the space became drenched in light. Emily ran over to the mechanical telescope mount.

'It's beautiful,' she said. 'I mean, it's just, beautiful.'

I made my way to the astronomer's chair, examining the array of notebooks on the desk.

'I'll keep watch,' Emily said, heading back to the door. She peered out into the garden. 'Hurry up though.'

I flicked through the pages of each book, the vast majority written by Simpkins. But then I found a few short sections of text. It had been written by Father. Little more than supplementary notes. Regardless, it comforted me. To hold the very pages once held by him. I put the book to one side.

Curiosity drew me to some drawers, hung below the desk. They were locked. I wanted to smash them open, but I fought the urge. I did not wish to upset Emily further. I found by lifting and rocking one of them, it could be positioned suitably to defeat the locking mechanism. This I did and the drawer slid open to reveal its contents. I rummaged through numerous star charts and sundries. And then I found it, a small black notebook hidden away. I flicked through the pages. Father's unmistakable handwriting, as neat and crisp as the day it was written. Every page, filled with his voice. It was a journal that spanned several years.

Emily faced me. 'George,' she whispered, 'we need to get out of here. Now!'

Sensing the urgency in her voice, I tucked Father's notebook inside my shirt and closed the drawer as best I could. Emily turned off the lights, plunging us into the shadows. I stood beside her, peering through a thin gap in the doorway. A restricted view across the lawn, towards the house. I could see the back door and part of the kitchen window, but that was all. Inside, the unmistakable figure of Mr Simpkins. I felt my throat tightening.

Emily took my hand. 'Get ready to run,' she said, 'as soon as he turns his back. Ready?'

My heart pounded so fiercely I thought it would leap clean from my chest.

Emily let go of my hand and flung the door open. She ran across the lawn, heading for cover behind the apple trees. Beyond them, lay the garden wall. I followed her, as fast as I could. Crossing no more than half the span of the garden, I tripped and fell over my own clumsy feet. I hit the lawn hard, winding myself. I looked up to see Emily. She had already broken free from the tree line. I watched as she vaulted cleanly over the garden wall. She turned her face to me. Her eyes fell on mine as I lay upon the ground some fifty feet short of her.

As I struggled to regain my breath, Emily began to gesture silently, frantically towards me. She was urging me to remain still. I tried to turn my head towards the house but the positioning of my body obscured the view.

I heard the back door being flung open. I looked back at Emily. Her eyes bulged wide.

'Run!' she screamed.

I never heard a girl yell so loud as I clambered to my feet.

She called out again, 'Bloody run!'

Scrambling across the lawn, I heard the voice of Mr Simpkins. He was running towards me.

'Come here you bugger!' he yelled. His voice boomed across the garden.

I did not dare to look back. I ran with such speed, I collided painfully into the garden wall. As I clambered over, Emily grabbed my belt and began lugging me over the brickwork. Within an instant, Mr Simpkins was upon me. I turned my face from him as best I could. He grabbed my ankle, pulling me back into the garden.

'Get here!' he yelled.

Fear took hold. Like a wild animal, I kicked and lashed out, connecting firmly with his chest. In a moment, his grip on me was lost. Emily seized the opportunity and pulled me over with such vigour, I slithered cleanly over the wall. I fell to the ground beyond, my hips sore and grazed.

Emily helped me to my feet.

We fled. I could hear the astronomer calling out, but I did not look back. Neither of us did. We just ran. We ran as fast as we could, all the way down to the junction with Barnett Wood Lane. Mr Simpkins did not follow.

We collapsed onto the grass verge, exhausted. To my surprise, Emily began to giggle. This confused me. Regardless, I found myself smiling, pleased to be in such company.

Emily's laughter stopped, ceasing as quickly as it had begun.

'Don't ever shove me like that again,' she said, hitting me in the arm. 'And don't ever look at me like that either.'

I nodded, too embarrassed to look into her eyes. And then she kissed me on my cheek. She got to her feet and made her way home. I sat alone on the grass for some time, watching as she disappeared into the distance.

I was alone. I usually like to be alone, but now I did not. With nowhere else to go, I went home.

I found a handwritten note in the hallway. It was from my mother. It said she was out shopping for food so I went to my bedroom and closed the door. The house was silent. I lay on my bed and opened the book. It smelt musty - as if every heavy odour had imparted itself into the binding. The pages were crisp but yellowed by age. My father's handwriting, neat and concise. I began to read, absorbed within the text. The forgotten voice of a dead man. At times it felt cold and distant, speaking of complex mechanical procedures and of tracking errors within the telescope mount. Yet, from time to time, it was as if Father was with me, in the room, talking solely to me. Father to son.

Much of the book related to operational protocols and the like. He used initials when referring to his colleagues. The letters *S.S*, standing for *Stanley Seabrook*, often appeared. Father had even reduced his own name, Alfred Engel, to initials. I took the letters *D.S* to be that of Mr Simpkins.

My attention was drawn to a particular entry. It was dated 20th December 1912. The writing was no longer neat. Rather, it had been reduced to a messy scrawl of untidy scratches across the page. I could not read all of it, but I was convinced this had been recorded on the night the three men discovered something strange about the star called Alnilam.

I learnt that through much of 1913 there had been many attempts to photograph the anomaly - brief brightness fluctuations. My father referenced hundreds of glass plates that captured the events. He wrote of one such incident:

Friday 12 September 1913.

Observation of Alnilam: 04:34 GMT R.A 5 Hours 31 Minutes 49.8 Seconds, Declination -1 degree, 15 minutes 13.1 seconds.

Stella flare commenced at 05:13:45, lasting 137 seconds. This is the 7th variable phase – again a prime number. At 05:14:30 and 05:15:55, light from the eyepiece was directed through a prism to image the spectrum. (plates 178a/b). These images show extremely strong emission lines across much of the range. Again, they do not relate to any known combination of elements. These are likely to be rapidly changing during the 137 second pulsing period. Unlikely to be a naturally occurring physical event.

A supplementary note from Simpkins read:

'Not a natural event! Deliberate, signal showing intelligence. Possible message content'.

The men agreed. To the best of their knowledge, no such signal could be produced so eloquently by the natural world. With every subsequent entry, they became ever more convinced. This strange phenomenon was the work of great minds. They believed the light to be deliberately transmitted, produced by immense levels of energy. A message from one civilisation to another. From across the great expanse of space.

I thought of the implications. The possibility of life existing elsewhere within the universe. The question *'Are we alone?'* There can be only two outcomes. Yes or no. Either life exists beyond the Earth, or it does not. Mankind may either be a small part of a wider community of beings or we are pitifully unique in our existence – a fluke of cosmic nature. Knowledge of either outcome would be monumental, an epiphany. Why then, had my father remained mute? Perhaps he saw Mr Simpkins as a fraud, a charlatan. Perhaps he found an error in their data. Whatever the reason, he had held his tongue. Silent until his very last breath at the foot of Box Hill.

It was clear from the journal, Simpkins was certain of one thing. Hidden within the flickering emission lines, during the 137 seconds of each variable pulse, there was a concealed message. A message transmitted by an alien race across the darkness of space. A simple greeting from one inhabitant of the galaxy to another. A courteous handshake across the void; you are not alone. A shiver passed down my spine.

I read how the astronomer attempted to image the mysterious light, to try and capture the data. To decode it. But the flickering pulses were too fast for photographic methods. So, it was my father who volunteered, to observe the pulsing light with the naked eye. Little had been documented of this first experiment. Nothing more than a few rough sketches. I saw them. Thick, grasping tendrils. They seemed to reach out from the page. And there, hidden in the darkness of the shadows, I saw piercing eyes. Familiar eyes. The eyes which once looked out upon me in the form of Emily Fenton. I knew then. I knew my father had experienced the same ghastly nightmare. I felt a connection with him, stronger than ever before.

Father wrote of an argument with Seabrook. The two men had become enraged. Father wished to continue in the observations but Seabrook felt uneasy with such research. Their anger came to blows, physical harm. Then Seabrook parted company.

The notes in later sections of the journal were scant. Illegible, save a few words here and there. But the sketches were frequent, disturbing. I did not wish to look at them, but when I did, I saw twisted, melting forms. The vilest depictions of debauchery and intemperance.

The final entry made by my father was dated March 20th 1914. It read:

Seabrook returned to the observatory unannounced. Angry confrontation with D.S and myself. Whilst D.S at the eyepiece, S.S. drove a thick nail into his hand – impaling him to the wooden observation seat. Having doused the telescope and platform in petrol, S.S ignited the observatory in its entirety and fled. The fire was intensely hot. It spread rapidly. I pulled D.S free from the seat – the action upon the nail tore his hand badly. We discovered that S.S had blocked our exit - barricaded from outside. An inferno took hold. The most horrendous of injuries to D.S. and myself. The fire showed no mercy. We burned. We burned like matchsticks - D.S was charred beyond recognition. As flames died back, I broke free of the observatory and dragged the remains of D.S onto the lawn.

Much of our photographic records were lost to the flames. It is of great comfort that some of our research notes and photographs remained safely stored in the Red House.

I watched, awe-struck, as our blackened flesh began to heal. It happened within the space of an hour. We had not perished in the flames. We had been reborn. All save for Simpkin's hand. It remained jagged and torn from its impalement. Dear God, what have we become?'

Chapter X

I was thinking about my father again. Memories of him drifted into my head with such ease. I did not discuss them with Mother. We hardly spoke these days, uneasy in one another's company. Regardless, from time to time, she would hint at some minor detail pertaining to his life. To a time when I was younger. When he was alive, and I was happy.

'He was a coward George, you know he was,' she stated. 'And he was weak for killing himself. That's a coward's way out. A selfish coward. Leaving me here with you, no financial support. And you with that damn gun.'

When dad had been around, we had been a family. A real family. I knew he wasn't a coward. He had done brave things in the war. But now he was gone, I wanted to run away, to never come back. But I was only a boy. What could I do?

After lunch, I went to my bedroom and rested. I distracted myself with my fossil collection. I kept a small display on the windowsill. I picked up a hefty chunk of rock and felt its dry, hard surface, the familiar contours and textures. This particular stone held the fondest of memories. Father and I found it on Box Hill when I was five; a fossilised crab. It was poorly preserved but it had caused my mind to burn wild with curiosity. How could such a creature become embedded in rock, so far from the sea? I wondered what Surrey looked like when this cold, hard rock had been a living, scuttling beast, millions of years ago. Through this fossil, I became transfixed by all things scientific. I no longer saw my surroundings as a fixed point in space and time. The Earth was fluid, transient. I felt its movement thundering beneath my feet. The universe was now a million colliding hues of purest light, dancing in my brain.

I laid back on my bed and examined the fossil. It was bathed in the sunbeams leaching through my window. The glint of tiny grains of quartz, trapped within stone. A glimpse of the distant past, the final seconds of a crab's life – preserved forever in rock. Its legs were fully extended from its body and its pincers conveyed the impression of motion, as if the creature were dragging itself upon its belly, seeking shelter. This had been its final act. A pitiful attempt to survive. Its failure, preserved for eternity. I thought about the glinting quartz. The crab wasn't real. It had perished aeons ago, its flesh and shell long decayed. This was merely a cast. A moulding produced by minerals, replacing the animal's exoskeleton over a vast expanse of time. An ancient shadow of a creature. And now I held it, illuminated by light from the sun. By the photons forged in the heat and pressure of a star's core. I looked upon the reflection of a shadow of a crab and saw nothing more than my own existence reflected back.

Christmas 1939 was a solemn affair. Rationing of some foodstuffs had now been implemented. This was supposed to ensure a fair distribution of essential supplies, yet the majority of shops held little stock. Rationing was all rather academic. School continued, despite the rather phoney war. Little had changed, except of course for the gas drills. But even this novelty had worn off.

By New Year, the classroom windows were adorned with large crosses of sticky tape. They were there to impede the effects of flying glass. Somehow they enlivened the drab décor of the classrooms, like perpetual Christmas decorations.

Throughout the spring of 1940, I avoided all contact with Mr Simpkins. This had not been difficult. As far as I could tell, not a soul had seen him, not for months. It was my opinion he was occupying himself with the study of Orion. Observing at night and sleeping at day, perhaps. The constellation had shone prominently throughout the winter months, but now it was almost lost to the sunrise.

By May, my chore of feeding scraps to the cooperative pig had increased. The beast had grown considerably and was constantly hungry. Many of the residents were beginning to consider drawing the procedure to its inevitable conclusion.

Mother volunteered me to collect door to door for the war effort. It was her way to get me out of the house. I was required to visit all the houses along our road. Read Road was a cul-de-sac of some ninety properties. I had not relished the task, so, I sought assistance from Emily. I was confident she would oblige. When I visited her house in the morning, Charles opened the door.

'Emily,' he called out, 'Your boyfriend's here.'

Emily appeared in the doorway, deliberately barged into him as she pushed past.

'He's not my boyfriend,' she said, 'so piss off.'

I felt dejected. If I was not her boyfriend, I did not know what I was. I pretended not to have been upset by her comment and did not raise the matter with her.

It took fifteen minutes for us to walk to my house. We chatted along the way, but I knew something was wrong. She did not wish to hold my hand but I enjoyed walking beside her nonetheless.

A wooden handcart had been loaned to my mother for the collections. It rested by our front gate. The cart was easy to pull but difficult to steer. We took turns knocking on each door, explaining to the resident how their household waste could be used for the war effort. Paper and card could be recycled to produce food cartons for soldier's ration packs or ammunition wadding for bullet cases. Bones could be crushed to make glue for the aircraft industry. Even glycerine could be extracted from the bones to make explosives. Scrap metal could be used to manufacture tanks and guns and shells.

We collected old rags to make blankets, uniforms and bandages. It finally felt as if the community was pulling together. Getting the job done. Supporting the boys in France.

By the time we arrived at Mrs Hegarty's house, the cart was full of the most wretched smelling boiled bones and such. Mrs Hegarty was a formidable woman and known for keeping the local children of the street well-disciplined. We felt it prudent to leave the cart upwind of her house. To my surprise, she appeared at the door in high spirits. Despite her stocky build and powerful arms, she greeted us warmly.

'Hello George dear, what are you two up to?' she asked, glancing over at the laden cart. She gave Emily a smile of recognition.

After I explained our purpose, the woman disappeared inside her house. I could hear her rummaging. She was gone for a while. Emily became fidgety so joined me at the door. When Mrs Hegarty reappeared, she was practically concealed in her vast entirety by a stack of old blankets and bedding.

'That's the lot I'm afraid,' she said, dropping the pile onto the doorstep.

We thanked her, but she was oblivious to our words. Instead, she turned to yell loudly at an unseen child somewhere within her house.

'Ernie,' she thundered, 'put that bloody thing down, this instant.'

Emily and I carried the rags clumsily back to the cart.

Mrs Hegarty faced us again. 'If you come back later this week, I'll have some bones to give you, what with that pig getting the chop.'

Emily stepped forward. A look of surprise washed over her face. 'What, the pig on the common?' she asked.

Mrs Hegarty grinned. 'That's right dear,' she said, 'I'm getting the head. It'll boil down lovely!' Her eyes sparkled with excitement before disappearing indoors.

I could tell Emily was upset about the impending slaughter. It was strange; I had been so eager to feed and make a fuss of the animal, I almost forgot its sole purpose was to die.

We loaded Mrs Hegarty's bundle onto the cart. It was stacked to capacity so we decided to leave the remaining houses for another day. Slowly, we pushed the meandering cart back towards the collection point at the top of the road. Emily still looked upset and I became self-conscious of my stares.

'It's just awful,' she finally said. 'That pig's the sweetest little thing. And that old bat wants to cut his head off. Boil it. It's barbaric!'

Despite having grown fond of the animal myself, I had been looking forward to eating pork. My mother was getting a knuckle to make ham and lentil soup. I had not equated the eating of pork to the slaughter of the pig. Still, I was hungry. I was hungry almost all of the time. Emily's family had not taken part in the cooperative scheme. They were not entitled to reap any of the rewards which its death would bring.

As we approached the top of the road, Emily looked tearful. I felt the urge to comfort her so I stopped pushing the cart. We both sat on the kerb. I patted her on the arm, not knowing how to console her.

'I can't believe they're going to murder that poor thing,' she said, 'What harm has he done?'

'None,' I said, 'I don't think it's personal. It's just that, well, people are hungry, and he's made of meat.'

Emily rose from the pavement and began pushing the cart further up the road. I stood and assisted her.

'Well, I'm not eating him,' she declared, 'I'd rather go hungry than eat that poor thing!'

The cart veered unexpectedly into the kerb. Emily quickly changed her hold, catching the palm of her hand on a twisted sheet of tin. She cowered, pulling her hand into her chest. The cart came to a stop.

'Let me have a look,' I said, reaching for her left hand. Reluctantly she opened up her fist. The jagged metal had cut across her palm. It was not a bad cut, only an inch or so long but it looked sore and it was bleeding. I do not know why, but with no thought, I dragged my palm across the same sharp edge. Blood dripped from my hand. Then I took hold of Emily's hand in mine. Her fingers felt warm and clammy. She tried to pull away but I held on tightly. Our blood mixing, sticky and wet.

'There,' I said, 'We're blood brothers now. Like in the Westerns.'

I let go of her hand. It dropped to her side. I thought she would wipe the blood off, but she didn't. Neither did I.

'I'll always look after you,' I said.

'I know,' she replied.

We deposited the contents of the cart at the collection point - the infant's school playground at the top of Read Road. Neat mounds of knickknacks surrounded a tree in the centre of the playground. We sorted our donations, placing each item onto the relevant pile before leaving the cart by the main gate.

With our chores done, we were free to play. Emily did not wish to visit the pig, worried she would upset herself further. We headed to the Rec instead. When we arrived, it was deserted. We had the entire place to ourselves. We played on the merry go round and the rocking horse and the big slide. Finally, we sat side by side, upon the swings.

I wanted to impress Emily so I showed her a handful of my poisonous Lords and Ladies berries.

'They're not poisonous,' she said, 'unless you have an allergy. They'll only make you ill. You'd have to eat loads of them.'

Disheartened, I replaced the berries into my pocket.

'That poor pig,' she said, 'I'm going to boycott anyone who has anything to do with it.'

'My mum's got a share in it,' I said. 'So has most of the village. He's going to be cut up soon, by Mr Hammond, the butcher. I could poison Mr Hammond if you'd like, with the berries.'

'Those aren't any good,' she said, 'We'd need something like deadly nightshade or devil's helmet. The woods are full of them.'

Emily was quiet. She was thinking about something. 'We should just set the poor thing free,' she said, hopping off the swing.

We walked together for a while, away from the Rec, just ambling along. When we arrived at the village pond the ducks were hungry but neither of us had anything to feed them. We spent a little time skimming stones across the pond but we got bored quickly so we wandered off again.

As we made our way along Woodfield Lane, passing the cricket grounds, we came upon five soldiers. They were LDV's, the Local Defence Volunteers. I recognised one of them, he worked in the village library. Stood beside them, a horse and cart. We made a fuss of the animal, which was friendly enough. Every time the beast tossed his head, Emily flinched.

We watched the men for a few minutes. They were trying to remove a metal street sign from its wooden backing. The sign read '*Crofton Close*'. Thick rivets fastened the sign onto two concrete posts. The soldiers did not appear to have any suitable tools to do the job justice. Instead, they resorted to the application of brute force.

Emily smiled at me as she petted the horse. 'I don't think there'll be much metal left by the time they've finished,' she said to me.

The librarian soldier turned towards Emily. 'We're not after the metal, Miss,' he said, 'We're removing all the street signs. To hinder the Germans, so they don't know where they are. You know, get them all lost.'

'Are you taking the one from Read Road?' I asked.

'Course we are,' he said, 'The whole bloody country's getting stripped out.'

'Do you think they'll really come?' Emily asked the soldier.

'Don't be daft,' he said, 'We'll be as safe as houses here, love. I wouldn't worry about it if I was you!'

After a while, I lost interest in the men and their horse. Emily did too, so we went about our way. As evening approached and darkness came, we headed back toward the common. We could see the pig from afar. A passing gentleman tipped a bag of kitchen scraps into the pen before continuing on his way. The offerings were eagerly received by the animal. It snorted and chomped loudly.

Assured that no others were present, we made our way across the damp grass, over to the iron bars of the pen. The creature had grown considerably over the last few months. It was not cute anymore. Its bulk was rather intimidating.

'If we let it go, it'll just get hit by a car,' Emily said, 'We need to take it into the woods. We could use this to lead it.' She began to untie the length of rope which bound the gate.

It was some two hundred yards from the pigpen to the treeline. The railway line separated the two. It would not be easy to lead the pig such a distance. I took off my leather belt in the hope it could be used as a collar. It was my Father's belt. I had added several extra holes to it with a nail so that it fitted me.

I clambered into the pen. The moment I was inside, the beast set upon me. At first, it tried to barge me into a tight corner with its body but as its confidence grew, so too did its aggression. At every opportunity, the pig sought to nip at my thigh or the back of my legs. I tried to push down on its snout but this only encouraged the animal to nip at my hands. I began to panic in the confines of the enclosure. My shoes squelched in the rancid smelling excrement and mud. Emily was giggling.

The belt barely reached around the pig's neck but I managed to attach it. I gripped the leather tightly and found I could steer its head away from my limbs. Emily passed me the length of rope. As I attached it to the belt, the pig dashed forward. It flung the gate wide open, knocking Emily backwards onto the grass. Her giggling stopped. The pig pulled me sharply to the ground, dragging me through the warm slurry. I was pulled clear of the pen before I could let go of the rope. The animal scampered across the common, lost in the darkness.

Emily helped me to my feet. I smelt awful and she was keen not to touch me. It was a ghastly mess that covered my front. Closing the gate, we set off across the common in search of the pig.

After a few minutes, four older boys approached us. They were following a narrow dirt track that led towards some houses near the railway line. They were lanky and boisterous. I expected them to bully me but they did not. They ignored me.

'Hello, Emily,' the tallest one said. He broke away from his friends and brushed past me to greet her. Emily's face lit up with a smile. She went to him. Embraced him. And then they began to kiss. I looked to the ground. The other boys began to cheer and tease their friend.

'Sod off,' the tallest boy said.

Emily took a step back.

'Who's your muddy friend,' the tall boy said to her.

'He's no one,' she replied, 'Are you off to Colin's house?'

The boy nodded and kissed her again, full on the lips. 'See you tomorrow,' he said.

Emily smiled as the boys headed off.

My heart was broken. I gathered the courage to look up at her. She was the happiest I had ever seen her. We said nothing.

Emily and I looked for the pig in silence. All the time, she was smiling. I watched her from the corner of my eye. We eventually found the animal near the railway line. It was sniffing and foraging on the ground. It was pitch black now. I took hold of the rope firmly. After a while, I found that I could lead the animal like a dog without too much difficulty.

'Dad's going to kill me for being out, after dark,' Emily said.

I did not reply.

We led the pig over to the turnstile by the railway bridge. The animal was too long and broad to fit through so we led it to a level crossing further to our left. As we approached, the pig saw the treeline opposite the track. It began to pull on the rope. I could barely hold on. Emily helped me keep control of it. Still, it pulled us across the track with such force, the rope dug into my palms. As we reached the other side - whoosh. A great steam locomotive thundered along the northbound line. It missed us by inches. The roar of the train startled the pig. It pulled free of our grip and dashed into the undergrowth, gone from sight.

'Well at least he's free now,' Emily said. She looked me up and down. 'You can't go home in that state,' she said, 'Your mum'll kill you.'

I said nothing.

'You can't be seen. Not like that. We'll have to change your clothes,' she said. 'Go and wait by the steam. I'll run home. Bring you back some of Charlie's old stuff.'

'Do you promise to come back?' I asked.

'Of course, I promise,' she said.

And then we parted. Emily headed back towards the common as I walked alongside the railway tracks, towards the station. Our relationship had changed. Things felt different now. I was sad to see her go.

The air raid blackout made my progress a slow and cautious affair. The stars, however, were spectacular. They helped me to forget about the boy on the common, the boy who kissed her. The boy who had made her smile again. The sky was so black. The stars were so bright. Ten thousand twinkling suns. Every single point of light emanating from a burning furnace perhaps a thousand lightyears away. In the space that lay between me and them, there was nothing. I had never felt so alone.

I wondered if the astronomer was at the eyepiece of the telescope. Orion was no longer visible so he would be unable to study Alnilam until the start of autumn. Regardless, the heavens continued to trail across the sky as the Earth rotated. The planet Venus shone brightly as it set low towards the west. It would be several hours before the moon would rise above the rooftops and illuminate the nightscape.

A clanking sound. A train was approaching from behind. I darted from the trackside and concealed myself amongst the weeds and brambles. Hidden by nature, I watched as a line of passenger coaches trundled past. They were slowing down. The train came to a halt at the station platform some two hundred yards ahead. I lay motionless, my eyes fixed. Much of the platform was obstructed from view but I saw countless soldiers disembarking. The locomotive drank from the water tower. Even this far away I could see the men were dirty and exhausted. Some carried a rifle, others held two. I saw a soldier barefooted, without a tunic. He strolled towards the end of the platform closest to me. He lit up a cigarette in the cold night air. The chaotic dance of jostling men behind him made no sound. For a brief moment, I sensed the barefooted soldier staring directly at me, eye to eye, from where I lay within the foliage. It was unnerving. He drew a final puff from the cigarette before flicking its remnants onto the track. He turned his back and became lost in the mêlée.

It took no more than ten minutes for the great locomotive to replenish its water tanks and for the troops to re-board. The train began to chuff off from the station towards London. It left the platform, still and deserted once more. Save for my memory of them, they could have never existed.

When I arrived at the little footbridge, I found the water in the Rye to be painfully cold. I stripped to my underwear and began to scrub my clothes clean as best I could. I shivered uncontrollably.

A sound. I heard it through the darkness of the night. It came from nearby, somewhere in the undergrowth. It was too dark to see anything. I kept still. Silence. Then the sound of rustling leaves. I strained my eyes, fixing them upon a patch of brambles by the stream. And then it appeared, the outline of a man. He stood, partly concealed within the twisted branches. No more than a silhouette. He may have had his back to me. He may have been facing me directly. I could not tell.

Forgetting to breathe, I let out a sharp gasp for air. Slowly, the figure retreated, swallowed up by the darkness. My hands fumbled on the ground until I located a stone of sufficient weight it could be used to defend myself. I remained still for five minutes or so but my crouching posture became too painful to maintain so I stood upright and stretched my legs. I listened but heard nothing. I wondered if I had imagined it. My eyes were tired and my body ached with the cold.

I wrung out my wet clothes and draped them over the edge of the footbridge, listening to the sound of the trickling water as it fell back into the stream. In the distance, somewhere in the woods, an animal cry. It was a strange and unfamiliar sound. Like nothing I had heard before. I tried to steady my nerves, but in my heart, I knew what it was. It was the sound of a monster.

A breeze picked up and my body ached with cold. A deep pain in the base of my spine forced me to seek shelter beside a hedgerow near the footbridge. I shuffled from foot to foot to keep warm. The sound of another train as it stopped briefly at the station. When it departed, another arrived promptly in its place. Their movements concealed by the dark blanket of night.

It was gone midnight when Emily returned. I felt embarrassed to reveal myself to her in my underwear. Eagerly I donned the fresh clothing she offered me. She had been crying. I could see it in her eyes.

'There was a train. Full of soldiers. At the station,' she said, 'when I came back over the bridge. I saw them. They were on the platform.' She was shaking. She looked much younger now, like a scared little girl. 'Some were covered in oil,' she said, taking in a deep breath, 'and one was with a nurse. I thought it was Louis at first. He was bleeding. He was bleeding so much.'

I did not know what to say, so I hugged her. She cried onto my shoulder. She cried so hard that she struggled to catch her breath. 'I…miss,' she said, 'him…so much.'

I froze. Over her shoulder, I saw the figure again. Standing amongst the foliage. Motionless. Silent. It stood perhaps twenty yards away. I knew it was Mr Simpkins. I knew immediately. But something was different. Something about the way he stood.

'What is it?' Emily asked.

The figure disappeared once more into the darkness.

'Nothing,' I said, 'I'm just cold.'

Emily wiped her eyes.

I didn't say anything to her. I did not wish to distress her any further.

We walked slowly across the common, towards the station. The trains were still passing through every twenty minutes or so. We waited until we were confident no more were due before crossing over the bridge. Emily kept her head bowed low, away from the station. But I looked, down onto the platform below. It was littered with bandages and assorted rubbish of every kind. A blood-soaked mop rested against the stationmaster's office door.

I walked Emily to her home. Not a word was spoken. We did not need to say anything. I knew. We both knew. Whatever happened in my life, I wanted Emily to be a part of it. I did not care about the other boy anymore.

I climbed into my bed at half-past two in the morning. I could not sleep. Hour after hour, I listened to the rumbling of steam trains as they clattered along the line at the foot of the road. The war had taken a new turn.

Chapter XI

A black unmarked car pulled out of Leatherhead police station onto Kingston Road. It headed off at speed towards Epsom. The low morning sun rested on the horizon, sending flickering shards of dancing light through the treeline.

'Ease off, Doris,' Porter called out to the driver. She glanced momentarily at the two policemen in the rear-view mirror. Constable Billet raised his eyebrow at her. The Wolseley reduced its speed.

'That's better, love,' Porter said, 'You don't want to be cleaning up vomit back here. I've only just had me breakfast!'

It was a short drive to the asylum on the outskirts of Epsom. The car lurched to the right as it entered the grounds of St Ebba's Hospital. It came to a stop beside an imposing brick water tower that marked the entrance.

Porter leant forward and patted Carol on her shoulder. 'Stay with the car, Doris,' he said, 'I don't want it getting scratched by any of these lot.'

Outside, the air carried the scent of fragrant flowers. A mosaic of colourful blooms lined the driveway as the two policemen paced towards the administration block. Dark red hollyhocks swayed gently among carnations, freesias and sprawling flowers of every colour. In the distance, across an open lawn flanked by two formidable villas, a solitary figure let out a primal scream. It was harsh and piercing, but in a moment, it was gone, replaced by the warbling buzz of a bumblebee.

'I hate this ruddy place,' Ported said.

The administration block, a smart Victorian gothic building, stood proudly to the right. It was partly shrouded by mature chestnut trees but the multitude of Georgian style windows suggested a bright interior. Two circular towers stood at each corner of the frontage. Outwardly, the structure had the appearance of a private school or, perhaps, a select country hotel. It looked welcoming.

Approaching the main doorway, Constable Billet felt obliged to remove his helmet out of respect for the grandeur of the place. Even Porter dragged his open hand over his head to flatten down any loose strands of hair.

Porter knocked on the door and stepped back. They were met by a stern, matronly looking nurse with thick, manly hands and sturdy shoes. Her voice though was surprisingly soft and pleasant.

'Hello Norman,' she said, 'back so quick?'

Porter grinned. 'Afraid so,' he said, 'I need to speak to Rollingson again. It's about, well, you know!'

The nurse invited the men inside and seated them in a cramped waiting room.

'I'll let the duty doctor know you're here. Just be a tick, dears,' she said.

Constable Billet studied the neglected décor and flaking grey paint on the walls. 'Wasn't this the old shell-shock hospital, back in the day?' he asked.

Porter nodded. 'And before that,' he said, 'it was an epilepsy hospital. They get all sorts in here now though. A right old mix.' The detective checked his wristwatch. 'Almost six-thirty,' he said, 'I hope our man's an early riser. Don't fancy pissing him off again.' The detective fidgeted with his shoelaces. 'Sergeant Wells takes over the investigation later today. Mare's right pissed off about it. He wants us to get some good evidence, enough to charge him and get Sergeant Wells off our back. Of course, if we rush in now, we could cock it all up. Still, if that's what the old man wants.'

'Good morning officers,' a confident voice greeted them. The two policemen rose and shook hands with the gentleman. He was a thin man in his late fifties with receding blond and grey hair. A frown of tightly knotted skin rested permanently upon the bridge of his nose, pushing his round spectacles forward and narrowing his eyes. He spoke softly, as if he were conveying his condolences to a widow.

'I'm Doctor North, the duty doctor. You're here to see David Rollingson, is that right?' he asked. 'He's already been cleaned and dressed. He's waiting for you in Thorn Villa. He likes visitors. He's been ready for you since about two this morning, I believe.'

The policeman followed the doctor through the building and exited into the rear garden. 'He wasn't too keen to see me the last time,' Porter said, 'He tried to lump me one.'

'Yes,' Doctor North replied, 'We'd amended his medication. It sometimes makes them agitated. It's nothing personal. Some of our guests are very ill, you know.' He gestured out across the expanse of lawn. 'That's Thorn Villa over there,' he said, 'Bit of a walk I'm afraid.'

As the men made their way, Porter stopped abruptly. He stooped to examine the underside of his shoe.

'I'm afraid some of our long term residents defecate on the grounds,' Doctor North said in a matter-of-fact way, 'We stopped their late-night cordial, because of the excess bedwetting. This is their little protest, you see. They'll soon adapt to the new regime quick enough though.' The doctor forced a smile as he watched Porter drag his shoe across the grass. 'The gardeners try their best, you know,' he said, 'but they tend to miss the odd spot. The residents can be quite imaginative when they put their minds to it. They can hide the stuff almost anywhere, you know.'

Thorn Villa was a welcoming looking structure. Robust window frames presented in crisp white paint. A mock dovecote crowned the centre ridge, adorned with a bold clock face. Long shadows of trees and border plants caressed the narrow gravel footpath that led to the entrance.

Inside, another nurse greeted the men and unlocked the door into a sparsely furnished hall.

'This is the day room,' Doctor North said, tapping the headrest of a high-backed armchair.

An elderly man sat dressed only in pyjama bottoms and socks, rolled his eyes. He turned in his chair and scrutinised the black buttons on Constable Billet's tunic.

'That's my jacket ya wearing,' he said, stretching out a frail, liver-spotted hand. Out of reach of the buttons, he slowly withdrew his hand and began to fidget with the elasticated waist of his pyjamas.

'Morning, sir,' Billet said.

The elderly man ignored him.

'Bernie is one of our longest-serving residents, aren't you Bernie,' the doctor said.

The man began to rock slightly to and fro, speaking in a low voice. 'Meanwhile. Meanwhile. Meanwhile,' he repeated.

Across the hall, another male resident slept in an armchair facing a window. Beyond, lay a small garden, enclosed by a six-foot-high brick wall.

The doctor gestured towards the garden. 'Rollingson is outside at the moment. He likes visitors but he does get rather anxious sometimes. The garden is the best place to keep him relaxed.'

The men peered through the bars of the window. Rollingson. stood alone outside. He was barefoot on the grass, his back turned. He stood awkwardly, as if his right knee might give way at any moment. Brown elasticated trousers hung loosely from his hips, displaying a band of filthy skin. He wore a dark green knitted jumper, too tight for his bulk. He turned and shuffled clumsily towards the window. A significant indent in his right temple distorted his features. His skull was lopsided, like a kidney bean.

Constable Billet turned away from the window.

The elderly gentleman, Bernie, rose from his chair and slowly shuffled across the floor. He made his way to the corner of the room, pressing his nose firmly against the wall. A stream of urine began to splash against heavy black-out curtains. The fluid pooled and frothed around his toes.

'He's a big old bugger is Rollingson,' Porter said, patting his colleague on the back, 'Best you don't aggravate him too much.'

Constable Billet handed his police helmet to the doctor. 'Do you mind holding this please,' he said, 'we won't be too long.'

The doctor took the helmet and turned the latch of a side door, pushing it open. The fragrance of cut grass drifted into the hall, concealing the smell of stale urine.

'Your visitors are here, David,' the doctor said.

Rollingson stepped back.

'Now, remember what we talked about earlier,' the doctor said, 'If I hear you've been rude to these nice gentlemen, I'll have to tell Nurse about it, do you understand?'

The doctor turned to the policemen. 'I'll leave you to it then. I'll be in the office, over there, if you need me. Just call out.'

Billet and Porter stepped into the garden. The door closed behind them, quickly followed by the sound of a sliding lock snapping into place.

'Hello, David,' Billet said, 'I'm Harry. Constable Billet. We haven't met before. Do you mind if we have a quick chat?'

Detective Porter stepped forward, ahead of Billet. 'And I'm Detective Constable Porter,' he said, 'I reckon you remember me, right enough.'

Rollingson nodded gingerly. He sat himself down on a wooden picnic bench, his back resting against the wall. The two policemen sat opposite.

Rollingson stared down at his empty hands. They were chunky and rough, like coal miners' hands.

'I'd like to talk to you about something,' the constable said, 'It's about the night you were arrested, at Epsom hospital. Do you remember?' The policeman continued. 'We just want to understand how you ended up there. Why you ran off from your carer. Can you tell me about that, David?'

Rollingson looked at the constable. His eyes, distant and glazed. 'I don't like…the carers,' he said, stumbling over his words. 'I like…to get away…I always come back. Always. I just want…to find Mary. She's in…hospital. I want to tell her that… the nurse is mean… to me. I couldn't find Mary though. Have they … moved her?… Where is…she?'

Billet removed his pocket notebook and pen from his tunic. He turned to a blank page at the back and slid it towards Rollingson. 'Do you think you could write your name down for me please?' he said, placing a pen onto the table.

'I ain't…stupid,' Rollingson said, grasping at the pen. He leant over the notebook, the bulk of his forearm obscuring the page. Slowly he began to write, his head bowed low, almost touching the page.

Porter looked at the wound on Rollingson's temple.

'That's an 'ell of a dink you've got there mate,' he said.

Rollingson sat up abruptly. He slid the notebook back to Constable Billet.

'See,' he said, 'told you I could…write. Look,' Rollingson said, 'That's my name, that is!' He relaxed against the wall again, smiling to himself. But then a look of concern formed on his face, as if a great worry had settled upon it. He began to gnaw at his thumbnails, already reduced to the stubby white lunula.

Constable Billet examined the clumsy scrawl across the page. 'Do you think you could also write down some swear words for me too please, David?'

Rollingson smiled again. 'Don't you know any then?' he asked. He paused, 'Are you trying to get me into trouble?'

'I want you to write the word *fuck* onto the page, please,' Constable Billet said, handing back the notebook and pen.

Rollingson concentrated as he dragged the pen across the page, 'F…U…G,' he said aloud before handing it back.

'I need to take a look at your pinkies,' Porter said, reaching into his pocket and placing a small wooden box onto the table. Rollingson stared at it.

'Your fingerprints, David,' Billet said, 'For our records. It's nothing to worry about.'

Rollingson placed both his hands onto the table, palm up. 'Then…can I see…Mary?' he asked.

Porter opened the box and delicately laid its contents onto the table in front of him. A solid block of copper. It shone in the morning light. Next to this, he placed a small rolling pin and a diminutive tube labelled '*Indian ink*'.

Rollingson watched with fascination as Porter squeezed a speck of black paste from the tube onto the block of metal. He ran the rolling pin across the block with some force. After a minute, the sticky ink had evenly coated the top surface.

Constable Billet reached into his tunic and produced a fingerprint form. He smoothed it out onto the table.

'Right then sunshine,' Porter said, 'let's start with your left thumb shall we?'

Rollingson stretched out his right hand towards the detective.

'No, mate,' Porter said, pushing the hand away, 'I mean your other left.'

Rollingson swapped his hands, keeping his left fist tightly closed. 'When…can I see…Mary?' he asked.

Porter did not reply. He took hold of Rollingson's hand and prised out the thumb. Holding the digit firmly, he rolled it slowly across the copper block.

'Why can't…I see…Mary?' Rollingson repeated.

The detective remained silent, placing the inked thumb onto the form and rolling it across, leaving a crisp, black rectangular thumbprint. Porter then took hold of Rollingson's index finger, pulling it towards the copper block as if it were an inanimate, unattached, object.

'I want…Mary,' Rollingson said, raising his voice, 'Now!'

Porter gripped the finger tightly, rolling it onto the copper. 'Well, you can't, mate. She doesn't want to see you, so that's that. Sorry.'

Rollingson looked rapidly between the two men. 'But she's my… girlfriend! Why won't she see me?' he asked.

'She ain't going to see you, David,' Porter said, rolling the man's finger across the page, 'And do you know why? Because you smashed her bloody head in with a fucking hammer. Now, stop wriggling.'

Rollingson rose. He grabbed hold of the detective's wrist as Constable Billet leapt to his feet.

'Let go, now,' Porter yelled, unable to pull himself free.

Rollingson stared blankly into Porter's eyes. His face turned red. He grabbed the block of copper from the table and swiped the detective across the temple with a clunk. Porter groaned and dropped to the ground, motionless. He then turned to face Billet, raising the metal block to shoulder height. The constable took a step back and withdrew his truncheon.

'Get back!' Billet yelled, positioning his truncheon, ready to strike.

The door to the villa swung open. Doctor North and two nurses ran across the lawn towards the men. As they approached, Rollingson overturned the picnic table, sending the constable tumbling backwards into a flower bed. Standing on a leg of the upturned bench, he began to scramble up onto the wall. He sat upon it, his legs straddling each side. The hospital staff tried to grasp his foot but he began to kick out wildly. A nurse took a blow to the face and yelped. She withdrew, blood spilling from a broken nose. Rollingson dropped to the other side of the wall, gone from sight.

Constable Billet got to his feet. He saw the doctor tending to the nurse's nose. He knelt beside Porter, rolling him on his side. The detective groaned, feebly pushing his colleague away.

* * *

I found it rather difficult to concentrate at school. Morning assembly was a solemn affair. The Major spoke of the current situation in Europe. He even suggested the Expeditionary Force might struggle to halt the German advance. He explained the importance of defeating Hitler and fascism. But from his musings, I could tell he knew no more about the situation than anyone else. He mentioned a place called Dunkirk. About the struggle to escape the beach. France had fallen. We would be next.

The Major, in his pompous grandeur, began to read out a list of boys names. Former pupils of the school, each fighting for King and country. I listened for Louis Fenton's name, but the list was long and I lost interest.

'You young boys,' the Major said, 'sitting cross-legged on the assembly floor. Some of you may well find yourselves head of the household. As such, you are to do your bit. Your duty. We must each face whatever strife comes our way.'

The Major looked stern. 'You are to keep your loving homes in order whilst the menfolk are away, valiantly fighting against this tyranny,' he said, 'But remember, they are not just fighting for the love of their country. They are fighting to preserve the love that exists in all our homes. We must all pull together!'

My left leg began to spasm. The Major described a household to which I could not relate.

'With this in mind,' he continued, 'it has been brought to my attention that the cooperative pig on Ashtead common has been stolen.'

A gasp rippled through the assembly. It was quickly dampened by withering glances from the teachers flanking the hall.

'If,' the headmaster continued 'any boy from Park House is found to have been involved in any high jinks of this nature, the consequences shall be harsh and the matter passed to the police, immediately!'

A voice called out from within the ranks. 'Chunky Evans ate it, Sir,' the remark causing much merriment amongst the other boys.

Without a single thought for assembly hall rules, I found myself turning around to face the commotion. I spied 'Chunky' Evans. He looked uncomfortable, demoralised. He briefly made eye contact and I took the opportunity to offer him a smile. He nodded to me in acknowledgement.

'Face the front, Engle!' a boy hissed at me with vitriol. I didn't know his name.

'Fuck off you filthy fucking rodent,' I replied, with no care of the consequences. To my surprise, the boy did not reply. Instead, he found himself teased and jostled by his friends sitting either side.

'Silence,' yelled the Major.

I turned to face the front as a hush fell upon the assembly. I could not help but grin.

For the finale, we all stood and sang *Jerusalem* by Hubert Parry. I mimed my way through most of it. When assembly ended, we filed silently out of the hall and off to class. Nobody tormented me in the queue. They did not even look at me.

I had gained very little in the way of meaningful sleep the previous night and my head felt heavy and prone to sudden unexpected jerks. This was particularly prevalent in my mother's lesson, after lunch. The history of Victorian glassware manufacture. Tedious drivel caused my mind to wander. I began to think of Emily and how upset she had been. Then I thought about her brother. Unlike Charles, Louis was a friendly chap. An athletic sort, always taking part in cross country runs and such. He used to turn a blind eye if he found me hiding in the library. But now he was gone. It was as if he never had the chance to be a little boy. Not for very long.

The lesson continued, Mother monotonously outlining the production methods of Stourbridge glass. My attention was momentarily captured by the mention of uranium. It was used as a colourant. But I soon began to drift again. I thought about Mr Simpkins this time. I had not seen him for over six months. I tried not to concern myself with the terrible nightmares that still filled my sleep. I was learning to cope with them. If I found myself thinking of such things, I would distract myself. I would dig my fingernails deep into my arm, draw blood if needed. Once, I took a drawing pin and pushed it into the palm of my hand. It helped detract from the torment. I felt more in control of my life now, less afraid.

My attention was drawn to movement outside the window. Several figures were making their way slowly across the far end of the cricket pitch. Five men, each in green battle dress. They moved hesitantly along the treeline. I watched as one produced a hand-shovel. He dug at the base of a tree trunk. First one hole, and then another nearby. And then a third. The other figures watched over the proceedings. They placed a small object into each hole and backfilled them, concealing the plots with ground litter.

In an instant, my attention returned to the classroom, intuitively aware of my mother's proximity. She stood beside me, her hand resting on my desk.

'Well, George?' she said loudly.

The entire class turned to face me.

'Explain why this can only be implemented at the start of the blowing process?'

I hesitated. Mother struck the back of my head with a wooden blackboard wiper.

'Pay attention, child,' she said.

I turned in rage and stared into her eyes. She looked shocked, inhaling sharply. Then she nervously broke eye contact with me.

The class sat in stunned silence.

Mother composed herself and returned to the front of the class. She looked pale and shaken. After taking a slow, deep breath, she continued the lesson as if nothing had happened.

The school day came to an end. I stayed back, giving Mother a head start. I never walked home with her. She always made her own way, alone. I watched from the main gate as the school grounds emptied. Wave after wave of schoolboys. Some glared at me but the majority were oblivious to my existence. A bluster of boys and teachers peeled left and right, into the street. I watched Mother as she faded into the distance. Within ten minutes the grounds were empty, save for the caretaker locking up the external doors. Then, even he was gone.

I rested my back against the low brick wall, listening to a bird chirping. It was a strange kind of call. I scanned the trees opposite the road, and there I saw it. A tiny, bright yellow budgerigar sitting on a branch. It chirped again before flying away.

Ahead, at the far end of the street, my attention fell upon a police constable. He was slowly ambling towards the school. As he drew near, I felt anxious, as if I were being judged. I did not wish to make eye contact with him, but I felt obliged to acknowledge his presence.

'Good afternoon,' I said as he passed.

The constable stopped and turned abruptly to face me.

'Any why,' he asked, 'is this afternoon good?'

The question caught me off guard and I struggled to find a reply.

The policeman was well turned out in his smart tunic. He reminded me somewhat of my father. He was in his early thirties, a lean built chap of some six-foot or so. With the police helmet adding extra height he was a formidable figure. Yet his voice, although authoritative, was more brotherly than custodial.

'So then, what are you doing hanging around here,' he said, 'Haven't you got a home to go to?'

I turned to leave but was stopped by a firm hand on my shoulder.

'Wait a minute,' he said, 'aren't you friends with the Fenton girl, what's her name, Emily, isn't it?'

'Yes, constable,' I said apprehensively, 'I'm George Engle.'

'I see, *you're* George Engle are you!' he replied, 'So, what can you tell me about this pig. You know, the one that's missing from the common?'

I felt my face redden. Self-conscious of this fact, they began to burn even hotter. 'Nothing,' I said.

'Hmm,' he replied, 'Only, you and the Fenton girl were seen by a group of boys, out on Ashtead Common on the very night the pig went missing! That's a bit of a coincidence don't you think?' The constable's eyes fixed on mine.

'We were just playing together, by the stream,' I said, 'We didn't see anything suspicious.'

The constable removed his hand from my shoulder. 'The boys say they saw something a bit suspicious,' the policeman continued, 'Do you know what they saw, George?'

I remained silent.

The policeman stretched his legs, giving the impression of increased height. 'Well, they saw you George, covered in pig mess.'

My heart pounded. 'My mum sends me there, to feed it,' I said, 'All our kitchen scraps. I fell in. You won't tell her, will you? She'll go mad if she finds out my clothes got dirty. The pig was still there when we left, honest. Maybe the boys stole it. Mum was going to make me pork and lentil soup.'

'Pork and lentil soup – very nice,' he said, 'Well, if you or your friend Emily Fenton happen to remember anything of significance,

I'd like you to tell me about it. Anything at all. Theft of food supplies is a serious matter you know, particularly during wartime! Pop into the Leatherhead station and ask for me, Police Constable Billet.'

I nodded. The policeman returned a dry smile then continued on his patrol. I stood motionless, breathing in short gasps until he was gone from sight.

After I while I remembered the playing field. I was keen to examine the area disturbed by the LDV soldiers. Confident I was no longer being observed, I headed over to the far side of the school grounds. A foraging blackbird betrayed the location as it eagerly searched for worms in the freshly churned soil. It chirped angrily as I approached, before flying off.

I knelt upon the ground and removed a loose chunk of turf resting there. With my bare hands, I dug through the soft soil. A few inches down, my fingernails scratched at something solid. I extracted it. An old glass bottle of some type, not dissimilar to a fizzy lemonade bottle. The cap was sealed with a daube of thick, red candle wax. The glass was clear and I could see it filled with a liquid. It had separated into two distinct colours of equal volume. The top liquid was a translucent yellow colour whilst the lower was opaque and white. Out of curiosity, I shook the bottle vigorously. The liquids remained well mixed.

I scratched the wax away with my nails, revealing a crimped metal cap. The word *'SIP'* was handwritten on it in black letters. The cap was too tight to remove by hand and the effort left a red mark on the palm of my hand. I studied the contents more closely and concluded it was home-brewed beer. No doubt the Local Defence Volunteers were keen to hide their illegal activity. Alcohol was bound to have some monetary value, to the right person.

I cleaned the bottle as best I could and placed it inside my satchel. A further scavenge of the area revealed two more bottles hidden in shallow graves. I appropriated these too. Excited by my hoard, I left the grounds. The glass clinked delightfully with each step home.

The following weekend I met up with Emily. We sat on the swings at the Rec and chatted about this and that. All the other children had gone to watch the cricket. There was not a single soul in sight. Confident we would not be overheard, the subject of the cooperative pig arose.

'A policeman stopped me outside school this week,' I told her, 'He asked about the pig. Said we were both seen on the common.'

'No one knows it was us,' Emily said, 'Don't worry about that. Martin promised not to say a word.'

I nodded slightly, upset at the mention of the boy's name. 'My mum's furious about the pig. She's been planning pork and lentil soup for bloody months,' I said.

Emily synchronised her swinging with mine. 'My dad gets the parish newsletter. It said someone saw it in the woods, living wild. Almost caught it. Even got the police looking for it.' She paused briefly, 'They said it could've been stolen by the I.R.A, to try and starve us!'

I hopped off the swing and helped Emily to her feet. 'Don't you Catholics need to eat too?' I asked.

'Want to play hide and seek?' Emily suggested, rather unexpectedly.

I nodded. We spent half an hour together in a playful mood, taking turns to seek. It quickly became a part of the game to hug each other upon discovery. Soon we gave less regard to our hiding than to our capture. I counted aloud beside the trunk of a sycamore tree, eyes tightly closed and giggling wildly.

A soft sound of crushed grass behind me. Then, two hands shoved me firmly from behind. I banged my head painfully against the trunk. My head ached as if it had cracked. I turned to face my aggressor.

'That's my girlfriend you bloody freak!' a boy's voice yelled. It was Martin. He stood close to me, his breath reeking of cigarettes and peppermint. In my heart, I felt the darkest welling of anger. It grew inside me. I squared up against the boy, two years my senior. Every ounce of energy surged through my fist. I punched cleanly into his throat. His knees buckled and he dropped vertically to the ground like a rag doll.

I felt joyful, watching him clutching at his neck, gurgling. Calmly I stepped over his body and dropped down onto my knees, placing my full weight into his stomach. A pitiful whimper popped from his mouth. His pathetic weakness enlivened me. Blood and rage pulsed through me. I began to punch each side of his head in alternating blows. Again and again. I revelled in his suffering. I felt alive.

I paused my assault momentarily to enjoy the sight of his wounding's. I struck him again, this time in his arm as he tried to shield his face. The strangest of sensations came over me. The boy was nothing. A slab of rotten meat festering in the heat. I pounded at his face again and again. I punched beyond his face as if I were smashing his brain into the back of his skull.

Emily appeared from behind the iron rocking horse. She ran over and shoved me clean off the boy. She was screaming at me. Or perhaps it was my own screams I heard. Perhaps it was the scream of the entire world. I did not care. I simply wished to kill him.

Emily knelt beside the boy. I rose to my feet with fists still clenched and anger in my heart. I took a step towards her. Our eyes met.

'Don't you dare!' she barked, raising a hand in defence.

'Bastard,' Martin spluttered as she helped him to sit up. 'Fucking bastard.'

I felt a warm drop of blood meander down my forehead. I walked over to the swings and seated myself. I glanced casually at his injuries. His eyes were swollen, red and raw. The skin around this throat was grazed and already beginning to bruise. I continued to swing, listening to the slow rhythmic squeak of the iron chains. He could have lived or died; he meant nothing to me. And still, I smiled.

Martin became agitated by Emily's fussing. He didn't want to look towards me, I could tell. He stumbled to his feet. Emily tried to steady him, but he pushed her away. I listened to them bicker. Their words drowned out by my inner jubilation. Something was said and then Emily shoved him in the chest. The boy turned his back on her. And then he left us, a distant figure across the Rec.

Emily came over and sat beside me on the swing. An awkward silence.

'He didn't deserve that,' she said, 'For a second I thought you were going to kill him. I thought you were going to hurt me too!'

I didn't reply. I allowed my swing to come to a halt. Together we sat motionlessly. Then, with the gentlest of touches, Emily wiped away particles of bark from my grazed head.

'I've never seen you fight like that before,' she said, 'He's twice your size.'

We strolled across the Rec in no particular direction. A soft breeze cooled my face. Emily stopped and looked up. She pointed into the clear blue sky.

'Look at that,' she said.

High above, fine white trails stretched out above the Earth. We lay down together on the grass and looked up.

'It's beautiful, don't you think?' Emily said.

I took hold of her hand. I didn't let go. We watched as the thread-like tendrils twisted and turned above us.

'Is it a dog fight? Is that what they look like?' she asked.

I nodded.

It was like cricket. We were spectators watching a game unfold. Too far from the action to distinguish friend from foe. A hundred fighters, twisting and darting chaotically through the heavens. Occasionally, the breeze would turn and we could hear the faint rattle of intermittent machinegun fire. That was our view of war, sanitized by distance.

After five minutes the cobweb in the sky drifted northwards, lost in the haze. As we got to our feet, Emily let go of my hand.

'My brother's been injured,' she said, rather catching me off guard. She looked down at her feet as we walked. 'Don't tell anyone, will you. I don't want people knowing. Not yet.'

Her face looked so pretty in the sunlight. A cluster of orange freckles dappled the bridge of her nose.

'Is he badly…' I said, before pausing.

'He's alright,' she said, 'but the Germans have him. Dad's furious.'

I reached out to hold her hand again, but at the last moment, she moved away.

'Do you fancy a drink?' I said, 'I've got some bottles of beer at home. I found them. The LDV hid them up.'

'No thanks,' Emily said, 'I tried some of dad's once. Disgusting.' She smiled at me and my heart quickened.

Emily sat down on the grass again as another wave of fluffy contrails became entangled over our heads. I knelt beside her and watched as she made a daisy chain for herself. She placed the delicate chain around her wrist. I gave her a nod of approval. The looming summer was in our hearts and the anger dissolved from my mind.

On Saturday morning, in mid-August, I ran a shopping errand for Mother. I visited Golding's the grocers to purchase our weekly ration of butter; two ounces each. It was an extremely hot morning already and I was keen to return home before it melted.

As I stepped out into the street, my ears were deafened by a terrific roar of powerful engines. So deep was the sound, I felt its resonance deep inside my chest cavity. Startled, I dropped the tiny package of butter onto the pavement. To my right, a magnificent fighter aircraft dashing along the length of Barnett Wood Lane, fifty feet above my head. The speed was terrific. A long trail of thick black smoke belched from its rear. In an instant it was gone, tainting the air with the stench of hot oil and cordite. Seconds later a Spitfire gave chase. The shadow of its elliptical wing momentarily concealing the summer sun from my eyes. I instinctively ducked as it passed, much lower than the first aircraft. Then it too was gone from sight, hidden behind the rooftops.

From the corner of my eye, I saw a small piece of metal cartwheeling along the gutter. It came to a halt in the road no more than ten feet from where I stood. Excitedly, I ran into the road and picked it up. A shattered bearing, still hot from war. I placed it into my pocket and returned to retrieve the splodged pack of butter from the pavement.

Chapter XII

I sat up in bed, awakened by the loudest of bangs. It was 11 o'clock at night. The sound of gravel sliding down the roof tiles. My bedroom door swung open. Mother stood in the doorway dressed only in her nightie.

'Shelter,' she said sternly, 'Now!'

Climbing out of bed and into the darkness, I barely had time to put on my dressing gown when Mother grabbed my arm. She pulled me down the stairs, through the house and out into the garden. I stepped out onto the lawn in bare feet. The cold air stung my lungs. The moon was full and crystal clear. It illuminated the garden, littered with fragments of branches, roof slates and shards of sparkling glass. It looked magical, like a dusting of snow on Christmas morning. My toes contorted with each stride, avoiding the glistening hazards as best I could. As we reached the shelter, I heard the distant ringing of fire-engine bells.

The Anderson was flooded, ankle-deep in water. As I entered, I inadvertently splashed the hem of Mothers nightie causing her to let out a profanity. I climbed onto my mattress, soiling my blankets with muddy water and grime. Mother, sat on her own bed plank opposite. She stretched out her dripping feet and rubbed them dry on my bedding.

'It's not a heavy raid,' she said, 'So go to sleep – you've got school in the morning.'

Mother settled herself down under her blanket, her back turned to me. It did not take long for her to fall asleep but I was unable to settle. I lay, peering out the narrow doorway, towards the house. The damp roof tiles sparkled in the moonlight. I strained to listen to muffled conversations between neighbouring shelters.

A man's voice spoke authoritatively.

'They've hit Barnett Wood Lane,' he said.

Another man's voice called out, 'I heard two go off,' he said.

A third man, more distant than the others, laughed as he called out. 'Well, your garden's such a bloody mess Bill, we'd never know if it ain't been hit or not,' he said.

* * *

The locker room was cramped and poorly lit. The early shift was changing from their civilian clothing into their police uniforms. Eight men jostled for elbow room. They fixed their ties in front of a single mirror hung from the back of the door. To their annoyance, the door swung open and the mirror was gone from view. Standing in the corridor beyond was Carol Barlow. She was already dressed for inspection.

'Oi, Doris,' one of the policemen called out, 'this is the bloke's changing room, sod off.'

She screwed her face up, 'Don't be such a prude,' she said, 'Nothing to see in here anyway. Certainly not with you lot.' She smiled at Constable Billet. 'Sergeant wants to see you in his office. Now, apparently.'

'Cheers, love,' Constable Billet replied, pushing his way through the men.

Sergeant Wells' office barely had room to contain his desk, chair and filing cabinet. Very little light filtered through the narrow barred window behind him.

'Come in Billet,' he said, 'You too Carol. Close the door would you, thanks.'

Carol shimmied her shoulders, forcing Constable Billet to offer her more room and lean heavily against the wall.

'It's Harry, isn't it?' the sergeant asked.

The constable nodded.

Sergeant Wells glanced down at some notes on his desk.

'As you know, I've taken over the Betty Stride investigation for the time being. Damn nuisance our main suspect has run off. Now, we're a bit thin on the ground at the moment though. B relief had a busy shift last night. A couple of strays fell on Ashtead.'

The sergeant glanced at a map of Surrey attached to the wall. 'Most of the shift has been at one of the scenes since midnight. Looking for entrapments,' the sergeant said. He looked at his notes again, 'Latest figures are one fatal, a missing infant, four serious and twenty-plus minor injuries. The four serious have been ambulated to Epsom District. I'll be taking some of C Relief down there in a minute to relieve the night turn.'

The sergeant picked up his tin air-raid helmet from his paperwork in-tray. He brushed it clean with the palm of his hand. 'I don't want this investigation to get side-lined. I've sent Detective Porter to Epsom hospital. Your man Rollingson might turn up there. He's done it before, apparently,' he said, 'Hopefully we can manage not to let a mentally incapacitated oaf out-smart us again, what do you think?'

Sergeant Wells rose to his feet. 'Right, Carol,' he said, 'The LDV, or Home Guard, whatever the hell they're called these days, has reported the theft of some ordinance. Home-made grenades or something. Bloody menace that lot. Now, our killer is pretty violent. That's the kind of thing he's likely to try and get his hands on, I suspect. I want you to speak to a senior officer or someone there. Find out what the bloody hell they're playing at. Bad enough the Germans are bombing us. We don't need a load of bloody geriatrics trying to blow us up too.'

Policewoman Barlow turned to leave but found herself unable to squeeze past Constable Billet.

'Harry,' Sergeant Wells said, 'Any update on that missing pig?'

'Not much,' he said, 'I spoke to a boy outside Park House School. He was hanging around the gates after closing. He may know something. He was seen on the common the night it was stolen. He acted a bit peculiar.'

Sergeant Wells donned his helmet and signalled for PC Billet to open the door. 'There's a memo from the Ministry of Food doing the rounds at the moment. They're starting to get twitchy about food shortages, theft and black-market goods. Might start to see some civil unrest if supplies stop getting through the blockades they reckon.' He stood in the doorway of his office. 'One other thing,' he said, 'Had a few reports that someone's living rough in Ashtead woods, near the common. See if you can find them and move them on. If there's the slightest hint they've eaten that damn pig, I want them nicked. Clear?'

* * *

It was an uncomfortable night in the shelter. Dawn broke at around five-thirty and I was eager to return to the house. Mother was still sleeping. I sat up and lowered my feet into the water. I clenched my teeth in freezing pain.

Standing on the lawn, I studied the debris strewn across the garden and surrounding rooftops. Most pieces were no larger than my hand although a large branch, some twelve feet long, had partially landed onto Dads shed. It had broken the spine of the roof, causing it to sag inwards. Even the frame was twisted, forcing the door to splinter and partially detach. It hung precariously from a single hinge. Fearful that Father's notebook was destroyed, I rushed in and searched through the chaos of fallen shelves and scattered tools. I found it safe, where I had hidden it, underneath the workbench. Even the three bottles of beer had been spared, save for being knocked onto their sides. I knew Mother would inspect the shed when she awoke so I removed the bottles and Fenton's clothing to the safety of my bedroom.

None of the windows of the houses had been broken. Upstairs, I looked through Mother's bedroom window at the front of the house. From here, I saw the full extent of the damage. Bricks and shattered wood lay strewn across the road. The worst of the damage was at the top, away from the railway line. I opened the window and lent out as far as I felt comfortable. It looked like the Baptist primary school at the top of the road had received a hit. The smell of burnt embers wafted in the air.

A swarm of grown-ups were below, clearing the road of obstructions. Some of the houses opposite had missing roof tiles and broken frames. I spied an upturned school desk, splashed in ink. It rested on its side on top a privet hedge.

By seven o'clock I had eaten breakfast and changed into my school uniform. I was placing my gas mask box around my neck when Mother came in from the garden. She looked unkempt and bedraggled. She glanced at me, and grunted 'Morning,' in my general direction.

I could not risk Mother snooping in my room before I returned from school so I placed the beer bottles inside my school satchel. I even hid Fenton's clothing in my sports kit bag. I would return them to Emily on my way to school.

Mother's gravelly voice followed me out of the door. 'Make sure you come straight back after school, do you hear! And you can clear this ruddy mess up too when you get back!'

'The Germans made it,' I said, 'why can't they bloody clean it up!'

Mother yelled at me. As I turned, she towered over me, her face scarlet with rage. A knot of veins bulged in her neck. 'Because,' she said, 'you're the man of the house now and you'll do what the bloody Hell I tell you to do! I'm fed up with you back answering me all the time. It's high time you grew up and started taking some responsibility around here!'

I could see the anger in her eyes but I was not afraid of her, not any more. 'I thought your new fancy man was head of the household,' I said, 'or has he run out of money now too?'

In an instant, she raised her hand to slap my face. She had such venom in her eyes. Instinctively, I grabbed her wrist with my left hand to block her. My thumb rested neatly under her wrist and my palm rested over her knuckles. I began to slowly apply downward pressure. I watched as she squirmed on her tiptoes, grimacing. I savoured the moment. I rejoiced in it. But then the moment passed. I released my grip and she collapsed onto her heels. The look of anger had drained from her face, replaced by something new. It was fear. We didn't speak. We didn't need to. She understood. Our relationship had changed, it had changed forever. I turned my back on her and left. I wasn't intimidated by her anymore. I could crush her like an aphid.

A piece of sharp, twisted shrapnel lay by the front gate. I placed it in my satchel as a souvenir. A few children were standing in the road, helping their parents to clear the street. They excitedly sifted through the dross for anything collectable. Kevin, a scruffy, sweaty little boy who lived next door, approached me with a broad smile on his face. He was two years younger than me and attended the Baptist school at the top of the road.

'School's been hit, smashed to pieces,' he said, hopping excitedly on the spot. 'It was a stray – bloody brilliant!'

* * *

Carol Barlow stood at the rear of Leatherhead police station, overlooking the prisoner exercise yard. She stubbed out her cigarette on the steps of the building. As she turned to head inside, Constable Billet appeared. He was retrieving a cigarette from his tunic.

'Heard about Porter?' Carol asked, with a smirk, 'He got thumped this morning, when he was over at the hospital.'

Billet shook his head. 'I didn't know that. Is he alright?' he asked.

'He's fine,' she replied, 'Just his ego that got bruised. Nicked his suspect though, Rollingson. Reckons he's god's gift to women now, silly sod.'

'Is Rollingson in the cells now?' the constable asked.

'No. Soon as HQ got a whiff, they moved him to Guilford. Think the big boys want to chalk up the arrest themselves. They've not told the press yet though. They'll want to make sure he's the right bloke first. Wouldn't look good if we've got the wrong man.'

'Where's Mare and Porter now?' he asked.

'They're briefing Sergeant Wells at the minute. Best stay clear of 'em love,' she said, 'It's a right show of ego's in there at the moment.'

Constable Billet drew hard on his cigarette. 'Fair enough,' he said, 'I'm off to look for some vagrant living rough in the woods. You're welcome to help if you want.'

Carol shook her head. 'I've got to go and do a door to door for a missing youth. He could be your vagrant in the woods I suppose. You know what children are like these days.' She pulled open the door, 'I've got to go and clean inside Porter's car now,' she said, 'His prisoner managed to smear shit all over the back seats. Filthy sod.'

* * *

I made my way along Read Road, towards Barnett Wood Lane. The primary school was in a dreadful state. The area was roped off around a precarious-looking wall that looked ready to tumble into the playground. Half the school was rubble. Not a single window left un-shattered. A ruptured mains pipe spewed water high into the air, creating a rainbow in the morning light. The tree which once stood in the centre of the grounds was split and burnt. Only a jagged trunk remained, the rest, strewn in every direction. Across the road, many of the shop fronts were blown in, their blinds dangled in tatters, swaying and rattling. Goldings the grocers had been hit the hardest. Mr Goldings himself stood outside. He was busy sweeping up fine glass and dust from the pavement. A chalk noticeboard beside the door announced '*Business as usual*'.

I felt sorry for Mr Goldings, he was an old man. With his wife already passed away some years back, he had no one to help out. I crossed the road and offered to sweep too.

'Thanks, son,' he said, 'but I've only got the one broom.'

The main window frame of his store had been pushed inwards, sending jagged cracks across the building. Inside, shelving and stock were spewed across the floor amongst the glass and splinters.

'At least no one was hurt,' Mr Golding said, giving a nod towards the primary school across the road, 'Not like Woodfield Lane.'

'Woodfield?' I said. The pit of my stomach began to turn.

'Yes lad,' he replied, 'A five-hundred pounder. Why? You got relatives down there?'

Adrenaline coursed through my body. Emily! I turned and began to run.

Mr Goldings called out after me, 'Wait You can't go there, it's not been cleared yet!'

I did not care. I could not stop running. I had to get to her, to see that she was alright. The faster I ran, the faster my heart filled with fear. I began to cry.

The ducks on the pond at the bottom of Woodfield Lane quacked angrily as I dashed through their midst. They fled noisily into the water as they dodged my feet. Already I could smell the cordite. In the distance, towards the far end of the lane, thick black smoke rose above the treeline.

'Bastards,' I cursed, watching the smoke drifting across the skyline. I ran past the cricket grounds. It was empty, silent. My pounding feet and wheezing lungs, the only sound.

Ahead, in the middle of the road, I saw vehicles. An ambulance, a fire engine and two police cars. They blocked the way ahead. To the left, twenty or so men were clambering across an immense pile of bricks and debris. Some were Home Guard, the new name for the Local Defence Volunteers. Others were emergency crews and civilians. Three houses, perhaps four, had once stood there. Now they were gone. Their innards spilt across the street and neighbouring gardens. Nearby trees stood barren, stripped clean of their leaves. Others were draped in shredded curtains and swashes of clothing like some ghastly Christmas tree. I squeezed between the police cars to get a clear view. I trembled, unable to tell which pile was Emily's house. I wondered if her body lay in tatters beneath the bricks.

A police sergeant, standing atop the destruction, calmly spoke out to those near him. 'I think it came more from the back this time,' he said, 'Definitely a groan.'

The sergeant was coated in fine dust as if he were a decoration on a cake. He looked tired. They all did.

I stood transfixed by the drama before me. To my left, standing upon a chaotic mound of masonry and smashed furniture, a dog scavenged through the debris. It was a skinny, rather neglected-looking mongrel. I watched as it noisily gnawed and chomped upon some such titbit.

The police sergeant pointed towards the animal and shouted, 'For the last time - get that bloody dog away from here!'

A constable nearby picked up part of a broken teapot and hurled it at the animal. The dog tugged its morsel free and scarpered past, brushing against my legs. Hanging from its jaw, the severed remains of a baby's arm. A tiny, perfect, little hand. An innocent new life, born into the madness of the world. The appendage flopped from the dog's muzzle, waving its last goodbye.

'You filthy fucker,' a soldier yelled out, hurling a brick in the dog's direction. The animal ran from sight, its gruesome prize still very much in its possession.

A police constable approached me. 'Is this your house, son?' he asked.

I shook my head.

'Well,' he replied, 'You'd better clear off then, hadn't you. Let us deal with this mess. Go on, bugger off you nosey sod, before I give you a thick ear!'

Squeezing my way through the parked cars, I continued onwards. I did not want to look for souvenirs. Ahead, I saw five detached houses with substantial damage. On one, the entire frontage had fallen away, revealing its contents like a doll's house. From the roadside, I could see into the remnants of the living room. Garish wallpaper lined the insides. I did not like the décor much. It was then I noticed Charles Fenton standing proudly by the front gate. Beside him, a pile of salvaged furniture and trinkets. I had not recognised the building. It was Emily's house.

'Is everyone alright?' I called out as I approached.

'Mum and Dad are out. I'm in charge. What do you want Engle?' he said. He looked stern, guarded his territory against the rest of the world.

'Is Emily alright?' I asked, trying not to sound unduly concerned.

Fenton smiled. 'You can see her, but it'll cost you,' he said, 'She was sleeping when the bomb hit. The floor gave way and she ended up downstairs in the kitchen – still in her ruddy bed!' Fenton looked ecstatic. 'She's the talk of the town at the moment. I'm charging everyone a penny to see her. I've made a shilling already, look,' he said, rattling a ceramic mug towards me.

'I don't have any money on me,' I said, 'You can have a bottle of beer though, if you let me see her first,' I said.

I flashed Fenton the neck of a bottle from my satchel.

Fenton's eyes widened. He nodded and gave me a sharp pat on my back. He led me to the rear of the house. The timber window frames at the side were charred and the glass blown inwards. The rear garden was surprisingly neat and tidy with very little damage.

Fenton opened the back door of the house. It was battered and stiff. It opened, revealing Emily, still in her bed. Two older boys stood watching her.

'Time's up,' Fenton said, 'Go on, clear off!'

Both boys left, giggling to themselves.

'Well then,' Fenton said, 'I'll leave you two lovebirds alone then. Don't forget about that bottle.' He left us, pulling the door closed.

I stepped up onto the wooden flooring which rested on top of crushed and shattered kitchen furniture below. The boards creaked and shifted as I made my way across to the bed.

Emily leant over in her nightie and gave me a tight hug. 'Thanks for coming,' she said.

I surveyed the damage. The bedroom floor had fallen in one unbroken section, flattening the entire contents of the kitchen below. The table, chairs and counters had all been presumably crushed flat. It was strange to see such a grand vault above my head. Light-green wall paint marked the area where Emily's bedroom once stood. High up in the wall, a picture hung at a precarious angle beside a closed door.

'Are you alright?' I asked.

Emily smiled at me. I could tell that her heart wasn't in it. Her blankets were coated in grey dust and bits of wooden splinters.

'Mum's gone to Epsom to register us as displaced,' she said, 'Dad's gone into Leatherhead. He's going to sign up as an ARP warden. He said it was probably just a stray bomb. He says if the

Germans can't find the airfields they have to ditch the bombs to save fuel, so they can still make it back to France.'

'At least you're all right,' I said.

'I don't want to leave Ashtead,' Emily replied, 'I was born in this house. Mum wants us to move away, further from London.'

I pulled Fenton's clothing from my sports bag and placed them on the end of the bed. Without a word, Emily reached over and began to fold them into a neat pile.

'Are you alright?' I asked.

She looked up at me and nodded.

The backdoor barged open. It was Fenton.

'Come on,' he said, 'Time's up – where's my booze?'

I reached into my satchel and tossed him one of the bottles. He froze.

'Bloody Hell,' he said, 'that's a bloody sip!'

Emily sat upright 'What's the matter, Charlie,' she asked.

His voice trembled. 'It's a Home Guard sip. Self-igniting phosphorus. SIP. It's a bloody grenade.' Fenton looked up towards the exposed cavity with a broad smile across his face. 'Thank you, Jesus,' he said, 'Thank you so very bloody much!' He looked at me jubilantly. 'Go on George,' he said, 'You can clear off now.'

'You had better go,' Emily said to me, 'Mum says I've only got a headache because of the bang. It was ever so loud. I still have to go to school. I can meet you at Park House after though, if you want.'

I nodded.

Fenton was smiling as he examined the bottle closely.

'Go on Engle,' he said, 'piss off!'

I clambered off the floorboard and onto the lawn, leaving Emily sitting in her bed inside her ruined home.

I felt rather uneasy during the first half of the school day. I was fearful any inadvertent knock to my satchel might cause the bottles to ignite. I hardly concentrated at all during Mrs Bond's lesson. It was on the 1846 repeal of the Corn Laws. By lunchtime though, I had almost forgotten about the bottles.

When the bell rang at the end of the school day, Emily was already waiting for me by the front gate.

'I got let out early,' she said, 'I had a nose bleed.'

We stood together as a swathe of pupils and teachers passed us. Some gave us scornful glares or teased us with remarks of marriage and such. When they finally dissipated, we were alone. Emily held my hand as we walked back towards Lower Ashtead.

'You should put the other bottles back,' Emily said, breaking the silence of our stroll.

I did not wish to part with them, no matter how dangerous they were. They gave me power. They gave me power over everyone I knew.

'They were buried on the school grounds. For the invasion,' I said, 'Expect the German officers will want to live in Park House.'

Emily gripped my hand tightly. 'Don't talk like that, George!' she said. 'I'd hate to think of them marching about in the school. I wonder where all the children would go?'

'I thought the village would never change,' I said.

Emily looked thoughtful. 'Dad says a German bailed out over Leatherhead last week. Don't know if he was burnt though.'

'I don't care if he was,' I said.

Emily let go of my hand. 'He's still somebody's brother,' she replied.

'I don't care,' I said, 'no one asked him to come here. I hope he did get burnt.'

'Charles has hidden his bottle in the village pond, under some rocks,' Emily said. 'He told me it's best to keep them cold. He says the phosphorus can burn your skin for hours. If you try and put the fire out with water, it burns even hotter.'

Emily took hold of my hand again. 'Mum says the council's housing list is getting longer every day,' she said, 'We're going to stay with the old woman at number six for a little while. Just until we get allotted somewhere.'

We arrived at the Rec. and played on the swings for a while. A small group of children turned up. I only knew them by sight. They became boisterous and I was worried they would knock my satchel. Emily looked at me as I wrapped a protective arm around it. Without a word, we left.

We took a short walk across the common to the brick footbridge. Emily giggled as I teased her about moving in with the gossiping old woman at number six. We were in high spirits when we arrived. I intended to stash the bottles underneath the bridge and conceal them with branches. However, several gentleman commuters were visible across the common as they made their way from the railway station. I decided not to hide them until after dark. We had a couple of hours to kill before dusk so we headed off into the woods to play.

I had a folding penknife in my pocket. It made me feel safer. I used it to fashion two wooden swords from a fallen branch. Despite my best efforts, Emily did not wish to engage in any duelling. Instead, we used the weapons as walking sticks and pretended we were lost explorers trying to discover an ancient African tribe. We enjoyed this game immensely and it was clear that Emily wished me to protect her from the unseen dangers of the wild.

We became so engrossed in our game that, by pure force of habit, I had led us into the clearing of the old Roman Villa. Perhaps I had deliberately led her there. I don't like to dwell on such things. Regardless, I felt uneasy the moment I stepped foot into the clearing.

'Are you alright George?' Emily asked.

'I'm fine,' I said.

Emily had never been to the villa before. She wandered about the clearing, exploring the ground for relics. I felt compelled to discreetly glance at the dog's final resting place. The engraved headstone still lay in situ, partly concealed by stinging nettles. But the soil around the headstone had been removed. The gruesome contents, gone.

'What is this place?' Emily said.

A flock of startled crows took flight. And then a man stepped out from behind a tree. A bedraggled figure of the greatest repulsion stood before us.

'It's the only link I have with my past,' the figure said.

This creature was, as far as I could tell, the rotting remains of Mr Simpkins.

Chapter XIII

The air smelt of death as the astronomer stood before us in the clearing. A rotten husk of a man, no more than twelve feet ahead. Emily stood behind me, her eyes widened at the sight of the thing. The beast of Mr Simpkins, a demon. The Devil himself. He stood upright, wearing the same drab and dated suit which the astronomer always wore. Yet this was just the shadow of a man. A veneer. I knew his soul was gone. The clothing was heavily soiled by foul-smelling grime. A darkly fluid, adhering to the suit, glistened around the upper torso and neckline. It was neither perspiration nor blood. Shards of thick drool dangled from his mouth and nose. Fallen globs, contaminated by dry leaf litter, clung to his trouser legs and shoes.

Protruding from the sleeves of the jacket, I saw two blackened, contorted hands. They were in a terrible state of decay. The left was missing two fingers and was most disfigured. A deep wound split the palm and, as far as I could see, continued upwards into the arm. It was almost crab-like in appearance. The other hand was discoloured, as if the skin had been burned away from the flesh. It was blotchy; some patches were dark red and others off-white. At first I thought it to be exposed bone. When the whiteness flexed, I knew they were layers of fat.

Held within the astronomer's grip was a length of rope. Tethered at the end, was a pig. A distinctive dark patch on its ear, together with my father's leather belt around its neck, identified the animal. It was in the sorriest of states. Its eyes were the saddest, most lifeless eyes. They held no hope. As the animal had grown, the belt had become embedded into its neck. Open sores wept freely around the wound. Periodically, the pig gasped for air. I was repulsed by its suffering. But the most ghastly inflictions were upon its side. Deep gouges cut neatly, deliberately. They formed a grid of rectangular lesions each an inch wide and several inches long. Towards the rear of the animal, some of these segments had been removed, exposing the muscle beneath.

The astronomer reached down. Slowly, he dug deep into the wound. The pig stood motionless, save for the twitching of its hind leg. In the cruellest, deplorable manner, the astronomer prised free a slither of skin. Lifting the morsel to his lips, he devoured it. The pig uttered no sound, accepting the inevitability of its perpetual suffering.

The transformation of Mr Simpkins into this vile beast was entire. His face was raw, as if the skin had been torn violently away. The nose was absent, save for a bloodied cavity that oozed snotty mucus. Sticky phlegm, adhering to facial muscles, dripped to his feet. The lips were torn jaggedly apart, permanently exposing his teeth and gums. Electric blue eyes bulging, like a wild animal. The astronomer chewed and sucked noisily upon the strip of flesh as strands of thick syrup-like drool dangled from his wet chin.

A dark patch slowly formed down my trouser legs. The astronomer smiled as I wet myself.

'Hello George,' he said, 'I see you've brought along a friend. Well, that's…nice.'

Emily stepped slowly forward and stood at my side, her shoulder touching mine. Her proximity comforted me. She looked pale, her mouth open, trembling. Trembling at the sight of this un-dead thing before us.

'Jesus,' she said quietly, 'What's happened to him. Is he a pilot? Is he one of ours?'

I shook my head. 'No,' I said, 'He's not a pilot. I'm so sorry.'

The astronomer grinned. 'I'm afraid I've grown rather tiresome of my skin,' he said. 'It was…necessary… to make some adjustments, you understand.' His wild eyes settled upon a patch of ground to my right. I followed his gaze to a discarded kitchen knife nearby. It was a vicious looking implement, its serrated teeth stained in blood. Next to it lay a wet slop of skin. A wisp of steam rose, dissipating into the evening air. I retched.

'Who is it, George?' Emily asked, tugging at my sleeve, 'Do you know him? Tell me who it is. What the hell's going on. What's he done?'

'You're disgusted by my purge,' the astronomer said, 'but you embrace war.' The corner of his mouth was upturned. 'Millions of men, women and children. They want to slaughter each other. I can feel it. They want to kill. They want to stab and slash and rape and burn. Mechanised slaughter. An efficient, economical process of elimination. It shall be exquisite. A thing of beauty. I shall revel in the carnage.'

The man smiled at me. 'And you George,' he said, 'what have you done to slow this tide? Collect rotting carcasses to manufacture explosives! You've done nothing but feed the fire. You want it to burn. You crave it. You're like me, in every imaginable way. Just as eager to celebrate the destruction of man.'

His eyes burned into mine. I was unable to look away.

Emily's breathing was short and rapid. I was grateful she was with me, but I was fearful. Fearful of what this vile thing may do to her.

'You've done nothing,' the astronomer said, 'Nothing but facilitate the industrial slaughter of life. The cleaners are coming, George, one by one. They'll release me from my human confines. Stop the voices. They'll set me free.'

'I can help you, Mr Simpkins,' I said.

Emily gasped. 'The astronomer?' she said softly, 'That's Mr Simpkins? Oh God, what the hell's happened?' She took a step backwards. 'You've been hurt Mr Simpkins,' she said. 'Badly hurt. Wait here. We can get help. A doctor.'

'No!' the astronomer yelled, 'I don't need help. I need… resurrection.'

With the most ungodly speed, the astronomer dashed towards me. He moved with such velocity and grace across the clearing, like a shadow. He seized the knife from the ground, grabbed me by my shoulder and drew me to his chest. I felt the earth sweep away beneath my feet. I was nauseous and disoriented. When I gathered my senses, I found myself standing awkwardly, held in his grasp, unable to move.

Emily stood some distance ahead of me. By her feet lay my abandoned satchel and carved wooden stick. The dreadful injuries inflicted upon this man had been no hindrance to agility.

'Let him go,' Emily shrieked, pausing to compose herself. 'Please,' she added softly.

I felt dampness seeping through to my skin. Its putrid odour found its way deep into my lungs. I retched. Then I felt the tip of a blade held tightly against my neck. A vein throbbed, blood held back by the obstruction of cold metal. I thought about the penknife in my pocket but I was too afraid to retrieve it. I awaited my fate with the same solemn inevitability as the pig. I took a deep breath and prepared myself for death. I was at the mercy of a demon. I fixed my eyes on Emily, finding comfort in her presence. I knew she would stay with me, that I would not die alone. I looked into her eyes and watched the tears run down her cheek. And then she looked away.

'Your father was fond of this clearing,' the astronomer said. 'It was inevitable you'd come here too, one day. I knew that you would, eventually.'

The pressure of the knife eased a little and a giddying wave of oxygen rushed to my brain.

'You see,' he said, 'these Roman remains are almost two thousand years old.' He sighed and I felt his warm, foul breath across my face. 'And the light from Alnilam is of a similar age. Curious, don't you think?'

Slowly, the man released his hold on me but I was too afraid to flee. Emily looked at me again, her eyes revealing the terror in her heart. Yet she was my only comfort.

The astronomer blew hard, extracting more muck and slime from his face. Wet clods somersaulted to the ground.

'The light from that star,' he said, 'holds purifying energy. Energy from another world.'

I focused on Emily, a girl of no more than thirteen years of age. She chose to stay with me in the clearing, in the presence of this monster. She could flee. She could save herself from this ghastly thing that stood before her. But she did not, she stayed. I hoped she had the courage to remain, until the end.

'Within the starlight was a soul. The soul from another being,' the astronomer said. He smiled at me. 'Such power. It was able to manifest itself, through me, as matter. E equals m c squared. Wisdom and knowledge, far too great to be contained within a single human skull. It has been shared out, you see. A gift to me, and others.'

The astronomer wiped the drool from his jaw with the back of his deformed hand. 'I need your help, George, please,' he said, 'You see, something was stolen from me. Something I need. A part of the message. A part of me. Your father saw the light of Alnilam too. He took energy from it. A portion of my soul. Like a missing piece in a jigsaw puzzle. He knew I needed it. That, and more. That's why he killed himself, George. To deprive me of what was mine.'

The man shuffled on his feet.

'There's a voice in my head,' he said, 'and it's tearing me apart. I'm in such pain. Damien Simpkins is still living inside my mind. Fighting me, tormenting me.'

The astronomer cleared the mucus from its face again. 'Your father failed to understand the beauty of the starlight. You see, the energy changes the very cells within the body. It's an exquisite process. To transport a life across the vastness of space, travelling at the speed of light. To be reassembled once more. Refabricated in the finest detail, using any available living material at the destination. The message was not given to me. The message became me. An alien soul. Delivered to the world, atom by atom. Your father knew. He knew I would need to devour him, to enhance my knowledge. That's why he killed himself. To deny me of a soul. But he was a fool, a coward. He could only bring himself to do half a job. So, the starlight message was preserved, passed from generation to generation. From father to son!'

The astronomer's eyes sparkled. 'My mind is full of such wondrous things. Such awe. Such vivid imagery. I have seen memories of distant lands, of power. I shall perform miracles, George. Terrifying, formidable miracles I shall make the world burn.' he said, 'It was the light that saved your father from the war, you know. Repairing his lungs as the gas burned his flesh. Preserving his portion of the message. Such a shame he couldn't appreciate the beauty of his salvation.'

Caressing his left hand, he continued, 'But he lived on regardless. Even siring his offspring. That, George,' he said, 'makes you an abomination of nature. You don't belong in this world. Seabrook thought it immoral. He attacked me, George, can you believe that? The filthy man tried to kill me.' The astronomer examined his left hand. 'He was deranged. As my mind filled with the message, he betrayed me. He took a hammer and drove a nail through my hand. He doused me in petrol and he made me burn, George. The pain was intolerable. He left me to die, to let the flames consume my body. Even your father was burning as he freed me. And then, a miracle. I was at peace with myself. Euphoric. You see, the excruciating pain of the fire ceased. My nerve endings had been shed. I could no longer breathe. The oxygen, consumed by the flames. Yet I lived on. Like a phoenix rising from the ashes. I was reborn. Reborn as Seabrook fled, turning his back on us. He left us to die. Too afraid to watch our suffering. Your world betrayed me. Now it's their time to burn!'

The astronomer raised his left hand. The wounded palm, only inches from my face. I looked upon the dreadful damage. The demonic, twisted claws of a devil.

'My stigmata,' the astronomer said, 'Like Christ's own suffering, don't you think. Nailed to the cross by mankind. Vile rodents of neither wisdom nor power. It is the one affliction that fails to heal. The wound of betrayal. Your father betrayed me, George. But I've waited, all these years. And now I'm going to hurt him. I'm going to hurt him, through you. I'm going to laugh as you scream in pain. As I rip you apart. As I tear your soul from existence. As I devour your flesh.'

Emily shuffled from foot to foot. 'Please Mr Simpkins,' she said, 'let us go and get help.'

'Don't you fucking talk to me you filthy fucking germ,' he yelled, his voice filling the woodland.

Emily dropped to her knees, her face turned to the soil, away from this torn, psychotic man. 'I'm sorry,' she said. She began to cry.

'You broke into my house, George,' the astronomer said. 'You stole from me. Your father's old notebook. You burgled my house no doubt too. Did you search my home? Rummage through my belongings? What about the kitchen? Did you look in there?'

'No,' I said, 'I only took the notebook. I never went into the house, honest. I'm really sorry Mr Simpkins. I'll return it to you in the morning, I swear.'

'But I left you a gift, George,' the astronomer said, clearing more sticky mucus from his face. 'Did you not see it? Did you not smell the stench of death?'

Emily tried to stifle her sobbing. 'We never went into your house, honest, Please, let him go.'

'Did you not look inside the cupboard, under the sink?' the astronomer asked, 'Were you not curious about the flies and maggots. They infest the kitchen you know. One of the true delights of the human disease. Their putrid rot. I kept him alive for so many hours. He begged me, George. He begged for me to end his pain. I did it for you, George. I killed the boy, James. Emily was so fond of him. I wanted you to have a companion, someone to be here with you, tonight. So you see, he had to die. He had to die so that Emily could comfort you in your final moments. Regardless of what you may think, I am merciful and nurturing. Besides, he was such a vile boy, don't you think?'

The astronomer turned to Emily. 'You really could have done much better than James you know, my dear. Still, it's all rather academic now, don't you think?'

Emily trembled. Her eyes looked distant.

'We need to leave now,' I said, 'please.'

'No, George,' the astronomer replied, 'you need to die.' Raising his rotting hand, he dragged his fingers through matted hair. 'You need to die,' he said, 'so that I may live.'

From the corner of my eye, I saw Emily move. At first, I thought she was going to run, to flee from the woods. But she did not. Instead, she seized the strap of my satchel. With a loud grunt, she hurled it forcibly in our direction. In a single bound, I leapt to one side. The satchel struck the trunk of a tree only feet away. An intense flash of light and heat threw me to the ground. There was a roar of flames. I rolled onto my side and looked back. The astronomer and the pig were alight, head to foot. A white-hot inferno of burning phosphorus. I scrambled across the ground to escape the heat. The astronomer stood motionless, his body engulfed in flames. I heard his flesh crackling in the flames. The pig let out the most dreadful squeal. It pulled free of its lead and scarpered through the undergrowth. The phosphorus on its back, igniting all that it touched. The fire was spreading. I watched the astronomer stagger a few paces forward before dropping to his knees, head bowed low. It was a dreadful sight. The air filled with the smell of roasting meat and chemicals.

Emily ran to me, helping me to my feet. The radiating heat was unbearable. It penetrated my clothing and scolded my skin and scalp. My trousers were dirty and beginning to smoulder. Emily, in her skirt and painfully bare legs, dragged me away from the blaze.

The flames which twisted and buckled around the astronomer began to envelop the trunk of an oak tree. It spread high into its canopy, growing in ferocity, leaping through neighbouring trees in a roaring frenzy. Emily, holding her carved wooden stick, ran towards the astronomer, plunging the tip deep into his chest. The burning corpse fell to the ground sending a swarm of sparks into the night air. They looked like a thousand stars returning to the heavens.

'We need to run,' Emily said, taking my hand.

The astronomer thrashed chaotically upon the ground. I watched as he gave up his grip on life. Thick smoke billowed from the blackened, mangled mass of limbs. Patches of phosphorus, splashed across his head and chest, continued to fizz, white-hot. It was a most wicked weapon to have been unleashed. Having taken my fill of the ghastly sight, we ran. We ran as fast as we could.

The sun had set below the horizon. In the fading light, we could not find the bridle path which led back to the Rye. The fire behind us continued to rage, casting long, dancing shadows across Emily's face like grasping fingers. The fire roared like a beast. Like the Devil himself.

Onwards we ran, darting between the trees, until Emily snagged her cardigan on some brambles and came to a stop. I watched as she tugged at the barbs, twisting and contorting her body in a bid to pull free. Her efforts only entangled her further. She looked frantic, vulnerable. I rested my arm on her shoulder. Ahead, in the far distance, the faint outline of the railway station.

Above us, the sky was obscured by the thickening veil of grey smoke. I looked back, towards the Roman villa. A mountain of orange flame stretched across the woods. It curled and twisted, leaping high above the treetops. I nudged Emily as she tore at the material to break free. Bent double, she removed her cardigan, leaving it ensnared. Out of respect, I turned my back. A sudden movement caught my attention. To the left of the forest fire, I saw a light. It was travelling through the trees, towards the railway station. It was running. For the briefest moment, the light stopped. It was an orange burning mass of flame. Within the flames, I saw the outline of a man, immune to the ghastly fire which engulfed him. It was the astronomer, resurrected from the depths of hell. He stared silently at me through the trees, through the flames. His head tilted to one side as if he were studying me. Then, without hesitance, he burst into motion once more. Behind, he left a flaming trail, igniting the woodland, cutting off our route towards the station.

Emily stood beside me in a clean white shirt. She had not seen the apparition and I had no intention of alarming her. We continued onward as quickly as we could. The fire was spreading all around. From time to time we adjusted our course, adapting to the ever-changing threat. We ran faster. We were running for our lives. In my frantic haste, I struck a tree square on and fell to the ground. I was badly winded.

Emily pulled at my arm. 'Please,' she said, 'we need to get out of here. I've killed him.'

I didn't know what to say to her, so I said nothing.

'We've gone back on ourselves,' she said as I got to my feet, 'Look, the fire's over there now.' She pointed towards the flicker of light through the trees ahead.

I nodded. 'It's everywhere,' I said.

Behind us, the flames licked at the sky like the vile tendrils of my nightmares. A thin trail of fire now arced away from the core, across our right flank, before blocking our route ahead. The only clear direction was to our left, deeper into the woods. Beyond the roar of the flames, the sound of emergency bells. They were distant and feeble.

'We should go that way, towards Oxshott,' Emily said, pointing in a vague direction. Then she turned to face me again. She smiled and hugged me. 'It'll be alright, honest,' she said.

Onward we ran as the fire encroached in every direction. It toyed with us. Taunted us. This was the Devil's fire.

The soft breeze grew into a gusting torment. I felt its heat pressing into my back like a scolding hand, wild and savage. I could no longer hear the sound of bells.

We pushed ever deeper into the woods. The smoke was dense and a whiff of chemicals hung in the air. Eventually, we found ourselves on a narrow bridleway. It was the main track towards Oxshott. We stopped to catch our breath. I hugged Emily. I could not help myself. I was euphoric. Emily giggled. Our relief was immense.

As we followed the track, I happened to notice a wooden marking post stuck into the ground. It was in bands of multiple colours. I had seen it before. A wave of excitement washed over me. The old bicycle, the one from the farmyard; I had concealed it along this very path! I began to race ahead of Emily. She called out after me, but I did not stop. I ran on, through the darkness. Dropping to my knees beside a familiar-looking tree, I began feeling through the undergrowth. Crawling on all fours.

Emily caught up with me. 'Are you alright?' she asked.

'Never bloody better,' I said.

When Emily saw the bike, she hugged me again.

'That's brilliant,' she said, 'Bloody brilliant!'

I mounted the bike and helped Emily onto the handlebars. She sat awkwardly as I began to peddle. The ground was rutted and I found it hard to steer with her back obscuring my view ahead. We only managed a short distance before tumbling to the ground. Emily cut her leg on the peddle. I saw a thin line of blood running down from her knee but she did not draw attention to it.

'You ride it,' I said, 'We can't both fit. I'll run alongside.'

Emily wiped the blood and dirt from her knees and nodded. 'If you're sure,' she said, taking the bike from me. She peddled slowly at first, allowing me to keep pace. At last, we were making good headway.

After a short while, the bridleway began to narrow, forcing us to travel in single file. Emily led the way, cycling as best she could on the rough track. The wind direction shifted and thick, acrid smoke began to envelop us. Emily coughed and the bicycle began to meander ahead of me. My eyes stung, forcing me to screw them tightly shut. I stopped for a moment and withdrew my gasmask from its box. I placed it over my head but found it offered no protection from the particles of smoke. My eyes still stung and my lungs continued to fill with the wretched filth. I felt claustrophobic in the mask, the rubber gripping tightly to my face. The smell of bleach made me choke and panic. I could not bear it any longer, so I threw the mask to the ground. I began to vomit. Each breath invoked a greater reaction to the vile air. I kicked off a shoe and removed my sock. I held it tightly over my mouth until the pain in my lungs subsided a little. Forcing my eyes open for the briefest of moments, I saw only thick smoke. Emily was gone. I tried to call out but with each gasp, yet more smoke invaded my chest. I was choking.

I staggered forward blindly, my barefoot splashing into a cold, shallow puddle. Kneeling in the darkness, I moistened the sock and covered my mouth. The air at ground level was less gritty. I called out to Emily but there was no reply.

I listened to the roar of the fire as it ripped through the woodland, destroying everything it touched. I felt giddy, exhausted. As I crawled on all fours, I heard it. The most wretched of howls. A primal scream - raw and enraged. It was an unnatural sound that did not belong to this world.

I tried to calm myself. I imagined Emily holding my hand. I tried to count the freckles on her face. Her smile. I moved slowly, one hand at a time, sipping at the filthy air. Onwards, towards Oxshott.

I struck my head on something. Reaching out, I felt a leg. I squinted painfully through the smoke. A blurred outline stood before me. The figure of a policeman.

'Come on George,' a voice said, 'you're alright now!'

The policeman picked me up and carried me over his shoulder.

Chapter XIV

My mind filled with the strangest dream. I was standing in the middle of the recreational ground. It was a warm summer day, without a soul in sight. Yet the Rec was somehow different. The lush green lawn extended far into the horizon, infinite in every direction. Above, a pale blue cloudless sky. And then I heard it. The gentle sobbing of a child. I turned to face the sorrow. In the distance, I saw her, a young girl holding her mother's hand. A set of empty swings slowly swayed beside them. The figures stood motionless. And then the little girl beckoned me.

In my head, I heard her voice. 'Please,' she said softly, 'Please!'

I went towards them. Jogging at first, then sprinting. Regardless, they remained beyond my reach, like the end of a rainbow.

I stopped to catch my breath, bent double with aching lungs. When I stood upright, the mother and child were beside me, inches from my face. Startled, I staggered back. The child's tears filled my head. I looked at her. No more than four years old, she wore a heavy, burgundy winter coat, despite the pleasant weather. But her face held no emotions. A blank, lifeless face, like a china doll. She stared at me with vacant eyes, emotionless.

I looked at the mother. She was a pretty woman in her thirties. Her face was full of anguish. I saw terror in her widened eyes. Thick streaks of mascara were smeared across her cheeks. Her bottom lip was turned down, like a pouting infant.

'Please,' the woman said, 'Help me. I want my daddy. I don't like mummy anymore.' The words of an infant, spoken from the mouth of the woman. She stood awkwardly in high heels. Unsteady on her feet.

I looked at the little girl. Her eyes boiling with rage as if she would tear me limb from limb, had she the strength of body to do so.

'Filthy scum,' she said, 'I want to purge you.' Globs of spittle flung from her mouth. 'I want to rip you from my mind. Rip away your filthy fucking stench.'

The mother raised her arm slowly towards me. The back of her hand was fused to that of the little girl's. Their skin, melted together, binding them.

'Please,' the mother said again, 'It hurts. I want my daddy.' She began to cry again. The inconsolable tears of a petrified little child.

The girl tilted her head to one side and smiled. Dagger-like, yellow teeth filled her mouth. She began to retch. I watched as a chunk of solid, human excrement emerged from her mouth. It spooled and twisted out of her face like a serpent. The stench penetrated my skin.

'Please,' the woman said, 'Please, kill me.'

I looked into her eyes. A child trapped inside the body of a woman. I turned my back on her and ran. But still, the voice called out to me. 'Please,' it said, 'don't leave me here. I want my daddy.'

Waking from the dream, I found myself laying in a hospital bed. The ward was quiet. Seven empty beds accompanied my own. I had been here for two weeks now. Every night, the same dream.

I stood up on the mattress and peered out of the narrow window set high into the wall. In the bright morning light, I could see for miles, right across the Epsom Downs. The greenery of Surrey was spectacular. My lungs no longer ached and my rasping voice had healed. I felt the warmth of the sunshine as it fell upon my face.

The Matron entered the ward. She marched briskly towards me. A stern and intimidating woman.

'Get down this instant!' she ordered, 'Staring won't help!'

I looked out the window again. This time I saw them. A twisting knot of white contrails set amidst the bluest sky.

Matron clapped her hands loudly. 'Back to bed now, quick as a flash,' she said, 'You've got a visitor.'

I settled myself under the blankets as she leaned across my bedside table, closing the blinds.

'Now then,' she said, plumping up my pillow, 'I hope you've been behaving yourself, young man. There's a policeman here to see you.'

Matron made her way over to the doorway. I watched as she whispered a few words to my unseen visitor standing in the corridor.

When Matron left, a policeman appeared in the doorway. He walked purposefully over to my bedside. It was Constable Billet.

'Hello George,' he said, 'You're looking much better now. How are you feeling?'

'I'm alright,' I said, 'I want to go home though. It's very boring here.'

'Quite an ordeal you've been through,' he said, 'You're lucky to be here. What on earth were you playing at?'

'Am I in trouble?' I asked, 'I was only playing with my friend.'

'Well,' the constable said, 'must have been a hell of a game. Half of Ashtead Woods burned down. Black as coal it is.' The constable removed an apple from the fruit bowl and sat down beside me.

'We didn't do it. We were just messing around,' I said. 'Was it you who found me?'

The constable nodded. 'Don't think you're out of the woods just yet, lad,' he said. 'So then, how come you and your friend Emily Fenton managed to find yourselves in the middle of a forest fire? Been messing about with matches have you?'

'We were just playing. Sword fighting and that,' I said, 'Then a man turned up. Mr Simpkins.'

The policeman lent close to me, 'Would that be a Mr Damien Simpkins, from Agates Lane, in Ashtead?'

I nodded. 'He was injured. Really badly. His skin was hanging off. We thought his house had been bombed or something. He started talking to us. I can't remember much of it though.' I said. 'There was a flash. Really bright and hot. Terrific heat. A stray or something.'

Constable Billet bit noisily into the apple. 'No reports of any bombs or incendiaries that night. In fact, the ARP's don't reckon the fire was enemy action. I wonder how, exactly, something like that could happen?'

I shrugged. 'The man just went up in flames. We ran away. Both of us. As fast as we could. It was really scary. We found an old bicycle hidden in the woods. Emily rode it to Oxshott. I couldn't keep up with her. That's when I found you.'

The constable placed the half-eaten apple onto the little table. 'I'm afraid I've got some bad news, George,' he said.

'Emily,' I replied, 'Is she alright? Where is she?' My throat became dry.

'I'm afraid we don't know yet, son. Not for sure,' he said. 'You see, she didn't go home. She's not been seen since the fire.'

My stomach churned as if I were falling. 'She's alright though, isn't she,' I said, 'She's not been hurt or anything?'

Constable Billet cleared his throat. 'No one knows where she is. Or your friend Mr Simpkins for that matter. He's missing too.'

'Emily was bombed out,' I said, 'Maybe she went to stay somewhere else. She doesn't like the old woman she's staying with.'

The policeman sighed. 'I'm sorry son, but there's something else you should know. You see, we searched the woods. Found a bicycle, among the ashes. The fire spread pretty fast, you know.'

'She must have ditched it and run,' I said, 'It was a really old bike. Didn't even have a saddle. She's a good runner.'

The constable began to fidget. 'We found something else too I'm afraid,' he said, 'A body. A child. I'm really sorry.'

In my heart, I felt nothing. I couldn't talk. I couldn't breathe.

Constable Billet placed his hand on my shoulder.

'Are you sure it's her?' I asked.

'Well, she's not been formally identified by her parents. The fire you see. But I'm sure…'

'It's not her,' I interrupted, 'I know it's not her.'

Constable Billet tossed the apple core into a waste bin and rose to his feet. 'Get your slippers on, son,' he said, 'We need to have a chat.'

I wiped a tear from my face and placed my dressing gown over my pyjamas. We left the ward and walked slowly, side by side, along the corridor. Reaching a row of wooden seats resting against the wall, we sat. A woman was seated nearby. She was nursing a young baby concealed beneath a soft white wrap.

'I have to ask you a few questions about Damien Simpkins I'm afraid,' the policeman said, 'You see, he's currently a suspect in a crime. A very serious crime. A murder in fact. The murder of an elderly woman. What can you tell me about his cleaning lady, Mrs Elizabeth Stride?'

I thought for a moment. 'His house is a mess,' I said, 'She couldn't have been a very good cleaner. Is that why he killed her?'

I tried to forget about the red house. 'Why has no one visited me,' I asked, 'Not even my mum. You're the first.'

The constable stood up. 'Your mother has her reasons, I'm sure,' he said, 'Did you know the authorities are sending children out to the countryside, for the duration. Just a precaution, you understand. I hear you've got relatives up north. Your mother wants you to rest in Lincolnshire. You have an aunt there, I believe.'

'Aunty Muckle,' I said, 'I don't want to go there. I want to go home.'

'But you're going there all the same, young man! Don't worry, you'll be alright. One of the porters will make sure you get there. You're leaving in the morning.' The constable paused, 'Don't worry, your mum will see you off!'

We walked back to my ward and I climbed into bed.

'Let me know if you remember anything else,' the constable said, 'Particularly about Mrs Stride or Mr Simpkins.'

The policeman then left me alone with my thoughts. Alone in an empty ward.

After a while, I went over to the book trolly at the far end of the ward. There was a reasonable selection of scientific literature available. I tried to read one on physics. It was a very complicated book. I didn't understand any of it. The author had the most peculiar and unpronounceable name.

I became bored with the book so took a nap for the rest of the day. No one came the entire evening. Not even to give me dinner. I was not bothered though. I had not felt hungry for days.

The hospital was silent. As darkness came, I fell asleep. I dreamt of demons and of Emily. She was frightened and cold, terrified. I sensed she was alone. Alone, save for something hidden within the shadows. Something terrifying.

I awoke. Bright morning light stung my eyes. To my embarrassment, I had wet the bed again. I changed into my school uniform and neatened the blankets as best I could to conceal the stained sheets. I sat on the edge of the bed and cried.

At ten o'clock a hospital porter arrived. I had already packed away my possessions, just some pyjamas and a dressing-gown loaned to me by the hospital. They had even provided me with a small leather luggage case and replacement gas mask. The box dangled from my neck, securely fastened by a length of string.

The porter was pleasant enough; no more than eighteen or nineteen years old. He picked up my luggage and I followed him.

'Why aren't you fighting?' I asked. I hadn't intended to sound accusatory but I was sure I did.

'I've done my bit,' he said, without eluding further.

As we continued to the exit, I studied him closely for signs of injury. I saw none. We stopped outside the hospital's main entrance. The sun was bright and the air was warm.

'Here's your travel pass,' the porter said, handing me a ticket. 'The 501. Takes you to Ashtead train station. Leaves every fifteen minutes. Are you going all the way to Lincolnshire on your own?'

I took the ticket. 'I think my mum is meeting me here or at the station,' I said, 'Do you know?'

'Sorry mate,' the porter replied, 'No one tells me nothing.' He returned inside the building, leaving me alone.

The wait for the bus was uneventful. A man in his fifties came and sat inside the bus shelter. He read a newspaper, his gas mask pushed to his side, keeping it clear of his turning pages. He wore a dark pinstripe suit and a bowler hat. A stuffy old bank manager or the like, I assumed.

After a while, a pretty woman sat beside him. She was smartly dressed in a red cardigan and matching skirt. She had a stern face though. They both ignored me so I did not sit with them.

When the 501 arrived, the man and woman began to gather their possessions. I boarded ahead of them, making my way to the top deck. The top was empty so I sat at the very front. It was a great view. I always like riding on the top deck.

The bus pulled off. It was a bumpy ride. I peered into the bedroom windows of passing houses. Every one neatly secured with crosses of white tape.

Once free of the outskirts of Epsom, the vista of Ashtead woods opened up on either side, beautiful and green. A tree-lined canopy formed a natural tunnel through which we passed. From time to time, birch and sycamore branches lashed out angrily. They struck the windows, clattering along the length of the bus like a xylophone.

We took a right turn into Craddocks Avenue. From here I could see the common. Beyond, the devastated woodland, reduced to a vast expanse of barren, charred soil. It stretched for miles, out towards the distant hills.

The bus turned into Barnett Wood Lane and came to a halt beside Ashtead pond. This was the closest stop to the railway station so I got off. Across the pond, underneath a weeping willow, a pair of swans gathered around their nest of twigs and roots at the base of a tree. The cob kept a keen eye on me as three young cygnets inquisitively swam over to investigate. It was such a peaceful part of the village. I wondered if Fenton's SIP bottle was still hidden beneath the water.

My grandfather used to write articles in the local paper about the pond. He kept the elderly, house-bound residents informed of the antics of the wildlife through the seasons. He told tales of swans and foxes and hedgehogs and ducks. Now the old man was gone, but the animals and the seasons continued regardless.

It took less than ten minutes to reach the railway station. The booking clerk was most despondent as he sat relaxed in his booth. I held aloft my rail pass at the hatchway but he showed no interest. Returning the ticket to my pocket, I made my way onto the platform regardless. A northbound train waited by the platform. It was not due to depart for half an hour. It was still taking on water and coal. A few passengers were seated on rows of iron benches. I scanned each of their faces. My mother was not among them.

Removing the gas mask box from my neck, I gently kicked and kneed the cardboard as it swung from the string. I quickly grew tired of this game, so boarded the train.

My carriage was at the rear. It was sparsely populated so I made myself comfortable beside a window seat. From here, I had a good view along much of the platform. As more people arrived, I scrutinised each one. Still no sight of Mother.

The platform soon became crowded and I could not keep track of each arrival. My carriage began to fill too. Mother was surely still cross with me. I had twisted her wrist, I had burned down half the woodland. She must be so angry. Too angry to see me off. That was it. She just wanted rid of me, to move me away, out of sight, until after the war. I could be gone for months for all she cared. She would have worked herself up into a frenzy. Now, she was sending me away for the duration without so much as a goodbye wave. Damn her then, I decided. I would never write to her during my exile. She could go to Hell for all I cared. I looked away from the window and ate my apple.

A whistle blew. The train began to jolt and lurch forwards. I looked onto the platform once more. Ashtead station slowly glided by my window. Indistinguishable figures and faces merged into one another as the train picked up speed. Then, in an instant, I caught sight of a familiar coat. It was my mother's best Sunday coat. She was standing at the far end of the platform. She was surrounded by a group of people. They were comforting her. She looked to be crying. I leapt from my seat and tried to open the window but it would not budge. I stood on my seat and called out through a narrow air vent.

'Mum,' I yelled, 'Mummy.'

She did not hear me.

The train continued to clank and clatter, picking up speed. I watched her blurred image as she swept by, oblivious to my calls. A second later and she was gone. I waved goodbye to nothing more than passing hedgerows.

I slumped back down onto my seat, staring scornfully at my fellow passengers. They would mock me if I cried, I knew it. Still, I could tell they now felt uneasy in my company. Sure enough, one by one, they vacated their seats and moved to other carriages. Only when I found myself alone, did I cry.

The world outside my window hurtled past. The familiar greenery and rolling hills of Surrey gave way to the London overspill and a wide expanse of bombsites. After half an hour, the train changed direction. We twisted and turned towards the northeast. The flat, featureless landscape of the Cambridgeshire Fens. Endless fields passed by. Some of corn, some of potato or cabbage. The soil was the blackest I ever saw. Black, like death.

With little fanfare, we arrived at Peterborough. It was a truly dismal place with no discerning charm or character whatsoever. I was to catch a connecting train from here. I remained on the platform for over an hour, kicking my gas mask box to pass the time. When at last the slow train to Lincolnshire arrived, I boarded the solitary carriage. It was daubed in thick flaking paint. Inside, the floor creaked and the air smelt stale. I was the only passenger. I ran noisily along the full length of the coach, yelling and hollering as loud as I could. I felt alive.

The sun was setting. It got dark quickly in the Fens. Outside, a whistle blew and my train was on its way. It stopped at three remote stations. Each deserted. No one got on. No one got off.

It was ten o'clock when the train arrived at Gedney village station. I stood on the platform. It was unlit, save a single lamp flickering above the exiting archway. Within seconds the steam train departed and I was alone. I listened to the soft thuds of a moth as it fluttered repeatedly against a lamplight.

It was years since I visited Aunt Muckle. She lived in Long Sutton, the next village along. Even through the darkness of night, I could sense the bleakness. Above me, in the eerie stillness, shone a crystal clear, moonless night, laden with ten thousand stars. They sparkled from horizon to horizon. So many, I could hardly identify a single constellation amongst the chaos. I rested myself on a bench and waited for my aunt to arrive.

An hour passed. Perhaps she did not know I was coming. Perhaps she did not want to take on the burden of another mouth to feed. Her house was a good mile away and I knew the narrow dirt tracks which led there were lined with deep, water-filled ditches. I did not fancy tumbling into them in the darkness.

I decided to sleep rough at the station. I could make my way to her house at first light. Besides, I did not wish to impose myself at such a late hour. So, I settled down on a cold iron bench. A barn owl, silhouetted on the station roof, called out to an unseen mate. This was my first night as an evacuee.

Chapter XV

My sleep, as always, was filled with such terrors. I dreamt I stood inside the sitting room of a stranger's house. I felt such anger and rage. A woman lay whimpering, half-naked, on a polished wooden floor. I stood over her. My right boot pressed down on her wrist. Her face winced as she tried to pull free. I knelt, pinning her elbow to the floor with my knee. The woman was hysterical, pleading for me to stop. She was pathetic. Her bulging eyes acknowledging the inevitability of her fate. I twisted my knee into her joint. She gasped in pain as I took delighted in her torment.

'Please, no,' she said.

I was ecstatic, euphoric. I could crush her. I could crush her like greenfly on a rose. Her life was nothing. The blight of humanity. From my belt, I drew a serrated steak knife. Her eyes followed the blade as it moved closer. I pushed the tip of the metal against the soft flesh of her shoulder and began to apply pressure. As the blade formed an indent in her skin, the woman shrieked. Convulsing on the floor, she tried to wriggle free. She was so helpless, so contemptible. Her skin yielded to the blade and blood dribbled from the wound. She screamed, her fingernails clawing at the floor. But still, she could not break free. Her cries and pleadings cajoling me. I dragged the blade through her wound. Slowly carving my words of hatred into her flesh as her feet twitched and thumped upon the floor.

I spied another woman. She lay motionless upon a rug nearby. Her eyes were open but lifeless. A dark puddle of blood flowed freely from her torso. The smell of death. The smell of iron. Iron forged from the heart of a dying star. I revelled in the exhilaration.

I sat up startled from the bench. The right side of my face was painful and numb. It was morning and the station was empty. I watched a blackbird as it sang from the railings. A delicate wisp of vapour drifted from its beak in the chilly air. Like a soul leaving a body.

My shoes lay discarded nearby. I put them on, despite missing a sock. I did not feel hungry but, nonetheless, ate my last apple. Strolling aimlessly along the platform, I kicked at the loose gravel sending it clattering onto the tracks below.

The station clock chimed seven times as I set off towards Long Sutton. The road was deserted, the street signs removed. I had been much younger when I last visited, everything looked so much smaller now. Except for the fields. I had forgotten how expansive they were. To my left and right, nothing but open farmland.

After a while, I saw a gathering of labourers working in a field. They were gathering in hay or some such. A horse-drawn cart was fully laden with its hoard. Ahead of me, the sun was low. Its brightness made me squint.

I passed a small scattering of houses. They were rustic and poorly maintained, not like the pristine and ostentatious houses in Surrey. Their gardens though were neat and colourful. Some had wooden stalls with honesty tins out front. They sold every type of home-grown fruit, vegetables and flowers. One even sold brightly painted wooden animals and knick-knacks. Another stall, laden with apples and tomatoes, displayed a chalkboard with the word *'Free'* written on it. The tomatoes were plump and red.

Marking the centre of the village, was the narrow spire of Saint Mary's church. It pierced the skyline ahead, like a giant arrow pointing towards heaven. I had fond memories of the church. I attended a candle-lit Christmas service there once. I had gone with Mother and Father and Aunty Muckle.

As I drew closer, the surrounding buildings took on an ever grander status. The wealth of the village, gravitating towards the church. My aunt's house was located away from the main road, along a stretch of dirt track called Lime Walk. I recognised the junction immediately, with its little stream flowing along its length. It ran as straight as an arrow, following the edge of the vast fields before disappearing into the distance. Beyond, lay the salt marshes on the banks of the Wash some four miles north. The sweet smell of apple blossoms filled the air. It looked so beautiful in the sunshine.

It was a short walk to my aunt's house. Set back from the dirt track, it stood proudly amongst nature. Its ornate chimney, large bay windows and formal rose garden tucked neatly behind a low walled garden at the front. I could not contain myself. I ran to the gate and pushed it open. The fragrance of the blooms hung heavy. I could taste their scent at the back of my throat. The front door was ajar. In devilment, I sneaked quietly inside, ready to pounce playfully when my aunt emerged. But I did not see her, the living room empty.

The smell of freshly baked bread lured me into the kitchen. A large table filled the space. It was coated in a dusting of flour and cluttered with an assortment of utensils and glass jars. The warm smell of the oven made my stomach rumble. The sink by the window was filled with soaking bowls and wooden spoons. As the sun shone into the room, a million drifting motes of flour became trapped within a sunbeam. Like a galaxy of stars in perpetual motion, they drifted in and out of the light.

I stood by the sink and looked out into the large garden. Beyond the holly bush and silver birch, where the ground sloped away, I saw the formal fish pond. And there, standing at the far end, was Aunty Muckle. I watched her, not wanting the moment to end, as she placed a handful of grain onto a bird table. A robin appeared. It darted around, pecking at the ground near her feet. A wood pigeon too, the boldest I had ever seen, rested on a branch nearby.

I continued to spy upon the woman. Her rough clothing and cumbersome black Wellington boots. Her ginger cat, Rusty, weaving itself between her feet, in a perpetual figure of eight. The cat paused from time to time, checking the proximity of the robin. The war was a million miles away. Then my aunt turned and looked back towards the house. A broad smile spread across her face.

As the days passed, I made myself comfortable in and around the house. Aunty Muckle spent a large amount of her time working on her allotment or arranging her flower displays for the vicar at Saint Mary's. With her sons away at boarding school in Lincoln, the house was quieter than I remembered. In the evenings she sat by the fireplace and read.

'I miss my mum,' I said, 'I haven't seen her for weeks. I think she's cross with me. She thinks I started the fire in Ashtead woods.'

My aunt closed her book and placed it onto a side table as her cat rubbed its face on her leg, purring contently.

'I'm hungry now, Aunty,' I said, watching as she stroked the cat.

'Come on then,' she said, 'I'll make you a nice dinner.'

I watched as she headed into the kitchen.

In the morning, Aunty Muckle and I walked off to her allotment further down Lime Walk. I played in the orchard whilst she dug over large areas of soil. She tended to her crops like a mother tending to an infant. Food was in such abundance here. It grew everywhere. I realised then how little we had in Surrey. Since the war, I had become accustomed to feeling permanently hungry. Aunty Muckle had never gone without. I did not feel hungry anymore, not here.

At the far end of her plot was a wooden shed. Inside were kept five egg-laying hens. They clucked noisily whenever I approached. They had a small enclosure to run in. During the day, they pecked and scratched for hours, finding every speck of food upon the ground.

In the adjoining plot, an elderly gentleman kept bees. I watched him with fascination as he donned his protective headgear. He wafted each of the hives with wood smoke, subduing the anger within the bees. Intoxicating them. Harvesting their yield.

'There you go dear,' Aunty said to the gentleman, handing him a basket of vegetables.

In exchange, he gave her two sticky jars of honey.

I felt rather melancholy. It was the first Saturday evening of September. I did not wish to upset my aunt so I hid away in the woodshed at the rear of the garden. I wanted to seclude myself from the world, to hide my face.

The smell of roast chicken wafted across the garden. The glazed, fresh honey filled my nostrils. It was cramped inside the woodshed with barely room for me to move. Two rusty lamps hung from the ceiling an inch above my head. I found that by burning one wick I could produce a low, soothing light without using too much of Aunty's paraffin.

I sat cross-legged on the dirt floor, running my fingers through the dust. I watched woodlice scuttle across the ground. The ones in Surrey would roll up into a tight ball if I harassed them, but these were different. They were flatter looking and I could not get them to roll up. As I watched the creatures, my eyes fell upon a small protrusion in the soil. I dug at it with my fingernails, pulling it free of the earth. I rubbed the mud away as best I could and polished it with spit. It was a lead soldier, sitting atop a horse. The horse was in full gallop, the soldier boldly holding his sabre aloft in a gallant charge. It was very detailed. The face of brave determination. It reminded me of the old man with the glass eye. At first, I wondered if it belonged to my cousins but it looked far too old. It had been buried for years. Then a thought - perhaps it once belonged to my father. Perhaps, like me, dad had hidden away in the woodshed as a little boy. Maybe he buried it deliberately; a prize to be unearthed the next time he visited. I held the soldier like a precious diamond. A tangible link to my father as a boy. A link to an innocent time, before the darkness. I could not help but cry. I placed the soldier into my pocket. I didn't play with it. I guarded it. I protected it. Its memory would never be lost again.

The following morning marked the first day of October. It was a bright, welcoming Sunday. I watched Aunty load her bicycle basket with flowers from the garden. They were for the church display. I did not feel like going there, so I stayed home. I waved her off as she cycled to St Mary's. She would be gone for hours and I was free to roam the house.

My dad had spent many holidays here as a child. He had told me how he would play in the attic with my uncle. Just tinkering. He enjoyed anything mechanical. The attic was bound to be filled with memories. I knew Aunty Muckle would not approve of me rummaging through her husband's belongings. I doubt anyone had ventured there since his death. Not in seven years. But she was not in the house now, I was.

My uncle had died unexpectedly. A simple graze on his hand whilst repairing a fence. Tetanus. It invaded his body, slowly destroying him. Within days he was barely able to swallow. By the third week, he was dead. I liked my uncle and I wanted to find a memento of his life.

Access to the attic was via a wooden step ladder. Rusty, the cat, was inquisitive as I climbed up. She did not follow me beyond the first rung. Instead, she remained on the landing, purring noisily as she paced back and forth. I scrambled through the hatch and located a string-pull to turn on the lighting.

Floorboards had been laid across the beams allowing me to move with confidence. I was rather disappointed by the lack of clutter. There was very little of immediate interest. A small collection of fishing magazines and parish newsletters were stacked against a supporting beam. The top edition was coated in fine granules of dust. I removed the lid from a wooden tea chest nearby. Inside, I found my uncle's clothes, each garment neatly folded away as if he were departing on holiday. On top, beside his flat cap and smoking pipe, lay an order of service. It was for a funeral. His funeral. There was a sketch of Saint Mary's church on the front. I felt uneasy looking at such things so I replaced the lid.

I searched the rest of the attic. In the corner, on the floor, I found a notebook. I wiped it clean with my palm. It was beautifully bound in leather and tied shut with two thin strands of string. I untied the bindings and the book fell open on its first page. Handwritten in the most exquisitely flowing black ink were the words:

'This book belongs to Alfred Engle, aged 12'.

I wiped the dust from my hands before running my finger along the text. I closed my eyes. For a moment I felt the spirit of my father standing beside me. I smiled. I had not smiled at a memory in such a long time.

I sat cross-legged and flicked through the pages. Each crisp, cream coloured page was blank. My heart sank. Not a single word had been recorded, other than the announcement of his ownership. I was heartbroken. A lost opportunity; the chance to become acquainted with my father's mind as an equal, schoolboy to schoolboy. I smelt the book. The odour of mould and the passages of time. He should have written something. He should have written something for me. I needed him now, more than ever.

I felt angry again. He had lost the chance to speak to me. To immortalise himself in the pages of a diary. And now he was gone, along with every single atom of his memory. I wanted to hurl the book across the attic. Hurl it into oblivion. I almost did. Instead, I sat and cradled it, close to my heart. As my anger waned, I decided to take ownership of it. Unlike my father, I swore to record my memories on each page. Not scientific facts or equations but experiences. The essence of my thoughts. An account of these most peculiar of events. An account of my dealings with this starlight demon. I did not wish my life to be lost on the blank pages of unwritten words. I want everyone to know what I have seen, what I have felt and what I hold dear. Thoughts and memories are what makes a person. They can be recorded, stored, immortalised. The body will rot and decay. Its function is only to protect the soul. The things that matter to me, I could see them all so clearly now.

There was a bang on the front door. Then another. I opened my eyes. The banging continued. It sounded desperate. I got to my feet and climbed down from the ladder. The pounding ceased. From the stairs, I saw the letterbox swing open. A pair of eyes peered through.

'Open up,' the voice demanded, 'I know you're in there! Open up now!'

I fumbled frantically to turn the latch as an unseen fist pounded the door once more. The door swung open, pushing me aside. The figure of a policeman towered before me. It was Constable Billet.

'Get in,' he said, ushering me back into the living room. 'Sit,' he demanded.

I sat in Aunty Muckle's armchair. The constable stood menacingly over me.

'Well then, George Engel,' he said, 'I think you had better answer some questions, don't you? And no bloody lies this time or I'll give you a thick ear. Now, tell me about your friend, Mr Simpkins.'

I began to tremble. I had never seen a policeman so angry. 'He showed me his observatory. That's all. I don't know how the fire started, honest,' I said, 'Is he under arrest?'

A bead of sweat glistened on the constable's brow.

'I'm not interested in the fire. I don't care who the hell started it. It can all burn for all I care,' he said. He withdrew a white handkerchief from his pocket and dabbed clumsily at his face. 'I want to know what happened to the girl, Emily Fenton.'

The constable placed his hands on the armrests of my aunty's chair and lowered his face to mine. 'And you're going to tell me,' he said.

A single drop of sweat fell from the tip of his nose onto the palm of my hand. I was too afraid to wipe it away.

Constable Billet stepped back.

'Look, son,' he said, 'All I care about is your friend. She's in danger. Grave danger. And I know it's got something to do with you.'

'Emily,' I said sitting up, 'You said she was dead. You said you found her body. You're a liar! You lied to me!'

The policeman sat down beside me.

'Look, George,' he said, 'The night I found you in the woods. I saw something. Something I can't explain. Something, not natural.'

The policeman rubbed at his left hand nervously. 'But whatever it was,' he said, 'I think it has hold of Emily. And I think you know it too.'

I wiped his sweat from my hand and nodded slowly.

'The burnt bicycle had a serial number stamped onto the frame,' the constable said, 'Reported stolen from Farrowmare Farm in Stoke d'Abernon a few months ago.'

'I was going to take it back,' I said.

Constable Billet rubbed at his eyes. He looked tired. Defeated.

'The police aren't looking for Simpkins,' he said, 'They've focused on the wrong man. I can't change their mind. But Simpkins, I think he's looking for you. I think he's using Emily as bait. Did you know the cleaners are coming?'

I felt a knot in my stomach tighten. 'The cleaners?' I said, 'What do you know about the cleaners? Mr Simpkins mentioned them, the very first time I saw him.'

'All I know is that they're coming, George,' the policeman said, 'They're coming to make him all shiny and new.'

'I want to go home,' I said, 'I want to see my mum.'

The constable rose to his feet. 'I've come all this way now, George. You're staying right here, in Long Sutton,' he said, 'I'm not letting you leave this village. Not now. Not until this is all sorted out.'

As I stood, the policeman placed his hand on my shoulder.

'I'm sorry son,' he said, 'but I think he's looking for you now. I think he's coming to get you.'

'He wants to kill me, doesn't he,' I said.

'Yes, I think he does. I know you're scared,' the policeman said, making his way to the front door, 'but so am I.'

As he left the house, he turned to face me. 'I'll speak to you later, George,' he said, 'In the village. Not in this place. You're not ready. Not yet.'

Chapter XVI

I stood on the little wooden bridge spanning my aunt's pond. Looking down at the goldfish, watching their ripples distort my reflection. I was thinking about Emily. The thought of her suffering tore at my heart.

Over by the house, I heard Aunty Muckle returning from church. I saw her through the kitchen window. Curiosity led me back towards the house. I peered secretively through the glass. She looked pale as she made a cup of tea and sat at the table. Unfolding a newspaper with trembling hands. I managed to glimpse the headline.

'Gruesome double murder in Upwell'.

Aunty held her hand to her mouth as she read. After a while, she folded the paper neatly and left it on the table. Wiping her eyes, she disappeared into the hallway. She would not want me to see her upset, so I waited until she was gone. I crept into the kitchen, listening to the sound of her footsteps as she headed upstairs.

I sat at the table and examined the paper. Two sisters found dead inside their own home. A remote house on the outskirts of Upwell, a small village no more than fifteen miles south of Long Sutton. Two ladies, both in their sixties. It had been the postman who discovered them. A vicious murder. A crime of mutilation. Obscene words carved into their flesh. Upon each face, were cut two letters. *'S.S.'* The reporter speculated this had stood for *'The Serial Slasher'.*

I did not need to read anymore. I knew who had done it. Simpkins wanted to send me a warning. He wanted me to know he was still alive. He wanted me to know he had killed the women, that he was nearby. He wanted to scare me. To let me know that I would be next.

Aunty Muckle spent much of her time at church. She busied herself attending to her husband's headstone. It was a rather endearing attribute of hers. She cared for the living and the dead in equal measures. I watched her for hours as she bound her flowers with crisp green and gold ribbon.

Back at her home, with no more chores for the church, Aunty sat quietly in her armchair, slowly thumbing through the pages of an old photograph album. I peered over her shoulder. Together we looked at captured memories. She ran her finger over the image of her husband, caressing his face. From time to time, the page would reveal a photograph of a vaguely familiar smile or shiny new motorcar which I once happened upon. Youthful relatives, almost unrecognisable to me. The people aged, but their house decor remained the same throughout the years.

Our attention was drawn to one particular photograph. It was of my parents, proudly holding a newborn baby in their arms. I looked into an image of my own eyes but barely recognised myself.

As the page turned, Aunty Muckle paused. A picture of two teenage girls kneeling on the lawn, playing with a pet rabbit. The girls, perhaps no older than fourteen or fifteen, were twins. They wore identical summer dresses with little daisies printed on them. Even their long hair which cascaded past their waists had been kept neatly in place by identical hair clips. Cheeky grins lit up their faces as the rabbit nibbled at their shoes. It looked to be a happy memory. That is why I was surprised to see my aunt so upset. With each turning of the page, the two girls aged. No longer teenagers but young women, off to work in a typing pool or the like. Another page and they were middle-aged, this time standing outside a house, still with the same mischievous grins. They were now in the company of a young gentleman. I did not recognise him. Perhaps he had been a passing boyfriend of one of the women. It was this particular photograph that upset Aunty the most. She sighed gently and closed the album.

A distant recollection of the twins drifted into my mind. Memories of a family reunion. Mother and Father were there. I was no older than five or six at the time. Aunty Muckle had been there too, along with her three boys. We had attended a funeral, my uncle's. We had eaten lunch in muted respect. Roast beef and Yorkshire puddings. It was followed by the most colourful trifle. And then I remembered them. The meal had been prepared by two identical women. The twins. The two same ladies in the photograph.

As the mood grew sombre, I had been sent out of the house with the older boys. They took me fishing in a nearby river. The first time I had ever held a fishing rod. Memories of the day dripped into my conciseness. We had stood upon a narrowboat jetty opposite a local fish and chip shop. The smell of frying chips had made my stomach rumble as we took turns to hold the rod. The boys caught roach which they kept in a bucket of water. When it was my turn, I had found it rather boring. Nothing happened for ages. And then my fishing float bobbed beneath the water and my heart raced. I had caught an eel. I felt so proud. As it dangled on the end of the line, one of the boys grabbed hold of it. He flung the slimy, twisting creature onto the jetty. I watched as it wriggled and contorted in its alien environment. Our environment. It did not belong here. Then, without hesitation, the eldest boy carved off its head with a penknife. Blood and slime coated the jetty where the headless eel thrashed wildly about. And then I remembered. We had been fishing in the little river which flows through Upwell. I knew why my aunt was so upset to see the newspaper.

In the afternoon I took a stroll into the village. Wednesday's were half-day closing. All the shops shut promptly at midday. Long Sutton was deserted. The air was mild and a pleasant breeze blew softly into my face. I paused outside the old derelict Bull Hotel, watching a swirl of dust briefly rise, trapped within a spiralling vortex. It billowed and danced across the courtyard beyond the coach's archway. I watched the twisting, convoluted shapes as they drifted. Had it not been for the presence of the dust, I would never have seen the wind. Then, in a fraction of a moment, it was gone and the dust fell to the ground. I wondered if any of it were real. Would the swirling air have existed without the presence of the dust, or my memory of it? To this day, I do not know the answer.

Across the courtyard, in the shadows of the building, I glimpsed movement. The figure of a man. He stood partially concealed. There was something familiar about his stance, how he held himself. For the briefest moment, I thought it was my father. I stared at the figure. I could not distinguish any of his features. The man stared back, scrutinising me.

I stepped out from under the archway for a clearer view. The man gestured for me to approach him. Slowly he turned his back and entered into the crumbling building. A sense of déjà vu, as though I had been here before, as though the ruins of the hotel were somehow familiar to me. Yet I could not recall ever being here.

I walked to where the man had stood. The door through which he had passed remained ajar. The small glass panes set into the upper section were dirty and cracked. A tuft of dandelions grew through the stone step, the only habitable niche in a barren desert of cobblestones. I paused, watching a black ant drag the lifeless body of another across the step. The horrors of existence, in miniature.

The door was rotten and bowed. I tried to push it open a little more but it would not budge. Squeezing myself through, I found myself in a bare, decaying room. A concrete floor, coated in dust, the air heavy with the smell of mildew and rotting wood. Most of the windows were boarded up. Those left exposed had been shattered by probing brambles and weeds. Nature was reclaiming its lair. In the corner of the room lay a filthy mattress. A bundle of rags and blankets piled on top. Around the mattress, the dusty floor had been swept clean by shuffling feet. And then I saw it, beside a makeshift pillow. A little lead soldier, riding a horse, his sabre held aloft.

The sound of movement. It came from behind an adjoining door. I felt the pulse of blood pushing through the veins in my neck. I glanced back towards the outside. I could flee, I could run away from Long Sutton. I could run away from everything. But I knew the dark thoughts and nightmares would always be with me. They would fill my head, burning the very life out of me. I knew I had to face my demon.

Placing my hand on the door, I pushed it wide.

'Hello George,' a voice said, concealed behind the open door, 'We need to talk.'

Stepping into view was a tall man. He wore a scruffy shirt and baggy trousers. Unshaven and dirty, as if he was on the run. I did not recognise him at first, but I knew who he was. It was the policeman, Constable Billet.

The constable spoke in a hushed voice, as if every syllable held a secret. 'Did you know Simpkins is here,' he said, 'Right here, in the village?'

I nodded. 'He wants to get rid of me,' I said.

The constable patted the side of my arm. 'Not yet,' he said, 'He's looking for someone else first. A woman.'

'He's mad,' I said, 'Completely mad. He's ill or something. Thinks there's aliens or monsters or something. You know, getting inside his head.'

The policeman smiled. 'I expect there's plenty of things trapped in that head of his,' he said, drawing a deep breath. 'Well, what do you think? Do you believe in aliens and monsters?' he asked.

'I think I killed a dog,' I said. The palms of my hands became sweaty. 'Mr Simpkins cut his own face off with a knife. Did you know that?'

The policeman nodded. 'Damien Simpkins is a very unwell man,' he said, 'He's been through a lot. What do you know about his actions during the Great War?' he asked.

I shrugged my shoulders but then thought better of it. 'He didn't fight,' I said, 'Not like my dad. He just stayed home. Worked on secret stuff. Telephone lines or something.'

The constable led me out of the building and into the clean open air of the courtyard. I followed him under the archway and out towards the main street of the village. 'Your father had a friend. A man called Stanley Seabrook. Have you ever heard of him?' the constable asked.

I nodded. 'He was killed in the trenches, before dad got gassed,' I said.

'Damien didn't go to war, his parents were German, you see,' the policeman said. 'He was registered as a conscientious objector. He didn't work on any secret projects. They wouldn't have permitted it.'

We both sat on a bench, outside Saint Mary's church. It was peaceful in the village.

'I went to his observatory,' I said, 'I saw the strangest thing. A light.'

I looked down at my arm. 'I can't explain it,' I said, 'I can't explain any of it. I had a dog bite, on my arm. A bad one. But the light, well, it healed me. I know it did.'

I tried to gather my thoughts. 'I don't know what the light was,' I said, 'Aliens, Jesus or even the Devil, I don't know. But the light healed me. Like a miracle.'

'I don't think it was aliens, son,' the policeman said. 'Look, I'm not a religious bloke. In this job, you get to see all sorts of things. Dreadful things. Strange things. But no matter how complicated things appear, it's the simplest explanation that leads to the truth. Now then,' he continued, 'It could've been little green men transmitting some kind of funny light from across the stars. Magic light that'll heal a dog bite. Light that can drive a man clear out of his head. Or,' he said, 'it could've been a very depressed man. An alcoholic man, wanting you to believe in his delusional fantasy. He's lonely, George. Not at all well.'

'Occam's razor,' I muttered.

'During the Great War,' the policeman said, 'a young lady, a total stranger, approached Simpkins, on Ashtead Common. Wanted to know why he wasn't in uniform. Why he wasn't fighting up at the front. Expect he stuck out like a sore thumb. Anyway,' he said, 'this young lady took something out of her handbag and gave it to him. Do you know what it was?'

I shook my head.

'It was a white feather,' he replied, 'sign of cowardice.'

The policeman arose from the bench. I followed alongside him as we slowly passed by the shop frontages.

'Of course, that wasn't the only feather he received you know,' Constable Billet said. 'Before the Great War, your father and Mr Simpkins spent their holidays in these parts. They met with two ladies, twins, in fact, Ethel and Hetty. Did you know your Aunt Hetty was engaged to Stanley Seabrook? After he was killed at Passchendaele she never married. Well, you know what they say about a woman scorned!'

The policeman glanced at his reflection in a shop window. He took the opportunity to neaten his hair. He still looked scruffy.

'It's awful, isn't it,' the constable said, looking away from the glass. 'Anyway,' he continued, 'towards the end of the war he got a second white feather. This time from your Aunt Hetty, and a third from Ethel. Expect the women gave him a hard time. Probably blamed him for Stanley's death. Apparently, it sent him into a right old rage. Your father calmed him down though. Took him back to Ashtead. Now then, did you ever see Mr Simpkin's new cleaning lady, Mrs Stride?'

'No,' I said, 'She'd left. That's why his house was so messy.'

'Mrs Stride was found dead a while back,' the constable said, 'Murdered. She had only cleaned for him a short while. Now then,' he continued, 'we think Elizabeth Stride was the very lady who gave him his first feather all those years ago, out on the common. Doubt she even recognised him. I expect she handed out hundreds of the damn things. Any young man out of uniform.'

The policeman escorted me to the end of the row of shops. 'Expect our friend Damien Simpkins recognised her right enough though,' he said, 'Doubt he would forget a thing like that. Probably brought all those memories back. Painful memories. I expect he got quite angry. What with his drinking and your dad no longer around to calm him down.'

'So he killed her?' I asked.

'Oh yes,' the policeman replied, 'he killed her alright. Rather enthusiastically too. And that leads me to the double murders in Upwell I'm afraid.'

'He carved Stanley Seabrook's initials into them, didn't he,' I said, not needing confirmation.

Regardless, the policeman nodded. 'I searched his observatory you know. Certainly liked keeping his records in order,' the constable said, 'I found some envelopes of interest. Four of them to be precise. Each one contained a single black feather, and a name, of course, written on every envelope.'

'What were the names,' I asked.

Constable Billet lowered his voice, 'Well,' he said, 'there was Mrs Stride, of course. He left that one with her body. And then there are the twins, Ethel and Hetty. And one other.' He paused momentarily, 'Dorothy Muckle,' he said.

A cold shiver passed down my spine. 'Then he might try and kill her too. Why aren't you protecting her?' I asked, raising my voice. 'You should move her away from here, as far as you can! Send someone to guard her, anything!'

'I'm afraid it's not quite as simple as that,' the policeman said, 'you see, he still has Emily Fenton. I doubt he'll hurt her. Not yet, anyway. He knows you like her, you see. But I need your help, George. I think he'll talk to you. We need to bargain with him. I need you, son, as bait.'

'Bait,' I said, 'He'll bloody kill me.'

'You'll be alright,' the policeman said, 'You won't come to any more harm.'

'When we were in the woods,' I said, 'he was like a wild animal. He wanted to kill me there and then. He's a demon.'

'He's calmed down a lot since then,' the constable said, 'He realises what's happened to him. When the time comes, I'll tell you what you need to do. But for now, you should just go home. Forget all about it all. Until it's time.'

I felt myself smirk.

'Don't try to warn your Aunt,' he said, 'We don't need to worry her. She needs to act naturally, not give the game away.'

We parted company in the street. The constable, in his drab clothes, headed back towards the centre of the village. I walked along the main road, back to my aunt's house. I did not know what to think. It all sounded so crazy. Mr Simpkins had murdered three women for suggesting he had been a coward during the Great War. What the hell did that have to do with me? And why would he take hold of Emily? My poor, poor Emily.

As I walked, something caught my eye. It was laying at the edge of the gutter, bright and yellow. It twitched and fluttered chaotically. An injured bird. A budgerigar. I knelt beside the animal and picked it up. I held the poor thing in my hand, trying to calm the creature. Warm blood leached from its tiny body. Both legs had been snapped clean off. Neat, almost surgical. Embedded into the bird's chest was a twig. Pushed into its body like a spear. The wound was fresh. I scanned the horizon for the culprit but saw no one. The bird flapped its wings, pitifully trying to break free of my hold. Not knowing how to save it, I placed it gently on the grass verge and began to walk away. My conscience got the better of me. I returned to the fluttering animal and stood over it, watching its suffering. And then I raised my foot and stamped upon its tiny body. A tangled mess of innards ejected from its tiny body.

I began to run. I ran as fast as I could. When I arrived at the junction of Lime Walk, I slowed my pace. The air smelt strange - metallic, like damp rust. As I opened the front gate to my aunt's house, something dripped down onto my chest. It fell from the tree above. Instinctively I wiped it away. A streak of wet blood smeared my palm. I looked up. Strung amongst the lower branches I saw a fury pelt. Higher up, the entrails of an animal dangled down.

At the base of the tree I saw a liver, shiny and clean. It lay beside two little lungs. The organs, laid out neatly and deliberately upon the ground. And then I saw it, the head of the animal, severed and spiked onto a branch. It was my aunt's cat.

I took a deep breath and entered the house.

Chapter XVII

The front room of my aunt's house was neat and tidy. I saw no sign of a disturbance. Cautiously, I headed into the kitchen. Despite the typically chaotic mess, nothing looked out of place. The house was silent. I searched every room in the house but there was no sign of my aunt. I checked the rear garden. Again, nothing.

Outside, it began to rain so I took shelter inside the woodshed. I went to light a lamp but it was gone, both of them. Through a gap in the wooden slats, I watched blackbirds scuttling across the lawn in search of worms. I sat on the floor, listening to the patter of rain upon the roof. At times it was rhythmic, soothing. Other times it was chaotic, like gunfire in a distant battle.

The birds sang as they ate their fill. Slaughter on a miniature scale. I propped myself against the pile of seasoning wood and closed my eyes. I dreamt of my father. I saw fields churned by shells and laden with shredded flesh. I saw the yellow mist of poisonous gas drifting across the land. I felt it burn my skin and eyes. But somehow it cleansed me. It stripped away the filth of humanity. I was left pure, invigorated, rejuvenated. The purge of man. And then I dreamt of Emily. She was so afraid. So cold and hungry and afraid.

I lay half-asleep. By now it was dark. I stretched my legs but it did little to alleviate my discomfort. A soft light shone through a knothole in the side of the shed. At first I thought my aunt had returned, but I was wrong. I got to my feet and stepped out into the garden. The sky above was thick with cloud and the rain lashed angrily at my face. The house stood in darkness. To the south, the sky glowed orange and red. It was a beautiful sight. The underbelly of the clouds, illuminated by a burning city below. An invasion was coming.

I stepped out of the woodshed. It was morning. The rain had ceased but the ground was damp as I peered through the kitchen window. The house was still empty. From the side of the building, I saw the front gate, wide open. A small cardboard shoebox lay by the apple tree, damp from the night's rain. I lifted the lid. Inside, the remains of the cat. The tiny, disrupted body, removed from the tree to preserve its dignity. I knew my aunt had placed it here. My poor aunt, such a gruesome discovery. She would be distraught. If she was not to be found in the house, I was sure she would have sought solace in the church. Mr Sipkins would know that too, I thought. He would have lured her there. A lamb to the slaughter.

A wave of dread. I found myself running towards Saint Mary's, taking the shortest route. I ran across the muddy fields that backed into the village park. From here I made my way through the graveyard behind the church. All the time, thinking of Aunty Muckle, of what that vile man may do to her. I felt sickened in the pit of my stomach.

I caught my breath beside a tree, looking out into the marketplace. The street had been closed to motorcars and numerous stalls erected in the road. A crowd gathered around them. The villagers mingled and chatted as stallholders yelled out their wares. Fruit, vegetables, flowers and animal feed. Tools, cockles, meat and bread. The people scuttled about like ants on sugar.

One stall sold bundles of samphire. A sign stated `freshly collected from the marshes'. People were jostling to get served by the old man.

A voice behind me.

'It's a different kind of life now you know.' It was Constable Billet. His civilian clothes looked more bedraggled and soiled than ever before. He smelt musty. Even his breath was unpleasant. He looked gaunt and unshaven.

'Something's happened,' he said, 'Something terrible. I didn't realise at first, but I know now,' he said. 'The darkness of it all.'

'You have to help her,' I said, 'Mr Simpkins, he's killed my aunt's cat. I think he's in the church now, looking for her.

The constable pointed towards a stall. 'You see that old man, the one selling samphire,' he said, 'That's Albert Couper. He's in the Home Guard. A private. You'll need to stick close to him when it all kicks off.'

I looked at the old man, he was in his late sixties with a weathered complexion with bushy grey eyebrows to match his cotton-like hair that billowed in every direction.

'But what about Aunty Muckle?' I said, 'You need to find her!'

I turned and looked towards St Mary's. Its tall, narrow spire stabbing at the blue sky. Sunlight glinted off a golden weathervane.

'Something terrible is going to happen,' the constable said, 'You'll have to be brave. See it through to the end.'

Crows squawked in the trees above. They were laughing at me again, mocking me. And then it happened. The bells of Saint Mary's began to ring. It was deafening. Terrifying. Within seconds the marketplace was a cascade of people, scattering in every direction. I had never seen anything like it before. The old man on the samphire stall vaulted cleanly over his counter. He turned and grabbed his tin of takings. He ran through the marketplace, weaving his way through the crowd.

'The bells,' I said, 'It's the invasion. What the bloody hell do we do?'

'Come on lad,' the policeman said, 'It's time for us to stop all this ungodly nonsense.'

Constable Billet took me by the arm and led me towards the heavy oak door of Saint Mary's. Letting go, he pushed the door open. Above our heads, the bells ceased. Long Sutton fell silent, save for the scurrying villagers. In the distance, I heard more peeling bells. News of the invasion was rippling outward, from village to village.

I followed the policeman inside. The church was empty. Our footsteps on the cold stone echoed loudly. Passing a row of wooden pews, I reached the main aisle leading to the altar. Out of respect, I began to genuflect. As I knelt, the constable grabbed the scruff of my collar and pulled me sharply to my feet.

'Oh no you don't, sunshine,' he said, 'not in this place.'

I smoothed out the ruffles in my shirt.

My Aunts floral decorations adorned the altar and the base of each stone pillar, each tied neatly in green and gold ribbon. Displays of yellow and white roses.

Then, somewhere to our left, a voice called out. It was the voice of an elderly man.

'Dear God,' the voice cried out.

Constable Billet ran. He ran toward the voice. It led him to a doorway. I followed.

Beyond, we found a stone stairwell. It spiralled up into the church tower. I could barely keep pace with the constable's broad strides. At the top, a heavy wooden door lay partially open. We entered.

We stood within the ringing room of the bell tower. My eyes fell upon eight ropes hanging down from the high ceiling into the centre. Each fluffy end of the ropes was coloured in the most striking flash of electric blue. Beneath, lay a body, convulsing on the floor. I knew it was Aunt Muckle, despite her turned face. Her body lay awkwardly. A pool of dark liquid drizzled from her chest, soaking into a beige carpet. Nearby stood the verger. He was an elderly man, his face ashen with fear.

This was a den of evil. An evil that had no place to be here. Knelt beside my aunt, was death. A wild, rabid animal, sickly and rotten. But despite the decay, despite the wretched state of its form, I knew it for what it was. It was not a man. It was the remnants of a man, of Mr Simpkins. A beast of darkness. A demon.

The beast was oblivious to our presence. Intent only in butchery. It lashed frantically at my aunt with bare, bloodied hands. From the centre of its drooling face, I saw a ring of yellowed teeth, sharp like daggers. Others were rounded like the tusks of a boar. But it was the eyes that frightened me. Bloodshot and raw.

The beast halted its assault. Delicately it rolled its victims head to face it. My aunt offered no resistance. Transfixed, I watched as this ungodly thing pushed its index finger into her mouth, between her front teeth. Then slowly it ripped open her upper lip. It dug deep into her mouth until it gained sufficient purchase. Holding a fist of flesh, it pulled away at her mouth. Her cheek tore apart and an open gash zig-zagged up to her left eyeball. The eye ruptured, squirting clear fluid across her face.

'Dear God, stop,' the verger called out, pulling at the beast's coat.

But the beast resumed its torture, unhindered by the verger's plea.

I turned to the policeman. He stood motionless. He did nothing to help. Nothing to stop this vile act. He simply watched silently, allowing the horror to unravel before us.

'Please,' I said, 'help her.'

The corner of the policeman's mouth began to turn upwards. It formed a smirk. And then he smiled.

'Help her,' I yelled, punching him in the arm.

'Damien, Leave her,' the constable said.

The beast paused. It turned slowly and looked at us. And then it looked at me, alone.

'Here,' the constable said, 'You can have the boy. He's almost ready.'

The policeman grabbed my arm, twisting my wrist painfully behind my back. He pushed me forward, towards the beast. My shoes splashed in my aunt's blood. Her limp hand tumbled forward and grabbed my ankle. She turned to face me. 'Please, help,' she spluttered.

The beast released its grip on the woman and she slumped back. Then it turned towards the verger. With unbelievable speed, it lept towards the old man, striking him across his chest with its fist. The force flung the old man across the ringing room. He landed heavily against the wall. Falling to the floor, he whimpered like a scalded dog.

The beast returned to where Aunty lay. It stepped over her twitching body and stood before me. It took hold of my hair, gripping my scalp in its fist. The constable stepped back as my face rested against the beast's rotting chest.

'You can have him,' the constable said, 'But only if you let the girl go.'

The beast spoke. It spoke in slow, almost silent words.

'Is that what you want, George?' it said, 'You would do that, for her?'

I did not wish to look at this vile, rotting corpse. 'Don't hurt her,' I said, 'Please.'

The beast shoved me, back into the arms of the policeman.

'He's tearing my mind apart,' it said, 'I want to be free of this nightmare. I need him gone.'

'Then let the girl go,' Constable Billet said, 'Set her free. And let the old woman live too. Prove you're merciful.'

Drool bubbled around the beast's mouth. 'If you free my mind,' it said, 'we can let them live. The old woman, and the girl.'

The verger tried to stand. He looked dazed.

'They'll come for you,' Constable Billet said, 'For the things you've done. Punish you.'

The beast wiped blood from its hands. 'I need more time. I need to be complete. You must convince them I'm dead,' it said.

'I'll see to it, I promise,' the constable replied.

'If you want the girl to live,' the demon said, 'you must do what I ask. The man, Couper, you know what to do?'

The constable nodded.

The beast moved, pushing me aside. Then, with an unnatural speed, it fled down the stairs, gone from sight. The constable did not attempt to stop it.

The verger crawled towards my aunt on all fours. He cradled her as she struggled to speak. He placed his ear to her torn mouth.

'Simpkins,' she spluttered, 'German.'

The policeman took me by my wrist. 'You don't need to see this,' he said, dragging me down the staircase.

I screamed and kicked out at him, trying to pull free.

'Aunty Muckle,' I yelled, 'Aunty!'

The verger paid no heed to my calls. He stayed by my aunt's side, comforting her as best he could.

As we stood before the altar, the constable flung my back hard against a stone pillar. He placed his hand firmly across my mouth and nose. I could not breathe. I panicked. From the corner of my eye, three Home Guard soldiers ran through the church. They wore tin hats and carried rifles. They did not see us as they scrambled through the doorway and up into the bell tower. When they were gone from view, the policeman kicked my feet from under me and I slid to the floor.

'If you want Emily to live,' he said, 'do every fucking thing I say. Do you understand?'

I nodded.

The policeman grabbed my hair and pulled me back up to my feet. He began to laugh. 'You still don't understand do you,' he said.

I pushed his hand away.

In an instant, the policeman grabbed my neck, holding me in a headlock. I tried to struggle free but I could not. His bicep flexed across my throat, choking me. My eyes bulged as I gasped for air. Even as my legs buckled beneath me, he did not release his pressure.

He led me, bent double, out of the church and across the graveyard. My feet dragged across the grass, through the flowerbeds. Then he flung me to the ground. I bashed my shoulder painfully against stone.

Coughing and spluttering for air, I pulled my shirt collar away from my throat. I felt giddy and dazed as if I would pass out.

'Look at it, boy,' the policeman said, kicking my leg sharply. The pain surged through my body. I looked up at the stone. Upon it were carved the words:

George Alfred Engle, 23rd September 1926 – September 11th 1940. Aged 13.

It was a headstone. My headstone, set upon my grave. I did not realise it at first. Then a knot in the pit of my stomach doubled me over in pain. 'No,', I began to cry, 'No!' I became hysterical. I could not control myself.

'You're nothing, George,' the policeman said. 'Your nothing but a memory. You don't exist. Neither of us does, not in the real sense. You see, we live inside the mind of a demon. Inside what is left of the mind of Damian Simpkins.'

The policeman pulled me to my feet. I cowered in fear.

'Don't you see?' he said. 'You're dead. We both are. He killed us. He murdered us, in Ashtead woods, in the fire. We've been dead for weeks,' he said. 'He ate your flesh, George. He ate your fucking soul.'

Chapter XVIII

Constable Billet led me away from the graveside, away from the headstone that bore my name. We stood under the shadows of an old oak tree. I was in shock, unable to control my trembling. Fear took hold. I felt so cold, so vacant. It could not be true. How could it? It was ridiculous for him to suggest such a thing. It was obvious. The man was a fool. An idiot to suggest such folly. And then I remembered my mother.

'What about my mum,' I said, 'She saw me off at Ashtead station. She was crying. Sending me away for the evacuation. You're a liar! You rescued me from the fire. You saved my life.'

'No, George, I'm sorry,' the policeman said, 'I didn't save you. I looked for you though, in the woods. But all I found was Mr Simpkins. He had a pig, tied onto a length of rope. The missing co-op pig. And he had a knife. I watched him, George. I watched him cut his own face off. I tried to stop him, tried to save his life, but I couldn't. It all happened so quickly. I thought he had punched me at first. And then I realised,' the policeman said, 'he had stabbed me. Deep into my chest. Your mind can play tricks you know, to protect you. You're dead George. You're dead, like me. Murdered. Murdered by an ungodly beast of a man. A demon. I don't blame you for not believing me. I didn't believe it myself. Not at first. But now I know. Now I know what that thing has done to us. What you've done to me.'

The constable patted my shoulder. 'Your mother saw you off, right enough,' he said. 'She was so upset. Watching your coffin load onto the train.'

And then I knew. Deep down I had known for a while. I felt a great weight lift from my shoulders. I caught my breath and looked across the graveyard. A display of fresh white roses and lilies rested neatly at the head of the plot. It was tied together beautifully by a length of green and gold ribbon. The same ribbon, used by my aunt. Every day she had come to this church. Every day, tending to my grave. I was dead and buried. I was nothing. I was dust, swirling in the vortex.

'Is she dead too?' I asked, 'Aunty Muckle?'

'She'll be alright,' the constable said.

'And Emily,' I asked, 'what about her?'

'Emily isn't dead,' he replied, 'She can thank *you* for that, George. But Mr Simpkins, well, he wants to do terrible things. I can feel it. But I think you have an influence over him, somehow. You and I, perhaps we could calm him. Stop him, even.'

'How?' I asked, 'What the hell could we possibly do now?'

I watched my hands trembling. This was madness.

I looked back towards the headstone. Flowers in memoriam. I felt uncomfortable in this place. It was unnatural. I was unnatural.

'I don't believe in heaven,' I said, 'Or ghosts. So what am I doing here? I want my mum!'

The policeman said nothing.

An ambulance arrived at the front of the church. We watched as two Saint John's men ran inside, carrying a stretcher.

'What exactly are we,' I asked, 'What am I?'

'Hope,' the policeman said. 'You're hope. Hope that we can stop him. This thing, inside the astronomer, this vile creature within Mr Simpkins. He's planning something. Something evil. I can sense it. Don't ask me how, but I can. Do you remember the starlight, George?'

I did not like to dwell on those memories. The nightmares were so terrible. So dark.

'He thinks there was a message, from a star,' I said, 'From Alnilam, in the constellation of Orion. Like a transmission. A message from an alien mind into his.'

'You saw the light too,' the policeman said, 'Such wonderful technology. Like magic.' He thought for a moment, 'or witchcraft,' he added.

'I think I want to go home now.' I said.

'George,' he replied, 'when you looked into the starlight, I think the memory of an alien mind was imparted onto you. Not all of it. I believe the bulk still resides within Mr Simpkins.'

'I have nightmares,' I said, 'terrible nightmares. Not just at night. All the time. They scare me. The things I've seen.'

The constable sighed. 'I don't think this alien chap is a good person,' he said, 'I think he was banished here. Sent as punishment for his crimes. Your father looked into the light too you know. Gained some of the message. I think he prevented this thing, inside Simpkins, from becoming whole. I think that's why he killed himself. To stop him. To keep him from that part of the light. The part which latched onto your father.'

I looked down at my feet. My knees were dirty. Dirty from the graveside.

The constable continued. 'But I think the message can be passed on,' he said, 'From one generation to the next. From father to son. You see, Simpkins needed it. And there was only one way that he could get it. He had to kill you. Consume your flesh. He ate your brain, your memories, your soul – even your fathers' memory of the light."

I felt shaky, as if I would vomit. I reached out and steadied myself against the trunk of the tree.

'After your death,' the constable said, 'you became embedded. Entrapped within his twisted mind. That's why you have such vivid nightmares, George. Visions of murder. You see, it's you. You're doing these terrible things. You murdered the twins. You murdered the young boy, James. It was you who attacked your Aunt Muckle.'

I covered my face in shame. The memories washed over me. I couldn't stop them. Memories of tearing skin, the screams, the sound of shattering bone. I had tried to keep them hidden, tried to ignore them. But they always returned. Always.

'You and I,' the constable said, 'exist only as thoughts inside the mind of Mr Simpkins. That's all that we are. Shadows of our lives.'

The constable tried to comfort me. 'Don't be afraid,' he said 'you're no killer. You're just a little boy. But you're trapped inside the mind of a killer. You're neither a demon nor a beast. You're better than that. Better than him. That's why he's fearful of you. Fearful of the memory of a scared little boy. You're burning him, George, burning at his conscience.'

I looked at Constable Billet. His eyes were watering as if he were about to cry.

'And me,' he said, 'I'm nothing more than your recollection. A shadow trapped within the memory of a dead little boy. A child's thoughts, contaminating the mind of a madman. I think I'm here just to comfort you. An imaginary friend for someone who has nothing.'

'So all this, it's happening inside Simpkins mind? Then I *am* a killer,' I said.

The policeman took hold of my hand. 'No,' he said, 'you're the voice of reason. You can stop this madness. If you're strong enough.'

The Saint Johns men returned from the church. They carried my aunt on a stretcher. The verger walked beside her, holding her hand as she was placed into the ambulance. He stayed with her, comforting her. I watched them drive off.

The three soldiers began to converse by the church entrance. I could not hear what they said. Two of them turned sharply about and jogged away, side by side. They left the churchyard and headed into the marketplace. The remaining soldier stood guard. With little ceremony, he fixed a bayonet onto his rifle. I watched him as he checked his ammunition magazine and cocked his rifle bolt.

The policeman patted my back. 'Come on,' he said.

'Where are we going?' I asked.

'Onwards,' he replied.

I followed the constable, walking by his side. I could barely keep pace. We passed the deserted market stalls and shop fronts before turning into Park Lane.

'Slow down,' I said.

'Why?' the constable asked, 'You still don't understand, do you? We're the same person. You can walk just as quickly as I can.'

I felt nauseous again. I wanted to stop and steady myself but the policeman kept to his stride. And then a peculiar thought occurred to me.

'Can they see us,' I asked, 'People, can they actually see us?'

The constable smirked. 'I told you,' he said, 'We don't exist. So no, they can't see us. But I bet they can see him alright,' he said.

Ahead of us, along Park Lane, I saw the two soldiers. We followed them discreetly. From across the fields, the wind carried the sound of church bells.

The soldiers came to a wooden hut along the lane. It was a boy scouts hut. They went inside, closing the door behind them.

'This is the place,' the constable said.

We stood to the side of the structure.

'We can hide up here for a bit,' he said.

Above the doorway, black stencilled letters.

Home Guard. Long Sutton (7c) Auxiliary Unit.

Constable Billet pushed his way through a dense privet hedge growing against the wall. We hid together among the foliage.

Through a narrow gap in the curtains, I peered inside. A captain of the Home Guard stood before his men in the centre of the parade hall. He was a thin, athletic-looking gentleman in his fifties. Behind him, a large wall-mounted map displayed the county of Lincolnshire and much of East Anglia. Seated before him were four soldiers. One I recognised. It was Mr Couper, the samphire man.

I pressed my face against the glass, listening as best I could.

'I've spoken to Spalding H.Q.' the captain said. 'They don't have the foggiest idea about the church bells. They think it's a false alarm.' He cleared his throat. 'But that's not to say Jerry isn't coming regardless, so we need prepare. Don't want to cause unnecessary alarm in the village though, but we must ascertain the battlefield situation.'

The captain shifted from foot to foot. 'Now, a flower lady at Saint Mary's was viciously attacked. It's possible she disturbed someone. A fifth columnist perhaps. The verger gave a brief description of the attacker. Not a great deal to go on though. A man in his forties, slim build. Scruffy, as if he's been living rough for some time.'

The other soldiers glanced at each other. They looked anxious.

'We believe the attacker is a man called Damien Simpkins. He's known to the victim. He's not from around here, he's a southerner, from Surrey. But he's of German descent. So, if he *is* a columnist, he may be here to cause disruption. Perhaps to divert us away from a main German assault, that kind of thing. Now, the attacks on our airfields stopped a few days ago. Fighter Command is pretty much at breaking point. Jerry has started hitting civilian targets pretty hard, particularly along the south coast so this could be the softening-up phase, prior to the invasion. Any questions?'

A sergeant raised his hand. The captain gestured for him to speak.

'Sir, if this bugger, Simpkins, wants to cause a diversion,' he said, 'shouldn't we just ignore him. Crack on with the village defence plans? Carry on regardless?'

'If this is a straightforward murder attempt,' the captain said, 'it's a matter for the police, not us. If he turns out to be a traitor, we have to stop him. Can't let a dangerous man like that run amok. He might try and sabotage our communication lines or transportation links, things like that. We've got to stop him.'

The captain pointed to the map behind him.

'Private Couper,' he said, 'I want you setting up a roadblock at the junction with Main Street and Chapel Gate. Private Hill, you're to block the T-junction at Pop-bottle Bridge with Bridge Road and Wisbech Road. No civilians in or out of the village without being challenged. Telephone through every fifteen minutes. Use the nearest civilian telephone. Understood?'

The two soldiers closest to my window stood and collected their rifles from the corner of the hall. As they unlocked the door to the hut, I dropped to the ground, concealing myself in the hedging. They stood outside, inches away. Constable Billet held a finger to his mouth. We were silent.

One of the men lit a cigarette and took a deep puff. He shared it with his colleague. The smell of tobacco drifted into my nose.

'I bet the Captain is loving all this,' one of them said, 'It's only a bloody assault and he tries to turn it into a full-frontal invasion. I bet this bloke was just trying to nick lead off the church roof.'

The other soldier grinned. 'God knows what he'd do if a Nazi Stormtrooper ever turned up in the village!'

The soldier flicked his cigarette butt into the hedge. It landed on the back of my hand. It was the strangest thing. I'm sure it must have burnt me, but I did not feel a thing. Not until I thought about it. Then it hurt.

The soldiers headed off towards the marketplace, their rifles slung over their shoulders. When they were gone from sight, I peered through the window again.

The Captain was still pointing at the map.

'Sergeant Proctor,' he said, 'I want you to join Private Moore over at the church. Commence a foot patrol in the south of the village between, let's see, the bus stop off Granary Road and Henry's fish and chip shop.'

The sergeant stood and collected his weapon. The captain turned to the last soldier. 'Mackinder,' he said 'you stay here with me. Answer the telephone and log all the welfare checks. Understood?'

As the sergeant opened the hut door, the Captain called out. 'Frank, come back with Moore in two hours. We'll rotate our positions every two hours!'

The sergeant gave a half-hearted salute before exiting. The door locked securely behind. Outside, he paused. Turning towards me, he stared through the darkness.

'Who's there?' he said.

Too frightened to move, I clamped my hand tightly over my mouth. Across the street, two cats fought. The sergeant turned and tutted to himself. Adjusting the sling on his rifle, he headed off towards the church.

Silence.

'Now what,' I asked.

'We wait,' the constable said, 'We see what Simpkins does next.'

I relaxed, leaning against the wall of the hut. It began to drizzle and I felt a cold mist blowing into my face. It cooled me, or perhaps I only imagined it did.

'I can't believe this is happening,' I said.

'I know,' the constable replied, 'Crazy isn't it. I shouldn't even be here. I should be at home, with my wife. I should be providing for her. Making sure she's alright, that sort of thing.' His lips thinned, 'Still, the police benevolent fund will see she's alright,' he said.

I began to think about home. 'She cried for me, at the station, my mother,' I said, 'I never thought she'd cry for me. Not ever. I always made her angry.'

I looked at the constable. He was fidgeting with his hands. With his wedding ring.

'I'm sure you meant the world to her,' he said.

'She never hugged me,' I replied, 'Dad did, but she didn't. Not ever.' I wiped some drizzle from my face, smearing it up into my hair. 'Do you think he'll tell us where she is, Emily, I mean?'

I thought for a moment. 'If we're really inside his mind, why don't we know where she is?'

'Look, you're a good boy, George,' the policeman said, 'You have a conscience. Right and wrong. That stuff. Simpkins doesn't. That's why you're so important. Without you, I think his rage would run wild. You can calm him down, you see. Stop him from hurting people. I think maybe you could even help Emily. Set her free.'

'But I don't know how,' I said.

Constable Billet put his arm around me. He said nothing.

I don't know how long we sat hidden. From time to time, soldiers returned to the hut to exchange their duties.

'It wants me gone, doesn't it,' I said, 'Out of its head.'

'Yes,' the policeman replied. 'You're tormenting it. I think you're a link to the old Mr Simpkins. You see, George, I don't think it can get rid of you. I think you and I have a choice. To leave its mind or to stay.'

'So, if I stay inside its mind,' I said, 'I can stop it.'

'Perhaps,' the policeman said, 'That's why it wants you gone. I think that's why it took Emily too. She's a hostage, you see. A bargaining tool. I think it's going to hurt her. I think it's going to do terrible, terrible things to her. And then it's going to kill her. Unless you leave its mind. If you leave its mind willingly.'

'If I go,' I said, 'will I be gone forever?'

'Yes, I think so,' the policeman said.

'Do you think it'll hurt, if I go?' I asked.

'I'm sorry, I really don't know,' the policeman replied, 'But it has to be your choice, George. I can't tell you what to do.'

The constable patted my knee. 'It's frightened you know,' he said, 'This thing inside Simpkins. This demon. I can tell it's frightened.'

'That thing,' I said, 'I doubt it!'

'Once,' the policeman said, 'only briefly, I saw into its thoughts. Don't ask me how, but I did. I knew then how frightened it was. How vulnerable. It didn't need to kill these women, you know. They were insignificant. It killed them because they had been cruel to Simpkins. Their murder was a gift to him, in exchange for his body. But now it needs him gone. And us. Gone, so it can acquire something else. Another victim of the starlight, just like you. A lady. Someone who inherited the last sequence of missing code from her father. The final segment of the message. It will make it whole again. Complete the process. The birth of a demon.'

'Who is she?' I asked.

'The daughter of a killer,' the policeman replied. 'I didn't make the connection at first. Not for a while. You see, I think this beast has been here before. Long ago.'

The constable began fidgeting with his wedding ring again, twisting it around and around his finger. 'Have you ever heard of the Ashtead Ripper?' he asked. 'He used to live in the red house, before Simpkin's. You see, I think it was the Ripper who first saw the light. He released the demon into the world. It lived inside him. Making him kill. Making him do terrible, terrible things.'

Constable Billet paused. 'The Ripper was never caught, you know. Never held to account for his crimes. I expect he died of old age. Or perhaps he couldn't cope with this thing inside his mind. Perhaps he chose to take his own life too, like your father,' he said, 'So, with the Ripper long dead, there was only one other way to acquire the missing sequence. Through offspring. He had a child, you see, the Ripper. A daughter. Must be in her forties by now. A grown woman. Still carrying part of the starlight message. That's what this creature wants now. This thing, inside Mr Simpkins. It wants it so badly. More than ever. It needs to find her, to devour her flesh. To be finalised. Powerful. But this creature, it has no idea where she is. The search is driving it insane.'

I said nothing. I barely moved. The drizzle stopped, but I still felt cold and vulnerable. We sat together, hidden by the darkness.

It was 11 o'clock. The Captain and Private Mackinder had already returned to the hut. At the far end of Park Lane, I heard someone running. The sound of boots drawing closer. It was the sergeant, in the company of a private. I recognised him, he had guarded the church earlier, his bayonet still fixed. The men were out of breath, struggling to compose themselves. The sergeant was wheezing.

Constable Billet nudged me.

'This is it,' he said in a low voice, 'They've seen them.'

The soldiers went inside. I stood slowly and listened at the window once again.

'In the marshes,' the sergeant gasped, 'Two lights. Out by the shoreline. We could see them from the embankment at the far end of Lime Walk.'

'Right men,' the captain said, 'He must be signalling to Jerry. This could be the landing point.' The captain removed his cap and dragged his fingers through his grey hair. 'Mackinder, call Spalding. Tell them that signalling lights have been spotted in the salt marshes. Possible enemy agent. Grid reference to follow. And for God's sake tell them to send reinforcements.'

Mackinder picked up the telephone receiver and spoke to the operator.

The hut door swung open. I dropped to the ground as the soldiers assembled outside. The captain inspected them.

'Right then, we'll pick the others up en route,' he said, 'We need all we can get.' He turned to face the open hut door, 'Hurry up with that call,' he said, 'and bring the Vickers!'

The three soldiers jogged off towards the village. The fourth emerged from the hut, struggling to raise a machinegun onto his shoulder. A belt of ammunition wrapped around his neck, the ends dangling by his knees. After locking the hut, he jogged after the other men.

Once out of sight, I stood and stretched my legs. I glanced at the window. The lights inside were off. And that was when I saw it. My face, reflected in the glass. My true image. The face of Simpkins, slashed and rotten. My own wild eyes stared back at me, cold and full of hatred. The face of the devil. I gasped, dropping to the ground, my hands held tightly over my face to conceal my shame.

'Help me,' I said, 'I don't know what to do,'

'You need to go to the marshes,' the constable said, 'to the lights. I can't go with you I'm afraid. I've done my bit.'

The policeman began to fidget again. 'I need it all to stop, you see,' he said, 'The pain in my heart. I'm sorry, but I need to go now. We're leaving, one by one. The cleaners are coming, for me. I want them to come. I'm ready now. Please, George, let me go.'

I nodded.

Slowly, we both stood. The constable's eyes looked tired and distant. The kind of look men have when they come back from war. I watched him closely. He was staring down Park Lane, towards the church. Staring at nothing. Staring into the darkness. And then I saw them. The silhouette of two figures. A mother and her daughter. They were holding hands. An unbreakable bond, as if they had somehow fused. A vision from a dream.

I froze. The fear of the inevitable. I knew what would happen. I knew because it was my intent. My own brain, bashing itself to a pulp. The filthy disease of mankind.

The mother and daughter began to move. They walked clumsily towards us. Awkward, jolting movements. Unnatural movements of the dead. The sound of high heels clip-clopping on the pavement. Ever closer.

I looked at the policeman. Silent tears fell from his eyes.

'I'm so sorry,' he said, 'I can't go on any longer. Not like this. I want it to end. I'm nothing. It hurts so much. Please!'

A shiver ran through me. The realisation of what I had done. To call a man into being for my own comfort. To protect me from the horror. The horror of my own mind. The darkness of the starlight.

The figures drew nearer. The cleaners were coming. Coming to purge the human filth from my mind. To cleanse me.

Constable Billet stood himself to attention. And then he closed his eyes. I blinked. And then, in the most ungodly way, they were upon him. Mother and daughter. They moved with such speed. Their screams pierced the night, deafening me. They clawed at the constable, pulling him to the ground. The sound of tearing flesh.

Unable to flee, unable to look away. I watched as sickly tendrils projected from the little girl's mouth. They gripped the policeman and pulled at his skin. They bore into him as he struggled. Twisting and contorting on the ground. His face was full of fear and pain. His hand reached out towards me.

'Help me,' he begged, 'Help me, mummy.'

The little girl's razor-like hands dug into him, tearing out his throat. Tearing away his life. A mist of blood sprayed forth, soaking my face. The constable fell silent. I watched as he lay twitching on the ground. Like an eel pulled from a river.

The cleaners stepped back. They smiled at me. Blood drizzled from the little girl's chin. She wiped it away with her finger and offered up the fluid to her mother. The mother sucked the girl's fingers with glee.

I knelt beside the policeman. I tried to stop the bleeding but it poured so freely. I comforted him as best I could. And then, when I was ready to let him go, he sighed. I watched as lifeless eyes rolled up into his head. And then he was gone. I stood, spitting his blood from my mouth. It was rancid and vile. Like the taste of rotten death.

The mother looked down at the dead man. She was pale, fearful. And then she spoke. The voice of a little frightened girl.

'Please,' she said, 'Help me. I want my daddy. I don't like mummy anymore.'

The little girl hissed at the woman. Her sharp teeth stained in blood. Then they turned their backs on me and departed down the lane. The fading sound of clip-clopping heels. The woman glanced over her shoulder at me. She was sobbing.

I looked down to where the policeman fell. He was gone. Not a trace of his existence remained. A dead man. Resurrected only by my memory of him. Obliterated by my willingness to set him free. The shadow of a man held within my imagination.

I felt dirty and vile. I looked at my reflection in the window once again. The ruptured face of the astronomer. It stared coldly back at me. Lifeless, soulless eyes. An unearthly, ungodly thing. A creature that crawled upon the Earth like a disease. I turned and vomited.

I began to think of Emily, of how I missed her. Of how I would never see her again. But I knew she was real. I knew she was alive. I knew she was so very, very frightened. If any good was to come of this unnatural hell, it would be Emily. My mind was foul. Filled with the rot of this devil. I knew then that I could not be saved from this hell.

I began to think of love. I began to think of friendship and compassion. Her mind is her own. Her beautiful, beautiful mind. The most wonderful thing to possess. The freedom to be free in thought. Her life is exquisite. Not just her life, all life. In every imaginable form. In all its complexities and in all its simplicities. I knew then what I needed to do. I would save her.

Chapter XIX

I ran as fast as I could through the night, scrambling over garden fences, across lawns and through flower beds. The night was silent save for my rustling. The sky had cleared. Ahead, above the horizon, I saw Orion. The constellation taunted me, the source of my torment. And there is shone, Alnilam, burning brightly in its centre. Two thousand lightyears separated us, but it was not enough. Not enough to inhibit the life that once spawned there. Now, this vile life lay imprisoned within the mind of an astronomer. A parasite, burning his mind and soul. And here I was, bound to its core. A billion electrical impulses of thought. A ripple of electrons along a nerve. I had been reduced to this.

Alnilam. I cursed it. I cursed its ungodly light as it shone down. I ran through the allotments, through my aunt's plot. Between the old man's beehives. Through ploughed fields. Through fields laden with crop. Onwards, towards the sea. Towards the great expanse of salt marshes that clung to the shoreline.

Clumps of soil adhered to my shoes. It weighed me down but it could not slow me. I was unstoppable. I ran like the wind, like a tempest. I had never felt so alive, so invigorated. My senses were burning. The smell of the soil, of the microbes. I felt the oxygen molecules in the air as they struck my face. The iron in my veins. Iron from the remnants of long-dead stars.

A sound. I paused to listen. Marching boots, no more than half a mile away. I could taste their sweat, carried on the air. The old men of the Home Guard, making their way to the marshes, towards the lights. Like moths around a bulb. The demon was luring them in. Luring them to their deaths.

I began to giggle. I could not help myself. They knew nothing of their impending death. Each step led them closer to their fate. I found myself mumbling. A nursery rhyme, no less. Teasing them. I could not help myself.

I know something you don't know, I know something you don't know... You're all going to die now, you're all going to die.

A memory jolted me. The smile of a little girl, of Emily. I punched myself in the leg to break the spell. An uncontrollable rage. I made a fist. My fingers tightly clenched before my face, fighting the urge to lash out at my skull. The sound of an owl hooting. I paused to listen. Wiping sweat from my forehead, I relaxed.

Onwards I ran. Leaping across ditches, through muddy fields. Onwards, until I saw the outline of the sea defence, an earth embankment stretching out before me. It followed the coastline for miles.

At the foot of the defence, I caught my breath. The clean air invigorated me. It pumped through my veins like electricity. Like a fire that could never be extinguished. I thought about Emily, about how she longed to have her brother back from the war. My moment on earth had ended. I knew that, now. But hers? Hers was only just beginning.

The embankment was steep, some fifteen feet high. I scrambled up to reach its crest. Crouching down beneath the stars, I surveyed the vista. Before me lay the salt marshes. Tufts of coarse grass blanketed a mosaic of muddy streams and dunes. They flowed out into the blackness of the night. Into the unseen ocean to the north.

Behind me, laid out like a miniature model, was Long Sutton village. The familiar spire of Saint Mary's church, pointing at the blanket of stars above. The arc of the Milky Way flowed like a river. Two hundred billion stars cutting the sky in half. How tiny and fragile it all was. How exquisitely beautiful. And then I saw it. A band of light reflected beneath the clouds, glowing on the southern horizon beyond the church. The soft red glow of London. A city on fire.

I lay flat in the long grass. The blades were laden with dew and their moisture soaked through to my skin. I looked out across the marshes, out towards the sea. Then, in the distance, I saw them. Two spots of flickering white light. They marked the shoreline. I knew they did. A trap set by the astronomer, by the parasite within his mind.

The sound of marching boots. The old men were nearing, making their way along a dirt track. My heart beat faster. I felt like a cornered animal; as if I were being hunted down, to be slaughtered. They wanted to kill me. To pierce my body with bullets. To rip apart my flesh. They would be relentless. They would not stop until they had destroyed me. Days, months, years. Whatever it took, they would find me and they would kill me. Not just them. Not just the old, grey-haired men of the Home Guard. Anyone. All of them. All of mankind. They would not rest until I was gone.

The soldiers came into view. I watched as they approached, breaking rank and spreading out into an arrow formation. They were difficult to see in the moonless night but from time to time a bayonet would glint under the stars. They were coming. They were coming for me.

On the north side of the mound, towards the marshland, a herd of sheep had gathered. They were uninterested in my presence but as the soldiers approached, they began to scatter. The men were clumsy and unfit. Unfit in body and mind. Worthless pathogens. When they reached the crest, they dropped to the ground. The Captain continued over the peak before taking cover in the grass.

'Don't bloody skyline,' he called out, 'Get down here.'

The other soldiers rose and advanced further before seeking cover on the north side of the embankment. They repositioned themselves in an irregular line, spreading out from the officer. The nearest man, no more than twenty feet from where I hid. He was looking out across the marshes too, out into the Wash.

'Alright, Mackinder,' the captain whispered, 'To your front, two enemy lights, nine-hundred yards, thirty rounds, short bursts, make ready.'

Mackinder raised the machinegun from the ground. The steep slope of the embankment proved problematic for the bipod so he folded it flush against the barrel of the weapon. Kneeling upright he rested the Vickers onto his raised knee. He delicately settled the gun to point naturally at his target, a white dot of light in the distance. He adjusted a vertical sliding rear-sight and took aim.

'Ready,' he announced.

'Fire!' the captain ordered. Two deafening bursts of gunfire pierced the night. The muzzle flashed, briefly illuminating Mackinder in the darkness, It cast long shadows across the grassland. A streak of red tracer zipped across the marsh. The gun fell silent. Half a second later, the distinctive thwack of bullets striking the muddy ooze of the marsh. Another burst of fire. And then another. The embankment filled with the scent of cordite. Smoke drifted over my body.

Silence returned, save for the slow tick-ticking of the Vickers barrel as it cooled. I looked towards the sea. The lights were still glowing, both of them.

'Out of range,' a voice called out, 'A good two hundred yards short.'

I turned my attention to the soldiers once more. I watched the sergeant crawl on his belly like a serpent, over to the captain.

'Sir,' he said, 'He could still be out there. Waiting to be picked up. A mini-submarine or something.'

'Perhaps,' the captain said, 'Either way, we need to put those lights out of commission.' He cleared his throat and called out to the other soldiers. 'Alright, listen in,' he said, 'Private Hill, I want you to head back to the Hut. Notify HQ of the situation. Find out when our reinforcements are due. Give them our six-figure reference.'

The soldier rose and ran back down the embankment, out of sight.

The captain called out again. 'The lights are out of range of the Vickers. We need to get down to the marsh and put them out at close range. Now then, that whole area has been mined. Not just anti-tank but anti-personnel too. Hundreds of them. Any ideas?'

'Sir,' one of the soldiers said, 'The Royal Engineers only laid as far as the high tide mark, I watched them do it. I know a route down. It's about half a mile to the east. I use it to get to the samphire beds. They grow pretty close to the tide mark. I could get to the shoreline easy enough. Then follow the tide line back to the lights. I could shoot them out, once I got closer.'

'I don't fancy sending any of my men into a minefield if I can help it,' the captain said, 'What do you think, sergeant?'

The sergeant removed his tin hat and rubbed his thinning hair. 'There could be a traitor out there, hiding up. He's likely to be armed. It could be problematic. But either way, we need to kill those lights.'

The captain turned to face the private. 'Are you alright with this Couper,' he asked, 'you'll have to go it alone, I'm afraid. Can't risk more than one man on this. If you see him, if you see anyone out there, don't give a challenge. Just shoot the bugger, soon as you get the chance. No warning shots. But get those bloody lights put out.'

Removing the pistol from its holster, the captain handed it to the private. 'You better take a sidearm too, Couper,' he said.

The samphire man pushed the pistol under his belt and secured his webbing and ammunition pouches. Slowly, he crawled down the embankment on his belly. He slithered close by me, unaware of my presence. He was so close. At the base of the sea defence, he got to his feet. I watched him jog along a narrow footpath that clung to the base of the embankment.

On the mount, the soldiers began to chat, passing a bag of sweets between them. I took the opportunity to drag myself silently down to the footbath. The soldiers were oblivious. I crawled on all fours like vermin. A rat. This is what they had reduced me to.

Out of sight, I got to my feet and ran. I ran in the direction of the samphire man. To my right, the grassy embankment. To my left, the muddy flats of the salt marsh. A barbed-wire fence separated the track from the marsh. Above me, a thousand stars looked down. Among them, Alnilam. Watching me. Judging me. Condemning me. It mocked my existence.

The samphire man, despite his age, made good progress along the track. Ahead, I could hear his boots pounding the dirt. His rifle magazines, clanking as he ran. I passed a sign nailed to the fence, a skull and crossbones.

Fifteen minutes later, the soldier paused. I took cover, dropping to the ground. The old man was examining a narrow gap in the fence. Tufts of greasy wool, snagged upon the wire. Slinging his rifle onto his back, he delicately manoeuvred himself through. The sound of material tearing.

'Fuck it,' he cursed, examining the hem of his trousers.

On the other side of the fencing, he knelt to pick up a glob of wet mud. He smeared it across his face, neck and hands. He even covered the insides of his ears. Regardless, he could not conceal his scent. The wretched stench of mankind. He moved on again, following a muddy track. It wound north, out towards the shoreline.

I got to my feet and followed. Now *I* was the hunter.

Eventually, the route gave way to an expanse of oozing mud. It smelt repugnant, like wet compost and sea salt. The mud clung to my shoes tightly. From time to time, when the wind changed, I could hear waves breaking on the shore. We were getting near.

The soldier stopped abruptly. I froze, fearful he had seen me. The old samphire man did not turn around. Instead, he looked down at his feet. I crouched slowly, no more than twenty yards behind. I watched him slowly dig his fingers into the gloop that encased his boots. Then he detached the bayonet from his rifle and pushed the blade into the mud. Probing obliquely into the slop, he pulled away at the sticky mess with his fingertips. He stopped again, deadly still. I saw a disc-like outline around his left boot, the size of a dinner plate. I knew it was a landmine. Anti-tank, too large to be triggered by the weight of a man. The soldier stood upright and flicked mud from his hands. Reattached the bayonet, he continued on. I followed him.

The terrain became increasingly slippy. With each step, I sank into the mud, passed my ankles. Progress was much slower now.

Eventually, after ten minutes or so, the ground became firm, replaced by a bed of shingle. I could hear the waves of the sea clearly now. The soldier began to run. The sound of his crunching strides gave way to splashes. I watched him as he stood in the water, washing off the heavy muck from his boots. Then he turned to his left, jogging along the tideline, back towards the distant specks of white light. Puffs of water vapour drifted from his mouth as the night air chilled his breath. I drew closer. Running behind him through the surf. I felt so free. So alive.

The soldier stopped again. He turned and faced me. He stared directly into my eyes. He looked startled, horrified even. He scrambled to shoulder his rifle, levelling the muzzle at my chest. Then, in an instant, a shadow appeared. It flung him to the ground. It was a wild man. A soulless man. The shadow screamed like a beast. Like the darkest beast of my darkest nightmare.

I watched the soldier's tin hat roll into the lapping waves, lost in the froth. I yelled out but made no sound. The unmistakable silhouette of the beast. It knelt beside the body of the soldier, pounding into the old man's face.

The samphire man gave no resistance. And still, the sickly blows continued.

'Enough,' I screamed. 'Fucking leave him.'

The beast ceased. It sat casually in the mud, beside the motionless body. I could hear the soldier breathing. It was laboured and hoarse. His face, splattered with mud and fresh blood.

The beast smirked at me.

I clenched my fists. Before me was a monster. The thing which had viciously attacked Aunty Muckle, that killed my two aunts in Upwell. The thing that killed Mr Simpkins and his housecleaner and the policeman. The thing that murdered James, that took Emily. The demon that destroyed my soul and imprisoned me within the mind of Mr Simpokins. And still, even through the darkness of the night, it continued to smirk. I ran at it.

The demon lashed out, kicking my feet from under me. I fell to the ground beside it.

'Don't be a fool, boy,' it said, 'You're smarter than that. You know what I can do. What I'm capable of.'

I rubbed my leg in pain. The soldier began to cough and splutter.

The demon examined the rifle lying beside the old man. It reached for it, detaching the bayonet from the muzzle, holding the blade in its hands, marvelling at it.

'Such a beautifully engineered tool of warfare, don't you think?' it said. 'So much more intricate than a simple fighting knife.' It ran a fingertip along its top edge. 'This section,' it said, 'is the rib separator. It's kept deliberately blunt. Designed to spread the ribs, to aid access to the vital organs. To prevent it lodging within a bone.' It held the bayonet like a precious heirloom. A thing of beauty. 'And this groove, running along the length of the blade,' it said, 'is the blood channel. To release the flow of liquids and air from the body, should it happen to penetrate the lungs. Without it, the suction force would grip the weapon, making extraction, problematic. Such exquisite craftsmanship for the purpose of murder.'

The demon looked up from the bayonet into my eyes.

'You're going to die now, George,' it said, 'I'm going to watch the life leave your body. Your filthy memory will drain from my mind. I shall feel the warmth of your breath as it leaves your body for the last time.'

The astronomer, this demonic madman, lent towards me. Its rotten stench of death.

'You see,' it said, 'I've done such terrible things. Things you could never imagine. Such magnitudes of murder. That's why I was sent here. But my captors, so appalled by the concept of death, could not bring themselves to execute me. Even after all that I had done; the scale of my debauchery. And now, here I am. An incomplete facsimile. So well hidden within a world on the brink of total war.'

'How ironic,' it said, 'It takes someone like me to show you compassion. I can save her you know. Emily. I can let her live. A sign of my mercy. I don't want to kill her. I don't want to rip the flesh from her bones. You've suffered so much, George. Let me help you. Together we can stop her from coming to harm. Perhaps you could be merciful too?'

The demon placed the bayonet onto the mud.

'Countless microbes surge through your body, George,' it said. 'Repairing the damage inflicted by man. But they aren't yours to keep. You know that, surely. They are mine. They carry memories of my past.'

I listened to the sound of waves breaking. The salty smell of the air. It was so beautiful. So fragile. Yet before me sat an abomination. A vile demon concealed within the form of man. Contaminating the very air I breathed. Every thought, every action, was abhorrent. And I was part of this madness.

'Do you know how you died?' the demon asked.

I did not reply.

'Well, after the girl doused me in flames, the burden of humanity was stripped away. I was left with nothing but the purity of my host. It was divine. I must thank her, don't you think? She burnt me like a candle. The fat beneath my skin, it bubbled and spat. The smell was, delightful. I chased you through the woods. Hunting you like a beast.

Like wild game. The sport of kings. And then I grabbed you. I grabbed you both. I pinned you to the ground, George, and I tore at you. I tore at you so deeply. You pleaded for me to stop. So much pain and fear in your eyes. It was exquisite. You cried and begged for me to stop. The anguish on your face. It was beautiful. And all the time, the girl lay by your side, holding your hand. Comforting you. It was very touching, in a way. And pathetic. I extracted your intestines when you were still alive. I placed them, wriggling, around your neck. Do you remember? You begged for me to end your life. To stop your suffering. You *wanted* me to kill you. I only did as you wished, George. You should be thankful. You were on the very cusp of death when I did it. I devoured your heart, beating raw in your chest. I ate your brain, too. Delicious. The message, hidden within the starlight. A million alien microbes, returning to my veins.'

I shook uncontrollably. Memories of Emily. I recalled the look of terror on her face as she watched me die, pleading for him to stop. She was so very, very scared. But she stayed. All that time. She could have run. But she stayed, comforting me. Until the very end. Until I become a part of the beast, entwined within its madness.

'She's still alive you know,' the demon said, 'My trophy. Our trophy. Something to be saved. Like the pig, don't you think? She's in such pain, George. She cries all night. Begging for help. Pleading. It gets very tiresome after a while. But nobody will come, George. You don't want them to come, do you! You want her to suffer. Why is that, exactly?'

'Help her,' I said, 'Please, let her go. Let her live. She means nothing to you. Not anymore. But she means everything to me. She's all I have. Please.'

The demon grinned and rose to its feet. It offered out its hand, helping me up. 'I want them to think I'm dead,' it said, gesturing in the direction of the Home Guard soldiers, 'I want them to forget about me, until I'm ready. I require one final acquisition you see, a lady. I need time before I can truly emerge. If I have to exist in this isolation, at least afford me some enjoyment. I wish only to observe. I want to watch mankind tear itself apart by war, and pollution and virus. Mankind is the real monster here. Not you or me.'

The demon placed its hand on my shoulder. 'I didn't mean for you to contaminate my mind. I'm sorry George, truly. You must be so afraid, so torn. Such anguish for a little boy. But I can help you. I can make it all stop. Please, let me help you. You've given me strength and knowledge George, thank you. I can see so much now. A universe at peace. The lull before the storm. It will burn, soon. Every mote. Every single filthy atom. I shall see to it. I shall make it happen. A perpetual darkness. All I need is the final portion of the message.'

The demon looked down at my trembling hands. It gripped my shoulder more firmly.

'She wants to live,' it said, almost in a whisper. 'Help me, tonight. Let the soldiers think I'm dead. I don't want to be hunted, like an animal. Do this, and she'll never be harmed. I shall protect her. Help her, George. Set her free. Let her live. Let her be, resplendent.'

A tear ran down my cheek. I knew how the beast had hurt her. How it tortured her. I wanted it to stop. I wanted it all to stop.

'I'm afraid this is going to hurt,' the demon said. It stooped down and lifted the limp body of the old man onto its shoulder.

I stood beside the creature as it carried the old man. We walked along the shoreline, side by side, through the darkness of the night. The stars above were beautiful, but I knew I no longer belonged beneath them. We stopped some twenty feet from the high-tide line, marked by deposited seaweed.

'There,' the demon said, 'Do you see it?'

I looked down. Protruding through the mud, three thin metal prongs. Each no longer than an inch.

'I'm afraid it will hurt, an awful lot,' it said.

Without hesitation, the demon dropped the soldier onto the prongs. A deafening bang. A tremendous blast moved up through my body. I flinched as a narrow jet of mud and pink mist travel ten feet into the air. My ears rang. Globs of wet mud and seashells fell to the ground around us. There was silence. Then ringing in my ears. It was quickly broken by the sound of groaning. I stood dazed, staring down at the ground. Grey smoke permeated through a round puddle a foot or so across. And then the screaming began. The demon staggered clumsily nearby. The mine had stripped away at its left leg and arm leaving soft slithers of skin hanging from its limbs. Its top lip was torn upwards and chunks of mud and grass were embedded in its mouth. The gums around its front teeth had been pulled away. They dangled from its teeth like half-chewed steak. Even the eyelids had been peeled outwards, its left ear, shredded.

My chest was wet and slimy. I panicked, fumbling hands searching for the wound.

The screaming stopped. The demon composed itself. Then it dug its fingers into its mouth and removed the debris.

'Relax,' it said, 'It's only mud on your chest.'

I looked for the soldier. I could not see him at first.

He lay nearby. A smoking upper torso, shredded and fragmented. Charred meat, entangled within strips of cloth and webbing.

In the distance, voices. They were calling out, yelling. It was the old men of the Home Guard.

My attention was drawn to movement at the sight of the blast. A marsh crab slowly dragged itself across the mud, away from the site of detonation. Behind, trailed an entanglement of innards, seeping from its ruptured shell. The pathetic frailty of life. I plunged my fingers into the oozing mud, scooping it in my hands. Then, I dumped it onto the dying creature, encasing it. Burying it. Preserving it. Perhaps, in time, it would become fossilized. Cast in stone. And then, perhaps, one day, tens of millions of years from now, it will be found again. A fossilized crab, high upon a mountain. Found within a world as alien to me as the one I now inhabit.

The demon removed its jacket, torn and covered in blood. It threw it down onto the earth. Its left shoe was missing. It cleared the mud and mucus from its nose and knelt beside the smouldering body. It pushed its hands into the slop, flinging aside chunks of skin and muscle. The discarded remnants of an old man. And then the demon found it. An automatic pistol, greasy from human fat.

The beast stood, smiling. It licked the barrel. Tasting the slime of mud and death.

I was disgusted by such action. The demon refrained, placing the pistol into its trouser pocket. Wiping the blood from its hands, it stooped down and removed its remaining shoe and sock. It flung them to the ground, near to the smoking puddle.

The demon shuffled towards the tide. We stood together in the cold water of the Wash. I reached out, holding its hand. The last time I paddled in the sea had been with my father. I smiled, warmed by the comfort of my memories. I closed my eyes and imagined him beside me. My father.

'They'll think I'm dead now,' the demon said. 'They'll think I was a traitor. They'll think the old man killed me. He'll be a hero. A posthumous hero.'

We walked, hand-in-hand, through the water, following the contours of the tideline. In the darkness of the night, the two lights ahead of us shone brighter than the entire universe.

After half a mile we reached them, two rusty lanterns placed on the shingle. I picked one up. I recognised it immediately. I had seen it before. It belonged to my aunt, they both did. They were from her woodshed. I had taken them. I had placed them on the beach. I had lured the samphire man to his death. I had done it. I had done it all. But now, I felt nothing. No anger, no regret and no shame. I felt no remorse for what I had done. I was ambivalent, cold. We left the lamps burning as we made our way through the night. The calls from the Home Guard were distant now.

We walked for an hour. By the time we reached the mouth of the River Nene, the sun was rising. A new day. A new era. And an ending. Ahead, two lighthouses, one on each side of the mouth of the river. They marked the entrance to the village port of Sutton Bridge.

Beside one of the lighthouses, we found a ramshackle hut. It was entangled in a mat of thorny brambles and ivy. I forced the door open and helped the demon inside. The beast collapsed to the floor, exhausted from its injuries. I tended to the wounds as best I could but they were deep and raw.

'I need you gone,' it spluttered as I sat beside the thing. 'So many voices. They're burning my head.' It turned to face me. 'Your father was afraid of me, of what I was. Of what I would become. I've looked into the starlight for so long.'

In the eyes of the demon, I could see the astronomer. He patted the back of my hand. 'Your father shouldn't have survived the war. He was a freak of nature. He belonged dead. Like a million other rotting corpses. But he lived on. To spawn you into being. Now, here you are. A thing that is a violation of the natural world. You should not be here, George.'

'The beautiful eternity of the universe,' he said, 'It lives in us. We're created from the dust of the cosmos.' For a moment, he studied the wet blood soaking through his trousers. The molecules of iron that turned his blood red. Atoms formed in the core of a long-dead star, spewed into the universe. The building blocks of the Earth. Of the Sun. Of mankind.

He stared at me with bloodshot eyes. 'All life in the universe is forged in the heart of dying stars,' he said, 'And the horrors of the universe, destruction and creation, are embedded in us all. We're linked to every creature in the universe, across all time. You, George, have been my sanity. But it's time for you to go. Time to crush you like the parasitic greenfly; so that the rose can bloom. Bloom across every inch of this wretched world.'

The astronomer took a deep breath. 'She's barely alive you know. I tore away at her. Such a pretty girl, don't you think?'

'Tell me where she is,' I said, 'I don't want her to die. She's all I have. She's just a little girl. Please. Where is she?'

'You know where she is George,' the astronomer said, 'You know exactly where she is. You know because you put her there. You stashed her bleeding body underneath the footbridge by the Rye. Gagged and bound. You cut at her skin, for pleasure. Do you remember? You should rejoice, young man. Rejoice in what you once were. In what I shall become.'

The astronomer looked down at his injured leg. 'I see a lot of you, in me,' he said, 'But you hinder me. Confuse me. And now, I think, I would rather walk alone than to walk with you in the wrong direction.'

I looked at the man as he bled. Pathetic and weak. Silence the rage that burned inside of him. But I was contaminated. Dirty and vile. Like the demon itself. I wanted no more of this unnatural life. I wanted to be free. Free of the torment and the nightmares and the fear. But above all, above all else in my heart, I wanted Emily to smile again. I wanted her to be back home with her family. A family that loved her. I wanted her to live the life I would never have.

'I think Mr Simpkins was a good man,' I said, 'I can help him. Keep him sane. Let Emily go. But let me live on too. Let me remind you who you are; Mr Simpkins the astronomer, not the killer. Not some alien thing. You're a good man, Mr Simpkins. I can help you fight the demon. The voices in your head.'

'I've tried to remove him,' the astronomer said, 'Tried to cut him out. Burn him from my body. I want to rid myself of Simpkins. His thoughts taunt me. Like a cancer. A filthy infestation.'

I knew then that the demon within Mr Simpkins could be destroyed. Not by me. Not by fire or bullets or bayonets or bombs, but by Simpkins. He still existed, somewhere deep within. He existed both physically and mentally inside the putrid husk of rotten flesh. I felt at peace. A great weight lifted. The destruction of the demon did not depend on me.

'Before life evolved here,' the astronomer said, 'there could be no fire. No flames burnt upon the Earth. Without oxygen produced by the first plants to grow on Earth, nothing could burn. And now, we find life is rampant. It colonised every crevice and pool on the planet. Belching out oxygen. Tainting the air with its perversion. Creating the ideal conditions for fire. For the flame to flourish. To burn. To cleanse. Life has created fire. And the flames shall destroy it. Everything will end. And I shall witness it. I shall instigate it.'

The astronomer smiled at me. 'I will flourish here, George. I shall revel in your wars. The thunderous exhilaration. Annihilation on the grandest scale. And mankind shall commit the act himself. I need to do nothing. Nothing but spectate.'

Outside the hut, I heard a sound. A rummaging of undergrowth. My heart leapt. The soldiers. The old men of the Home Guard. They had tracked us down, followed us. And now they would despatch us. Butcher us. End the vile torment that burned inside.

The astronomer turned to face the door. 'You can come in now,' he called out, 'Don't be shy. I know you're there!'

The little wooden door pushed open. A man walked in. He tentatively looked around the shed before closing the door behind him. He was a big man with broad, powerful shoulders. He wasn't a soldier. He was a civilian, in dirty civilian clothes. A common labourer. One side of his head looked peculiar. A large dent. It covered much of his temple.

'Hello, David,' the astronomer said.

The man nodded but said nothing.

'This is Mr Rollingson,' the astronomer said, 'He's been helping me out with a few errands. A bit of a vagrant I'm afraid. You see, he's on the run. He owes me a favour. I managed to free him from a police cell. It all got rather messy I'm afraid. You've been looking after Emily for me, haven't you!'

Rollingson looked around the shed blankly before settling his gaze once more on the astronomer.

'I've found her, the woman,' he said, 'I know where she...lives. I know...everything!'

'That's splendid, thank you,' the astronomer said.

'Now then,' the astronomer said to the man, 'I'm going to ask another favour. I want you to go back to Leatherhead. I want you to show the police exactly where the little girl is. Where you've been keeping her. Do you understand?'

Rollingson nodded again. 'And then...' he stuttered.

'Yes, of course,' the astronomer replied, 'Then I'll take you to Canada, to be with Mary. You'd like that, wouldn't you!'

Rollingson gave an awkward smile.

'Well, off you trot then.' The astronomer said, 'Chop-chop!'

Rollingson left, closing the door behind him.

We sat in silence. In the distance, I heard seagulls calling. Flying free above the Earth. Free of the horror of war. Free of the horror of mankind.

'It's curious, don't you think,' the astronomer said, 'that you never realised you were dead. Yet outside these four walls, mankind doesn't realise it is alive.'

'If the starlight message was passed onto me by my father,' I said, 'Why did you make me look through the telescope? I didn't need to suffer like that, did I?'

'No,' the astronomer replied.

'You could have just killed me. The very first time you saw me in the woods, before the war,' I said.

The astronomer nodded. 'Yes, I could have,' he replied.

'Then why didn't you?' I asked.

A smile formed across his face. 'Don't you ever like to play with your food, George?'

'What will happen to me,' I said, 'when I die?'

'Nothing,' he replied, 'You will no longer exist. Your memory will be gone. You will be nothing. Worthless.'

I began to sob. I could not help myself. 'But I wanted to live,' I said. 'I wanted to grow up.'

'You live only for as long as you are remembered,' the astronomer said. 'You have been an asset to me, George. A part of me. My life was preserved in starlight. Shone across the void of space. From Alnilam to Sol. I understand what you have gone through,' he said, 'I empathise with you, truly. Perhaps, I think, it would be fitting if your life were preserved too, like mine. Not in light, but in ink. You could live forever. Not in this world. Not trapped within my mind, but free. Free within the pages of a book. I can grant you that. I own you this much, at least.'

I reached into my pocket and removed my father's notebook together with Stanley Seabrook's fountain pen.

The astronomer placed the pistol by my side. Still soiled in the blood of the dead soldier.

'You know what to do,' he said, 'when you're ready. I'll look after the book, make sure that you're remembered. You can live again. In the minds of many. But as a guest, not a prisoner this time.'

'Thank you,' I said.

The astronomer closed his eyes and drifted beyond my reach. His body was frail and broken. Yet the ripped skin along his left side was already rebinding. As he slept I watched him heal. Only the tattered and bloodied clothing draping his body stood testament to this ungodly man. He was to be restored, save for the familiar wounding on his left hand. He could never heal the damage caused by a true friend, one who had tried to save his soul. I knew there was hope. Hope that, somehow, the madness that filled his body and mind could be driven out. My father had taken his own life. One day, perhaps, Simpkins would do the same. One day.

I ran my fingertips across the pages of the notebook. Retracing the outline of my father's name. I do not know the nature of this great technology hidden within the starlight. Its dark magic is a mystery to me, and I want no further dealings with it. Yet, to transport the mind of some creature from Alnilam into the skull of a man, to heal his body from the most dreadful of injuries by means which I could never understand, is miraculous. This demon will not be destroyed by war or by technology or by faith. It will be destroyed, in part, by the memory of a frightened little boy trapped inside the pages of a book.

I examined the pen. It was beautifully exquisite, crafted in blue and green enamel with a gold nib. The raised initials of Stanley Seabrook. I began to write. I wrote with speed and fluidity. The memories of a murdered little boy, held within the tortured mind of a man and a demon. But I write not just to Simpkins. I write to you, so that I may live again. Inside your own mind.

A new day was born. But for the light to dawn, there must first be darkness. And the darkness was ready to return. The blackest of black. Approaching figures outside. I was not afraid. I felt proud of my father's actions. I had feared my mother but I had loved her too. And then I thought of Emily. My dear, dear friend. My heart was broken. Our friendship no longer ran parallel. Yet I was sure Mr Simpkins would save her. My life shall end, but hers shall go on. She shall live, and she shall be beautiful. In every sense of the word.

I looked down at my journal. Each page filled with the recollections of a dead boy. A life recorded forever, beyond the physical confines of entropy. I placed it beside the astronomer. In its place, I seized the dead soldier's pistol. The wooden door flung open. A mother and daughter stood before me. Two more lost souls, incarcerated within the madness of hell. I reached into my pockets and withdrew a handful of berries. Dried berries from the *Arum maculate* plant. Lords and Ladies, taken from Ashtead woods. I ate them. I ate them all. I ate them to be free. To be free of this terrible, unnatural binding. The little girl let out a piercing shriek as she lunged for me. I held the pistol to my head.

The balance was restored. $E=mc^2$.

Chapter XX

The steam train bound for Brighton pulled into Ashtead station. A smartly dressed woman looked up from her paperback novel and glanced out at the busy platform. She saw little of interest.

The compartment door slid open. A suited gentleman stood in the doorway. He smiled politely as she studied him.

'Sorry, do you mind,' he asked, 'all the other compartments are taken!'

The man brushed droplets of rain off his suit.

The woman nodded slightly, watching as he placed his damp leather suitcase onto the overhead storage shelf.

'You don't mind do you,' he asked, pulling down the blinds to the passageway beyond, 'The sun's awfully bright, don't you think.'

The woman did not object. She watched silently as the gentleman settled himself opposite. Paying little regard, she returned to her novel.

The gentleman watched her. He studied her closely; her free hand resting upon a gas mask box by her side. She looked elegant. Educated, even. Not unattractive. In fact, she looked quite pretty, in a certain light. The gentleman cleared his throat, catching her attention once again. Reluctantly she closed the book and looked up at him.

'Excuse me,' he said, 'I couldn't help but notice. You bear a striking resemblance to an acquaintance of mine.'

'Really?' the woman said, in an uninterested tone.

'Yes,' the gentleman replied, 'Although I must admit he was an acquaintance, unfortunately, I never had the opportunity to meet in person.'

The woman looked up at the gentleman curiously. He was a pleasant enough looking man in his mid to late forties. He wore a smart tweed suit but it had seen better days. It was worn and faded. Old fashioned. His clothes were damp from rain, his black leather shoes splattered with mud.

'Excuse me, sir,' the woman said, 'I don't quite understand.'

The gentleman smiled. But it was a forced smile. The kind of smile which did not rest naturally upon his face.

'Forgive me,' he said, extending a gloved hand, 'Damien. Damian Simpkins.'

The woman shook his hand. Mr Simpkins held it tightly. She tried to politely pull free but he held her with both his hands as if he were greeting a long lost friend.

'Delighted to meet you, Florence,' Mr Simpkins said, 'I've been looking for you for so long. Several years in fact.'

'My hand,' she said, 'have you quite finished?'

The gentleman released his grip.

The woman sat back in her seat. She looked agitated. Unsettled. 'I'm sorry,' she said, 'have we met?'

Outside the carriage, on the platform, a whistle blew. The train lurched forwards. Slowly, it pulled away from the station, heading south.

'Oh, I know all about you, Florence Jones,' Mr Simpkins said.

'Actually,' the woman replied, raising her tone, 'It's Mrs Sydenham. Jones was my maiden name.'

The man lent forward. 'Now, we both know that's not strictly true now, don't we!' he said, taking hold of her hand again. He held it firmly this time. She grimaced at the force of his grip. Turning to face the compartment door, she took a deep breath. Before she had the chance to call out, he was upon her. His gloved hand pushed hard upon her mouth. She began to struggle but found herself unable to prevent herself from being dragged to the floor.

The man rose to his feet. He towered above her. In an instant, he drew back his leg, kicking her forcibly in her throat. She coughed, ejecting a mist of blood into the air. It stippled the carriage floor.

'But that's not your real name is it,' the man said, 'You're Florence Ambrose, aren't you. I've had quite a job finding you!'

The woman groaned as blood dribbled from her mouth. Mr Simpkins squatted beside her. He grabbed her hair, pulling her face away from the floor to face him. 'You're nothing,' he said. 'You're nothing but the whore child of the Ashtead Ripper. But in your veins, coursing through your vile body is something which belongs to me.'

The woman began to splutter. 'Please,' she said.

Mr Simpkins pulled harder on her hair, tilting her head back to expose her throat.

'Within your flesh, dear Florence,' the man said, 'lies a code. The last code in a sequence. My sequence. A code to describe every atom, every memory, every detail. I'm going to be born again Florence. Born anew. Complete. Untainted by the filth of humanity.'

Slowly, softly, he kissed her forehead. Her blood smeared upon his lips. He lent in again, this time biting her, pulling at her flesh. Devouring. She struggled, contorted. Regardless, her attack continued. She knew her fate. She knew she was dying. Fixing her gaze upon the carriage window, she watched as a blur of treetops melted into the rain-filled skies over Surrey.

The train clattered onward, passing over a level crossing. The lady stretched out her arm towards the window. She sighed one last time and was at peace.

* * *

Two police cars waited beside a barrier as the southbound train hurtled past. The rain pounded the ground in shards. When the barrier raised, the black Wolseley 14/60 motorcars clattered over the level-crossing at speed. Turning off-road, they drove onto Ashtead common, towards the woods. The leading car, its headlamps choked to narrow slits, began to slide across the wet grass. Clods of earth flung skyward as it lost traction. It came to a stop. The second car swerved sharply to avoid it. It too became stuck, its wheels spinning hopelessly.

A passenger door flung open. A police sergeant appeared. He wore a heavy cape to keep the rain from his tunic. The police crest adorning his helmet darkened for the blackout.

'Don't just sit there,' he called out, 'Get yourselves fell-in!'

Six constables decanted from the vehicles. They formed a thin line, an arm's length apart. They began to pace slowly forward, towards the bridle path that led into Ashtead woods. The downpour was relentless. Their trousers were soaked, their capes splattered with mud.

'Emily!' the sergeant called out. Nothing could be heard over the pouring rain. Again he called. And again, only the sound of the rain.

The line of policemen began to bottleneck as they reached the brambles that grew chaotically on either side of the track. It led over the low brick footbridge across the Rye. The sergeant traversed the short span as the remaining men peeled left and right. They scrambled and slid down the embankment until they each found themselves standing ankle-deep in the cold stream. The water flowed quickly, despite the narrow outflow pipe under the bridge being partially blocked by branches.

The pipe was no more than two feet wide. One of the constables, a thin man, not yet in his twenties, began to remove the blockage, allowing the foliage to drift downstream. Crouching down, he peered into the darkness of the tunnel.

'It's alright love,' he said. Reaching into the tunnel, he took hold of a hand. 'You're safe now!' he said.

Another policeman, standing in the stream, called up. 'Sergeant Wells,' he said, 'We've got her.'

The sergeant scrambled down and joined his men in the water. The thin constable, still holding the hand, tugged gently to help free the child. As he stood, the limb slid freely from the pipe. He stumbled backwards, splashing in the water. He looked mortified.

'Christ!' he said. A severed arm and shoulder hung from a mutilated head.

One of the policemen removed his cape and placed it on the bank. The grisly remains were placed on top.

'Is that her?' one of them said.

There was no reply.

'There's more bits in here, sergeant,' the thin policeman said, covering his mouth from the wretched smell, 'but I think we'll need a shovel.' He peered into the darkness of the pipework.

'Hang on,' he said, 'Something's moving. Pass me a light, mate.'

Another policeman offered up a torch. 'Careful Turner,' he said, 'it'll be rats. Filthy buggers.'

Shining the torchlight into the darkness, the thin constable saw two bloodshot eyes peering back at him. Cowering in a foetal position, lay the battered and gagged body of a young girl. Her eyes darted wildly in terror.

'Hello, Emily,' the constable said, 'It's alright now. Out you come, love.'

The girl was gently coaxed free from the bridge. The policeman wrapped his cloak around her shivering body. The thin policeman picked her up in his arms, out of the water. Carefully, he carried her up the embankment as the rain fell. The little girl tried to talk but could only draw sharp intakes of breath. As they approached the Sergeants car, the rear door opened. The thin policeman placed the child inside, seating her beside a uniformed lady.

'There you go, Carol,' he said.

As the thin policeman closed the car door, he smiled at the little girl through the glass. Her wide, petrified eyes stared back. Another policeman stood beside him. He looked over towards the furthest car. They both did. In the rear, sat two policemen, either side of a bulky man. The bulky man sat motionlessly. The side of his head, indented.

'He'll ruddy hang for this,' the thin policeman said. 'Bloody maniac!'

The other policeman nodded. 'Makes you wonder what goes on in their heads sometimes. All he does is just ask to see some bird called Mary, whoever the bloody hell she is.'

Over by the Rye, Sergeant Wells examined the human remains laid out on the embankment.

'Phillips,' he said, 'get the snow shovel out. Scoop the rest of this mess up before it's all washed away.'

The body was in a frightful state of disruption. The side of the head smashed in on one side to reveal an empty skull. Leaning over the remnants, the sergeant took hold of a corner of the cape and pulled it over to protect it from the deluge.

'Stand down, Billet,' he said under his breath.

Turning his back to the rain, he lit a cigarette.

LONG SUTTON

Bapt. Ch.

P.H.

Chapel Br.

The Beeches

M.P

P.H.

The Warren

LITTLE DEREHAM

Fox Cottage

Delamore Slaughter Ho.

F.B.

Park Lane

Hall

Market Place

P.O.

Sutton Ho.

Church

⑪ ⑫ ⑬ ⑭

About the Author

Born in Surrey, England, I studied Astronomy and Planetary Science at university. After serving in the British Armed Forces, I settled down to a long career in Emergency Response planning; preparing the United Kingdom to recover from natural, accidental or malicious major incidents.

An elected Fellow of the Royal Astronomical Society, I am eager to promote the sciences to a wide audience. I have taught astronomy and physics to college students as well as contributing to some publications. In my spare time, I am a keen astrophotographer - regularly photographing galaxies, nebula and planets from the dark skies of Lincolnshire where I now live with my wife and two young children.

If you enjoyed this novel, please consider telling your friends and family. I am most grateful to those who take the time to leave a fair and honest book review.

If you wish to be kept informed of other novels in the pipeline, or wish to contact me directly, please consider visiting the author website or subscribing to the mailing list.

Acknowledgements

I would like to offer my sincerest thanks to the following people for their help and support: Robert Nix (Texas, USA), for his continued advice and guidance on all things literary, Melanie Weighill (Florida, USA), for her expert proof-reading skills and my beautiful wife Sarah-Jane (England), for her love, keen eye and patience.

https://atrichens.wixsite.com/author

Printed in Great Britain
by Amazon